Welcome to the Wilson Family

HOT RAVES FOR *HOT BOYZ*

"What makes this work is it shows you a side of life that you may not know: what wealthy and famous African-Americans may go through, and their similarities and differences from the common man. A classic Los Angeles novel, HOT BOYZ is erotic, funny, and a contemporary page-turner -- Marissa's most ambitious work yet."

-Cydney Rax, Book-Remarks.com

"The author does a fantastic job drawing you into the character's lives while keeping you guessing on their next move. Get ready to be entertained because you won't believe what happens in the end."

-Loose Leaves Book Review

"HOT BOYZ is chock-full of absorbing characters and riveting, nontraditional plotlines. A true ensemble cast, no one character's tale overshadows the rest. Instead, each contributes to the sum of an extremely unique romance."

-Romantic Times

"The characters are so real and every person can relate to something in this storyline. Not many authors have the ability to entertain and give a message all at the same time. HOT BOYZ does just that!"

-Erika Ware

"HOT BOYZ is an intriguing contemporary tale that showcases the downside of success in which if the person is not careful he (or she) could lose sight of what matters in life."

-Harriett Klausner, The Best Reviews

"HOT BOYZ rings with passion and realism which draws readers into the character's lives and shares the healing that comes only through honesty and love. This is a powerful novel of the commitment to and the sanctity of family."

-RAWSISTAZ Reviewers

ALSO BY MARISSA MONTEILH

May December Souls
The Chocolate Ship
Hot Boyz
Make Me Hot
Dr. Feelgood
Something He Can Feel
Turnabout Is Fair Play
The Six-Letter Word
You've Got It Bad: Dr. Feelgood Sequel
(2012)
L.A. Husbands and Wives: Hot Boyz Trilogy
(2013)

HOT Girlz

THE *HOT BOYZ* SEQUEL

MARISSA MONTEILH

4D Publishing Paperback Fiction

Copyright © 2011 by Marissa Monteilh
Reading Group Guide © 2011 by 4D Publishing

The quote on the front cover is from a Marissa Monteilh review written by Anna Burns for Library Journal

The quote on the back cover is from a review of Hot Boyz in May 2004 written by T.L. Burton for Romantic Times

Cover design: www.vondahoward.com
Cover photograph: www.gregorymaxx.com

ISBN 13: 978-1-61793-837-5

Printed in the United States of America

This book is dedicated to my gorgeous, smart, loving daughter Nicole – a daddy's girl who is the epitome of the perfect wife and mother. I want to be just like you when I grow up.
I love you infinity!

ACKNOWLEDGEMENTS

First and foremost, I thank God for my gifts and for allowing me to live my word-passion for eleven years. My seventh grade English teacher was right!

I wanted to write a book that my sons, in particular, could enjoy: a family novel with parents, grandparents, kids, pets, God, love, life, sports, faith, and drama. I believe I've achieved that with *HOT GIRLZ*: the *HOT BOYZ* Sequel.

A major thank you to my children – Adam, Ron, Nicole, and my son-in-law, Darrien - you all make me so proud. Forever love!

To the grand ones whom I'd give my life for - my grandchildren, DAJ, ASJ, AIW. You each light up my life! And grand kisses and to my Guap-puppy, who the Wilson's dog, Nadia, was mirrored after!

To my brother Greg and his beautiful family, and to each and every one of my beloved friends – thank you!

To my KP, my biggest supporter who lends me his ear over and over again whether I'm happy or frustrated or experiencing writer's block. I love you!

My dear author friends - there are far too many to name – this includes my fellow Georgia Peach and Novel Spaces authors. I cherish the shop-talk and camaraderie and say to you all, write on!

To the editor of five of my titles, Karen Thomas, for acknowledging my talent years ago and believing in me. I owe so much to you. You are appreciated!

My agent, Andrew Stuart, I am thankful for your expertise and pep-talks. And Latoya Smith, my editor at Hachette Books - you are amazing.

MM - you are my sister and my rock!

The book clubs are the pulse of the literary world. Thank you for selecting my titles, supporting my works, showing such hospitality, and buying my books.

Shout outs to Written Magazine and Michelle Gipson - Cindy Hurst and Urban Knowledge bookstore in Columbia, SC - Ft. Benning management and staff - Malik at the Regional Library and Linda at the Central Library in Georgia - Mocha Ocha and the NAACP Author Pavilion - Radiah and Charles Hubbert with Urban Reviews - Ella Curry and EDC Creations - TaNisha Webb and Fall Into Books - Curtis Bunn and the National Book Club Conference - Carol Mackey and Black Expressions - Cydney Rax and Book Remarks - Tee C. Royal and RAWSISTAZ - Vonda Howard and Black Literature Magazine (my talented cover designer) - Kim Knight and Between the Lines Bookstore - Kym Fisher and Victoria Christopher Murray with A Chapter A Month.com - Bryan Cleveland with CT Concepts (my web designer) – Yolanda L. Gore with Inspirational Literary Circle and Designs (my virtual assistant), and more.

To my valued Facebook and Twitter friends, I'm having a blast with you! And to you, my cherished readers everywhere– muah!

I hope that this continuation of the lives of Mason and Mercedes, Claude and Venus, and Torino and Sequoia entertains and satisfies you. I present to you, the Wilson family in my very first sequel . . . *HOT GIRLZ*!

Much love!

Marissa Monteilh (Mon-tay)
www.marissamonteilh.com
www.facebook.com/marissamonteilh
www.twitter.com/divawritermm
www.gapeachauthors.blogspot.com
divapublishing@aol.com

Ladies first!

HOT Girlz

1

Mercedes

"... the seven year itch ..."

He was younger.
Pop!

There he goes, popping into my head again, Mercedes Wilson said to herself.

He was probably the same age that the female Titleist representative was when Mercedes's husband of almost two decades, the father of her two children, the one and only famous pro-golfer Mason Wilson, decided to cheat on her seven years ago while on tour in San Diego at Torrey Pines.

Mercedes figured it out while watching a professional golf tournament on television with their daughter, Star. Mercedes noticed the bright red hair of the white woman who followed Mason like a love-struck puppy. Seeing the woman made the hairs on the back of Mercedes's neck stand straight up. The hairs on the woman's head and the strands of hair in Mason's red Benz were exact. Mason won the U.S. Open Golf Championship that day, but he nearly lost his wife. He claimed to have had casual sex with the woman whenever he lost a tournament. Win or lose, Mercedes made it clear that his behavior was unacceptable, and that sex with someone other than one's spouse is never casual.

After intensive family counseling and much prayer, Mercedes forgave him. She warned him that if he ever violated their marriage vows again, she would take the kids and leave him in a heartbeat. Nevertheless, she had to accept the fact that after all the years of their union, her famous husband, Mason Wilson, was an adulterer.

And now, it was Mercedes who played hide-and-seek with the notion of infidelity herself.

Things would have been fine if that young member of the Los Angeles City Council would have simply stayed the heck out of her head.

She tried convincing herself that what happens in Vegas stays in Vegas . . . and what happened in Vegas was that she had an encounter with an elected official named Ryan.

She wanted to still believe she could practice what she preached seven years ago about being faithful. Mason may not have had another affair since then, but this time, the seven year itch was biting the hell out of his wife, and it bit hard.

Pop!

"Good morning, Cedes." Mason greeted his wife using the nickname he had given her when they first met in college back at U.S.C.

The sound of Mason's voice propelled Mercedes from the past into the present on this summer morning in July. The sun hadn't quite shared its offspring with the world. There was not a cloud in the azure sky. The usual summer breeze from the Pacific had not yet breathed its usual breath.

From the backyard, the barking from their new blue-pit, one-year-old, blue-eyed Nadia, served as their regular good morning hello. Their chocolate lab, Kailua, who was a true family member, passed away at the age of eight from lymphoma. Though devastated, the family decided it was best to get another dog right away, and it seemed that the new dog, Nadia, bonded to Mattie more than anyone else. Mattie, the beloved matriarch of the family, mother to Mason, Claude, and Torino Wilson, was bedridden for years and living in Mason and Mercedes's home, suffering from vascular dementia.

Sporting a cognac-colored shoulder length bob and wispy bangs, Mercedes spoke while heading to her oval desk in the downstairs office of their five-bedroom home. She was dressed in an off-the-shoulder purple dress with gold high heels.

"Hey there. You're up mighty early, aren't you?" Her oversized chandelier earrings shook as she spoke. She set her purse on the desk.

"I am." Mason, now forty six years-old, had retired from golf to spend more time with his family. He had been home for the past two years, and was now working on his second book. The first book, *Shadow on the Green*, was his auto-biography about his experiences with racism and what he called the true color of money. The title made the New York Times bestsellers list. And now he was half-way through the last title of his two-book contract about how to relate the execution of golf to the execution of life, called *Grip It and Rip It*.

Their new home was smaller than the previous, yet equally as immaculate. Back in 2003, the girlfriend of Mason's brother, Claude, was murdered on the front porch of Mason and Mercedes's home on Thanksgiving Day in front of the entire family.

To Mason, moving was a no-brainer. They had thought about moving outside of Los Angeles, but after being in Ladera for more than a quarter century, they decided to stay in the 90056 zip code, moving from their custom home on Bedford Avenue to a newer home on Ladera Crest Drive, also in upper Ladera.

It was Claude, owner of Wilson Realty, who found the dramatic, architectural style four-thousand square foot home. It had vaulted ceilings, two stone fireplaces, and distressed oak hardwood floors. The first floor library had a wet-bar, and his-and-her desks positioned smack dab in the middle of the room, with bright red leather couches against opposite walls.

Mason sat on the sofa reading the *Wall Street Journal*, sipping from a coffee mug. He wore his black Nike fitted cap and matching sweat suit. He had already been out for his morning walk. Though Sean John was Mason's clothing sponsor during his career, Nike was now Rashaad Wilson's sponsor. Mason had handed over his golf club-baton to his very popular and successful young son.

Mercedes asked, "You're usually right back in the bed by the time I leave. Weren't you up late, writing?"

"I was, but I got on up while you were in the shower. I have a meeting this morning. Needed to get in some cardio, get my adrenaline going." He placed his coffee mug on the end table and looked at his gold watch. "I've gotta be downtown by eleven."

"Really? Why?"

"You know Elijah? Elijah Cummings, former head of the Urban League?"

"From Maryland. Of course I do. We saw him and his wife last year on the cruise we took to Barbados."

"He called me last week. Said he read *Shadow on the Green*. He mentioned there's a vacated seat coming up on the Los Angeles City Council. I guess the current president of the council, Eric Garcetti, discussed the vacancy with Elijah."

"Okay." She waited for more.

"So, Eric wants to meet with me to discuss the possibilities."

"As a city council member?"

"Yes."

Pop! "Wow."

"Wow, what?"

"It's just that I didn't know, I mean, we didn't discuss it, and here you are on your way to a meeting about a career in politics."

"I didn't confirm until yesterday. You got home late and by the time you ate and we chatted for a second, you knocked out before I could get out of this office. I should've talked to you. I'm sorry."

"Mason, it's all good. We've both been busy. But think about it. As far as you making a move like this, I mean, you basically have no background in politics."

"Cedes, you know I was studying government at S.C."

"Yeah, but that wasn't your major. Honey, don't get me wrong. I'm happy for you. Just the fact that you're even considering it is very cool." Mercedes opened her briefcase and rummaged through the files.

"Listen, you know I've spent most of my life hitting a golf ball. From the time I was young golf had me hooked. It was unpredictable and that was my thrill. Now, my life is as predictable as it gets. I sit here, day in and day out, writing most of the time, checking up on Rashaad and his pro-career, checking in with Star and her new job with the symphony in Atlanta, and watching you continue to grow your modeling business. I try the best I can to spend time with Mom. Turns out I worked right through the kids being home when they were younger. And now that I'm home, they're gone, living their own lives. I just really need something new. I need something challenging. And besides, I think public life would agree with me. Tell me you'll support me on this." His last sentence sounded like a question.

"Oh, you know I will. I just want to keep it real as far as the background that's needed, that's all I'm saying." She closed her briefcase.

"All that's needed is that the candidates live in the district, which is District Eight for this spot, that's us, and that they are qualified voters. From what I read, the pay is just under two-hundred-thousand, plus a car and other incentives, which is not even my motivation. I'd still need to make money in other ways. I'd just do it to see where it leads. To see if I can make a difference with my radical self." He took another sip from his coffee mug.

Mercedes nodded and was all ears.

He continued, "What I'm doing today is having a meeting at City Hall with the president of the city council and a couple of people on his staff. It's just a meeting. Bernard Parks is vacating his seat in May so it depends on how many applications they get from people who want to apply for it. It would be temporary until the regular election in 2013, and at that point I'd need to campaign. We're talking about spending some money to campaign and I'd need to go door-to-door if need be." He focused on her hips. His eyes were suddenly flirty. "Maybe you could be my campaign manager."

A chuckle escaped her lips. "Yeah, I think I could, and I would. And you know I'm happy for you. I'm proud of you. And I support you. I'm sure Eric Garcetti knows who you are, not to mention the Mayor, and actually, with the number of people who are fans of yours, name recognition alone would get you elected. And of course I have complete faith in you if this is what you want. Anything I can do to help, I'm here."

"Everything's good. I'm just happy to be getting up and out of this house. Writing all day can drive you mad. These four walls are working my nerves."

"I'm sure. You know, maybe you can hire a ghost writer. I'm surprised the publisher didn't offer one."

"No, thanks. I'm good. I'm too independent for that. Just need something different to add to the mix right now."

"Okay. I did notice that you don't even get out to the fairway with the guys anymore. That's not like you."

"Sometimes I do."

"Not like you did when you first retired."

"Deadlines got me tied down, Cedes, I'm telling you. Not for long, though. I should be finished soon."

"Okay. And as far as the meeting, will you call me when you're done? Let me know how it goes."

"I will."

"Good." Mercedes took hold of her purse.

"Have you checked in on Mom yet this morning?"

"Not yet."

"Lucinda tells me Mom hasn't spoken a word in days."

She said, "I noticed. It's bad enough she can't get out of bed on her own or even turn over. And she has to wear that dang colostomy bag and diaper. But I think with her not being able to speak, that's the worst part. It's as hard on her as it is for us to see her lose her abilities. Mamma's always been a talker. They brought up the topic of the non-verbal stage of the disease at the last Alzheimer's board meeting. I think it might be time to get her to the doctor for a checkup."

"I agree."

"I'm on pins and needles when it comes to her."

"I know you are. Thanks for taking care of my mom, well, our mom, yours and mine, like you have. I'll head into her room in a minute. Maybe I'll take Nadia in with me."

"Good idea. It seems that besides Star, Nadia's the next best thing for Mamma." Mercedes turned around to unhook her phone from the wall charger.

Mason's eyes went from her back, to her behind, to her legs, all but licking her down. "Damn, you're hot, wifey."

"Well, thanks, hubby." She gave a tiny grin and then turned to stand before him.

"I'd say hot enough to be a political wife."

She replied, "Oh really? I'd say you look good enough to run this entire town or the country, any day of the week if you choose to."

"We'll start with the council seat first." He came to a stance. Bowlegged and over six feet, he picked up his coffee mug and took a seat at his large mahogany desk.

"Deal." Mercedes turned toward the door as though ready to head out.

"Plus, I was just thinking about getting our taxes audited." He clicked the mouse, eyeing the computer screen. "You know how the world of politics can be. And also, keeping our noses clean is critical." He perused the page, reading a new message. "Here's an email from Eric Garcetti's assistant." He paused and read again. "She said the first person I'll be meeting with is Ryan Germany. I've heard of him. He represents the Ninth District."

Pop. Pop. Shit!

Mercedes stopped and cleared her throat. "Okay." She faced him again. "Good luck."

"Thanks. You gone?" He looked over at her.

"Yeah." She walked back to him and leaned down, giving him a kiss. She noticed the subtle trace of alcohol. Possibly cognac. She kissed him again just to be sure. *Damn. Not again.* She shook her mind out of its trickery and asked as she turned toward the door, "You gonna feed Nadia?"

"Yep. I've got her." He then said as she walked out of the library, "Love you."

"Ditto." Their trademark reply.

If ditto meant *me too*, Mason was in for a rude awakening, and a very dirty political nose.

And Mercedes was in for a reality check revisit from a twenty plus year-old monster.

2

Venus

"... does your husband know ..."

Years ago, Claude Wilson's girlfriend, Fatima, was murdered on the porch of Mason and Mercedes's home by a jealous ex who had followed her around for days. He had called her fifty-two times in a row before he shot her in the head at point blank range. He then shot himself in the chest. But he survived.

The night before Fatima was killed, Claude, Fatima, and her best friend, Venus, had a threesome together. Fatima had asked Venus to do it as a favor, as a birthday present to Claude on the eve of Thanksgiving.

Little did Claude know that Fatima was being stalked by her ex, Owen Chambers, whom she had still been secretly sleeping with. Fatima had asked Venus to keep an eye on Claude, and on her son, Cameron, if anything ever happened to her. Venus agreed. But she never imagined the fact that because she and Claude had shared their mutual grief together, things would lead to him popping the question while they were in Vegas. Claude and Venus were wed less than one year after Fatima was killed.

Claude adopted Fatima's son, Cameron, who at first would not accept Venus because of her betrayal to his mother. And even Claude began to have concerns about his decision to marry Venus, especially after visiting Fatima's murderer, Owen, in prison. Owen told Claude that Cameron was his birth son, and that Venus knew about it all along, but never told Claude.

So, not only did Claude find out that Cameron was Owen's son, he also found out about the agreement between Fatima and Venus for Venus to be with Claude, and also that Fatima was still sleeping with Owen. The friction between Claude and Venus and the guilt that Venus felt every time she would make love to Claude outweighed their bond. Venus moved out. Especially after old-fashioned Claude forbid her to work.

Claude found the strength to forgive Venus and ask her back. He had sent flowers and left messages that she ignored, until finally after both Claude and Cameron invited her to Mason and Mercedes's home on Thanksgiving Day, Venus came back, standing on the very porch where her best friend was killed. By the next year they had their own child, a baby girl named Skyy. And Venus kept the job she had gotten as a director at the Make-A-Wish Foundation.

Fast forward, after work on the last Monday in July, Venus Ortiz Wilson picked up Skyy from pre-K class at Knox Presbyterian on La Tijera. They had only been at their yellow Senford Avenue home in upper Ladera for about fifteen minutes when Venus answered her Blackberry.

"Hi, Claude."

"Hey. I'm on my way home. Are you there yet?" There was a pep to Claude's words.

"Yes, honey," Venus replied. Her tailored white suit fit her slender figure like a glove.

"Good. I just finished signing a contract on a house on Corning."

Half-Latin with long, curly hair, Venus stood in their open area family room while six year-old Skyy sat on the huge mocha sectional, holding the remote, watching cartoons.

Skyy had a heart-shaped face. Her dark, curly hair hung down her back just like her mom's hair. She was focused and still.

Venus sounded excited for her husband and said, "Good for you. Congratulations."

"Thanks. You know who Mary is, right? The new sales agent I told you about who just started at the office?"

"Yeah."

"She had a conflict in schedule again. She's already missed a few caravans and meetings. She has a young son and her husband travels a lot. My office manager hired her, but I sure can't say I would've. I'm not sure it's gonna work out. But hey, we got the house sold today. It'll be a good chunk of change for the company, and for her."

"Good. And Claude, don't think I don't know where you're going with this." Her tone had warning. She took off her blazer and hung it on the coat rack near the front door.

"I'm sure you do. It's just another example. I think if a husband and wife can afford it, there should be one parent who is home with the kids. That's how my mom was."

Venus focused to keep her voice down. "Anyway, I've only been home for a hot minute. I'm gonna try and figure out what to make for dinner. I haven't even changed my clothes, let alone taken off my shoes."

"I'll just say this and leave it alone. You need to stay at home and look after Skyy. Not some nanny like before when we had someone helping us out."

"What are you talking about? We had a caregiver here when Mattie lived with us, but she still left here at four o'clock each day. She wasn't a nanny. I handled Skyy by myself, basically. Back then when the family decided Mattie needed a full-time nurse, Mattie went back to live with Mason and Mercedes. We no longer had a need for anyone. Claude, let's not do this again. I already stopped working once."

He just listened.

She continued, saying, "Honey, we've been through this before. You know it's not the money that makes me wanna get up and go to work. It's a career. I need that. Just because I work doesn't mean I love Skyy any less." She looked over at Skyy again and paced the marble entryway. "Besides, I do meaningful work." She took a breath. "Do you know that yesterday we were able to work out a deal with an organization called Destination Joy? They've decided to donate a ton of celebrity member's frequent flyer miles so we can get the kids flights booked for free. I'm excited about that."

"That's great. I know you love what you do. I can hear it in your voice. But, you know I'd prefer that you put our kid first, at least just for a little while. Skyy's been at Knox for a few years and now it's time for her to go to kindergarten. Because she was born in January she's already a little older than those kids in pre-K. I'm just talking about her having you home and available now that she's going into elementary, and then she won't have to do the after school program. At least not until maybe fourth grade."

"That'll be a while. Besides, what if I asked you to quit your work?" She kicked off her shoes and then stepped barefoot as she walked to the gourmet kitchen, taking a peek into the fridge, and then the pantry.

"That's very different. I own my own company. I've got people who can run it for me so I can take time off. And maybe I should work from home more often. My point is, no one can look after Skyy like we can."

Venus let out an audible sigh. "Claude, I need to start getting dinner ready."

"No need. I was gonna tell you that I'm headed over to our soul food place. What do you want?"

She managed a smile. "Oh, that's sweet of you." She thought for a second. "I'll just have the catfish with whatever sides you have. And get Skyy the smothered chicken. She loves it. With veggies."

"Okay, I'll be there shortly. And Venus, I love you. I've got you."

"I know you do. I love you, too. See you in a minute." As soon as Venus disconnected she tried to shake out her mind. The phone rang. She eyed the display. "Hey there, Cam. How are you?"

Cameron's words were rushed. "I need to talk to Dad right away."

"What's wrong?"

"Mom, I just called Dad's cell and he didn't pick up. Is he with you?"

"No. We just hung up. He's in the car about to stop and get dinner. What happened?" Venus removed her tiny hoop earrings and placed them on the porcelain tile island.

"I'm in the counselor's office at school. My coach is here, too. They're kicking me out of school."

"Kicking you out? That's crazy. Let me talk to your coach. Put him on the phone."

"I've gotta go. That's Dad on the other line." He clicked over fast.

"Oh my God." In thought, she paced back and forth from the kitchen to the family room and back. She called Claude. No answer.

Skyy called out, "Mommy. My favorite movie, *Shark Tale,* is on. Can I watch it?"

14

Venus dialed Claude again, talking as she listened to his voicemail greeting, telling Skyy, "Oh, sweetie, no. Wait until later." She hung up.

"Please?" Skyy's voice was soft. She aimed the remote at the screen and searched for more shows.

"No. Maybe after we eat." Venus walked into the family room and took the remote from her daughter, powering everything off. "In the meantime, come on and go outside with me for a minute. Then we'll read a book and talk."

Wearing jean shorts and a flowered Gap tee, Skyy hopped off the sofa and headed to her mom, taking her by the hand. Skyy's purple flip-flops were at the front door.

"Here, slip these on."

Skyy did just that. "Mommy, is my brother okay?" She didn't usually miss much. And calling Cameron her brother was like her own loving nickname for him.

"Yes, sweetie. Cam's just fine."

"Is he coming home? I miss him." She looked up at her mom.

"He'll be home soon enough. Maybe you can talk to him later."

Venus and Skyy walked down the porch steps and along the circular driveway. The concrete was warm upon the soles of Venus's feet. The late afternoon prepared its handoff to early evening.

Venus took in the view of Ladera Heights, known for its well-manicured lawns, fancy cars, and sprawling estate homes. The look and feel and essence of the upscale neighborhood from the outside seemed perfect, with towering, strong palm trees lined up along the street. But Venus knew that chances were, inside of the homes themselves it was quite possibly anything but.

She walked toward the custom brick mailbox they had built at the curb, hurrying to the strip of cool grass.

Skyy had let go of her hand, running back and forth along the front lawn. "Mommy, catch me." Her voice was playful.

"Hold on, let Mommy get the mail." Venus reached into the mailbox and shuffled through the few pieces of mail: a power bill, a credit card bill, and a letter that was addressed to her maiden name, Venus Ortiz. The return address was the California Men's Colony in San Luis Obispo.

Curiously, she opened the letter and unfolded a long white sheet of notebook paper. Her mind held its breath. The words were scribbled, small letters, with the sentences all running together without benefit of much punctuation.

Hey sexy I miss you I can't wait to be with you again the way I turned your girl out and blew her mind with my mouth How's my son Soon it will be the three of us cutie pie Soon enough

By the way does your husband know you wanted me the whole time when I was with Fatima Does he know you and I had sex and Fatima never knew Does he know you've always liked what Fatima had How you stole her college boyfriend years ago How you'd sneak and call me back when I first met her I hope your husband doesn't have a close friend because you can't be trusted Now that Fatima is dead and you already have what she had I'm thinking that won't be enough You'll go buck wild soon enough So I say you and me should just correspond and maybe you can even come and see me Wouldn't that be sneaky Right up your alley Tell my son I said he can come and see me too Oh that's right I'm willing to bet he doesn't know I'm his father yet right Your husband's ego wouldn't allow that Maybe I'll just have to find a way to tell him myself I guess I'll chat with him on the Bureau of Prison's Corrlinks I'm sure I can find his email address I sent a link request to your job but it bounced back Oh well Till next time Love Owen

Venus fought to close her mouth. She darted her eyes over toward Skyy, who was still playing on the front lawn. Venus began to sweat. She swallowed hard and her heart shifted with fright.

"Skyy, let's go inside. Now." Venus ran to Skyy and picked her up, hugging her tight, looking all around, and heading back into the house, closing and locking the door, fast.

Venus set the alarm and stood in the entryway and took a deep breath, putting Skyy down.

Skyy asked, "Can we read now?"

Venus shook her head and made herself focus on her young daughter's question. "Sure. Go and get a book."

Skyy skipped to the staircase and headed up to her room.

Venus went straight to her cell and called Claude. He still did not answer. She then called her sister-in-law, Mercedes, and tried her best to simply focus on having as normal a voice as possible. She placed the mail atop the island. "Hey, there." To her, from inside her convoluted head, it sounded like her own voice was cracking.

"Hi, Venus. How are you?"

She fought harder to stay calm. "I'm okay. Yep, I'm okay. So, how's Mattie?" She leaned against the island, hoping her small talk didn't sound fake.

"Mamma's about the same. I made an appointment for her to go and get a check up next week. How are you? And how's Skyy? I still can't believe you and Sequoia now have the young ones, when my Star and Rashaad are all grown up and out of the house."

Venus tried to force a smile but couldn't. "We're fine." She inhaled and exhaled huge. "Mercedes, I need to talk to you." Her hands shook.

"Sure."

She thought twice, and switched problem-gears. "Something's going on with Cam. I mean, he called, and I guess they're talking about kicking him out of school. I have no idea what happened. I think he talked to Claude after he called me, but I haven't heard from either one."

"Venus, I'm coming right over."

Venus spoke quickly. "No. I want Claude to tell you and Mason about this himself. I haven't even talked to him yet. You know how private he is."

"I do. Okay. Still, I can't imagine what the deal is. Cameron's a good student. I'm sure it'll all be ironed out."

Skyy came downstairs. "Here, Mom." She handed Venus a thick book of fairy tales.

"Okay. Just give Mommy one minute." She gave the book back to Skyy and held up one finger. "Go take this and sit on the couch. I'll be right there, I promise."

Skyy walked away, hugging her book, looking sad. "Okay."

"Mercedes, I just wanna know what's up with him. Not knowing is worse than knowing."

"Listen. How about if I come over anyway? Claude doesn't even have to know why I'm there."

"Mercedes, I don't want to interrupt your evening. Is Lucinda there to stay with Mattie?"

"Yes. Both she and Mason are here. She's basically a live-in now though she does go home every now and then. I'll be right over in a few. You know I'm just a few blocks away."

"Okay. See you in a minute. Thanks."

"That's what family's for."

Venus and Mercedes hung up.

"Here I come, Skyy," Venus said to her pouty-faced, awaiting daughter.

Skyy had quickly changed focus. She rubbed her eyes. "Mommy. Can I have pancakes?"

"Oh, Skyy. Daddy's on his way with food. Chicken and veggies, okay?" Venus sat down next to Skyy and placed another call to Claude. No answer. And then she called Cameron. No answer.

"You said my brother was okay." Skyy flashed her eyes toward her mom.

Venus prepared herself to reply when she heard the garage door open and the sound of Claude's sports car pull in. She stood and headed to the kitchen.

"Daddy!" yelled Skyy, with an instantly perky tone while she ran toward the kitchen door that led to the garage.

"Wait, sweetie." Venus heard the garage door close, and the car door open and close.

Bluetooth to his ear, baldheaded Claude opened the door frowning and talking fast, cradling two bags against his NBA-type body frame. Two seconds after he stepped inside, the security alarm went off with a major screech.

Skyy jumped and held her ears. It was piercing.

"Hold on, sorry," he told the caller. He said to Venus loudly, "Why'd you set the alarm so early?"

"No reason." She hurried to the keypad and disarmed it.

He placed the bags on the breakfast nook table and kept talking. He wore a white shirt with obvious sweat stains under his arms. He walked to the island and set down his keys. "So, look Sampson, we need to talk to the school administrators right away. There's no way my son violated any school policies about cheating, or student Internet policy, or plagiarism, let alone this crap about him having someone to write his essay. What's all that mess about? I need to know how they reached these bogus conclusions. My son does not lie. Plus, he's just about to graduate. It's taken him more than five years, but he's ready. I will sue the school and the whole damn city if I have to. Say what? . . . Leave school in the meantime? Oh, no, he won't unless we make a decision like that on our own. I'll head out to Berkley tonight if necessary. My brother Torino is an alumni there. He made that school a lot of money playing football . . . Oh, you know it. Look, like you said, go ahead get on this and call me right back. In the meantime, I'll talk to Cameron again . . . Okay. Thanks." Even his forehead was sweaty.

Venus walked over to him as he stared only at his black Porsche mobile.

He took a step back. "Not right now." He walked past her, touching the screen of his phone while holding a red folder.

"Claude, it'll all work out."

He said nothing.

"Daddy," Skyy called out, standing behind Venus.

Claude smiled at his daughter. "Hey, Skyy. Daddy will be right back." And he told Venus, "I'll be in my office for a while."

"Okay. Thanks for getting dinner, honey." Venus began taking the containers from the bags. The soulful smell of Claude's rib dinner, greens, and rice hit her nostrils. "Smells good, huh, Skyy?"

Skyy nodded.

"Here. Sit down. It's time to eat."

"My stomach hurts, Mommy." Skyy now moved like molasses.

Claude said with volume as he walked toward his office, "She should've eaten already. And you wonder why I want you to stay home." He shut the door firmly behind himself.

Venus sat down at the kitchen table next to Skyy in deep thought. *It's only six-thirty.* "Say your blessings, sweetie."

Skyy started to pray, with Venus joining in, "Bless us O Lord, for these thy gifts, which we are about to receive, from thy bounty, through Christ our Lord. Amen."

"Good girl." They both began to eat. "So, how was school today?" Venus asked, just as the doorbell rang. Venus got up. "Just a second, Skyy."

"Who's that?" Claude yelled from behind his office door.

Venus yelled back. "I'm sure it's Mercedes. She said she was coming over."

"Does she know about this?"

"No," Venus yelled again, opening the door. Mercedes stepped in and they hugged. She toned down her voice. "Hey, girl."

"Hey, Sis." Wearing faded denim, Mercedes put her powder blue Coach bag down on the entryway table and headed toward the kitchen. "Is Claude here?" she asked quietly.

Venus nodded in reply. "Did you drive?"

"Yes. You know I'm lazy." She grinned Skyy's way. "Hi, Skyy, girl."

"Hi, Auntie." Skyy swallowed her food and grinned back as Mercedes kissed her on her cheek.

"Don't you look cute? Looks like you're getting a tan." Mercedes brushed her hand along Skyy's forehead.

"I went swimming."

"You did? You're just a little fish, huh?"

"Yep. I love to swim."

Venus just stood over the table, arms crossed, looking blank.

Mercedes took a seat across from Skyy. "Relax, Venus. Finish eating. You know how it is. This is the world of the Wilson brothers. Enough drama for your momma. But, I'll tell you one thing. Things are gonna have to start slowing down a little. Mason's thinking about running for office."

"What?" Venus walked toward the double-sink when she stepped on her earring that had fallen on the floor. "Ouch." She picked it up and placed it back on the island next to the other earring, noticing that her stack of mail that was atop the island was now gone, including the letter from Owen.

Venus was white as a ghost, and she was completely speechless.

Though Mercedes chatted using some words that were suddenly inaudible, sounding like blah, blah, blah, all Venus's ears zoomed in on were Claude's words coming from the other side of his office door, talking extra-loud to Cameron.

3

<u>Sequoia</u>

". . . there's only one Torino Jr. . . ."

It was all about the eyes.

After all these years, Sequoia Wilson couldn't get it out of her head that Colette Berry, crazy former girlfriend of Sequoia's husband Torino Wilson, had a son named Kyle Jr. who looked just like Torino, and not a bit like his hazel-eyed father, Kyle Brewer.

Actually, to Sequoia, little Kyle Jr. looked like he could be the big brother to her and Torino's five year-old son, Torino Jr.

And that had nagged the hell out of Sequoia for years.

Colette was light-skinned with light eyes herself, and Kyle was the spitting image of Derek Jeter, yet Kyle Jr. was chocolate brown with dark brown eyes.

Kyle had been Torino's best friend, until Torino, who owns the nightclub called Foreplay, fired Kyle for pocketing door money. That was right around the same time Torino's then girlfriend, Colette, got kicked out of the club for acting psycho after catching a case of her usual jealousy fever. When Torino got off work at three in the morning, he drove by Colette's apartment and saw Kyle's car parked outside.

Revenge sex was something Colette told him she believed in. And it was clear to Torino that it was on.

Months later, pregnant Colette tried to pin the paternity on Torino. Once she found out Torino was dating Mercedes's best friend, Sequoia, Colette showed up at Mason's house during a family dinner, holding a knife to her belly, threatening to end her life and her unborn child's life if Torino didn't stop seeing Sequoia.

Claude and Torino talked her out of it, she seemed to move on with Kyle, and for the most part she had been quiet. But when the child was nineteen months old, Sequoia saw Colette, Kyle and Kyle Jr. at Magic Johnson's Fridays in the Ladera Center. It was just a feeling. Maybe instinct. But Sequoia became convinced that Kyle Jr. was her husband's son, though Torino still denied it.

Today, having traded in his long dreads for a low, Mohawk haircut, former football player-slash-retired playboy Torino sat on the gray loveseat in the den next to Sequoia. They'd just finished playing *Scrabble* on their laptop in their Spanish-style, three-bedroom, lower Ladera home on Halm Avenue just around the corner from Mason and Mercedes's old house. It had Brazilian hardwood cabinets, coffered ceilings, and a lap pool with a lanai. It was built in 1929 and was worth more than nine-hundred-thousand dollars when he bought it in 2005, but now it was only worth about seven hundred-fifty, which was the norm considering the economic slump. But forty-one year-old Torino was doing very well for himself. After all of his years of financial setbacks, he now had amassed a good amount of savings.

Most of the money he made was from managing the rapper, Lady Di, who he discovered in the club years ago. But last year she signed with Epic records, got a new manager, and moved on. Torino swore he would focus his attention on real estate, and shift more of his efforts into the club he bought from Mason and his business partner Cicely, who also turned out to be their half sister.

Last year, Torino, who was named after his father's 1975 blue Ford Torino, opened a new club in El Segundo called Wilson's. Both clubs catered to everyone from the occasional nightclub person, to the actors, athletes, and musicians of the world. He also owned second house on Shenandoah that he rented out for five-thousand per month.

It was a Friday night.

A smooth Hiroshima CD played.

Sturdy, curvy Sequoia, wearing only an oversized white tee shirt, just the way her husband liked it, spoke like she had just won a round of Jeopardy on television. "I beat you again. Face it; I'm just smarter than you." She bounced up and down as she sat on the sofa in their den, shaking her brown, straight hair back and forth.

"Why is it that you can come up with words no one's ever heard of?" he asked, sitting right next to her, dressed for work in a blue suit.

"Sore loser." Her pear-shaped solitaire sparkled as she waved him away with her hand. "Poof, be gone."

"Cheater."

"Oh, so I'm making the game give me points? I'm in cahoots with the Scrabble game makers? Torino, how would anyone cheat on a computer version of Scrabble?"

"I don't put anything past anyone who comes up with the word gelation."

"The process of gelling, Torino. I told you."

"That's bogus."

"You're a trip."

"I'll get you next time. You and that damn computer."

"Yeah right." She popped her lips.

He told her, "You went away to Vegas with Mercedes and ain't been the same since."

"Whatever."

"Yeah, you're trippin' all right. Right TJ?" TJ was Torino Jr.'s nickname.

"Yes, Daddy," TJ said, with his dark brown skin, hair in a tightly curled Afro. He sat on the floor playing with his racecar set, making *vroom, vroom* sounds.

Sequoia placed the laptop on the coffee table and sat back, watching her son. "I did miss you guys while we were gone." She patted Torino along his thigh.

He kept looking at her thigh. "I never asked you, but how'd the fashion show go, anyway?"

"Great. You know Mercedes is an expert at that. She can do all that in her sleep."

"What else did you guys do? Gamble and hit the nightclubs?"

"We did. We went out. But it was nothing like Foreplay or Wilson's."

"Good answer." He scooted forward after noticing the clock and then stood. "Hey, I'm gonna see you later tonight. I've gotta hold down the fort at the club."

"Okay. I'll see you later."

"I might even cut out early." He grabbed his keys and wallet from the end table and then patted TJ on his head. "Goodbye, TJ."

"Bye, Daddy."

"You be good. Listen to Mommy."

"I will."

"He's always good," Sequoia said, curling her legs under her, getting comfortable.

"See you later." Torino eyed her down, looking at her legs. "That's some sexy shit right there." He leaned into her and gave her a peck on the lips.

She returned it with tongue until she heard, "Daddy. Leave Mommy alone." She pulled back laughing. "Yeah, Daddy."

"It's a conspiracy. My own son is blockin' me."

"You just bring it on back home so we can continue," she said just as her cell rang from the sofa table.

26

He headed to the door and blew a kiss, exiting as she grabbed her phone.

She said, "Hey, Mercedes. What's up?"

"Hey there, not much. You?"

"Torino just left. He's headed to work."

"Okay. I thought he might leave around this time."

"Where's Mason?"

"He's in the bedroom watching TV, taking a break from his book. He'll get up again and go back in the office."

"I still can't get over how much he's home now. He was never home before."

"That's what retirement will do for you."

"I guess so. You talk to Claude and Venus lately?"

"I stopped by the other night. Why?"

"Why? Why do you ask why? Just the fact that you asked why, means you must tell me why you asked why. What is it that you're trying to see if I know first by asking why?"

"Oh, no. You are so wrong."

"Please. I know you."

"Not."

"Yeah, well, whatever. You being all secretive and stuff. Anyway, from what Torino tells me, Claude's still trying to get Venus to quit working. And while I can't say I've always been a fan of Venus, he needs to lighten up. She's got a dream job."

"She does. But some women wish they had an old-fashioned man with those types of rules. A man who doesn't want you to work? Please."

"Claude isn't old fashioned. He's controlling, and you know it."

"That he is. But she knows what she's got. It's working."

"Is it? I mean, maybe something might be up over there between the two of them. So, what's up over there, huh?"

"Sequoia, stop fishing."

"You stop tripping."

"I'm not."

"Are, too. Forget you. Listen, I know what I wanted to tell you. I think I'm going to spend some time with Mattie tomorrow, maybe around noon, if that's okay."

"Sequoia, you don't have to ask. You come by anytime. If we're gone, Lucinda will be here with her."

"Good." Sequoia paused. "Girl, you know I'm still thinking about Vegas."

"Really?"

"Did Mason ask for details?"

"No. He knows it was work. No biggie."

"I'm talking about him asking you if we did anything else."

Mercedes sounded like she knew her man for sure. "No. Mason doesn't care about stuff like that."

"How do you know?"

"He trusts me."

"Well, Torino asked me."

"About me?"

"No. About us. About the show and the trip. I told him we went out for a minute."

"You did?"

"Yeah."

"Why'd you tell him that?"

"Why not" I thought you said Mason doesn't care."

"What else did you tell him?"

"That you had a grind-fest with a boy-toy."

"No I didn't. That's not even funny."

"Oh, excuse me. It wasn't a grind-fest. It was straight up sex on the dance floor."

"Sequoia. You know it was not that deep. It was just dancing."

"Okay. But I didn't go into all that. That's for you to tell. I'm just saying, it's not like you two went any further afterwards, right?"

"Of course not. When would I have had time to go further than that?"

"Beats me."

Suddenly, TJ asked, "Mommy, will you play with me?" sounding tired, actually yawning.

"Now how are you going to play when you're about dozing off, TJ?"

"I'm not tired."

"Oh, Lord. A child's famous last words before they conk out. Listen, girl. I've gotta go put this boy to bed. I'll talk to you later. Maybe I'll see you while I'm over there tomorrow."

"Okay. Talk to ya. And watch yourself, with your big mouth."

"Wow, if that ain't the pot calling the kettle black? You're Wilson family central."

The clock struck three in the morning when Sequoia heard Torino walk in their master bedroom and then head to the bathroom.

There was an amber light shining next to Torino's side of the bed. The room smelled like her angel-food body oil.

Torino took off his clothes, all but his boxers, and before Sequoia could even turn over to look his way, he came back out. He headed to their walnut-framed bed and got under the covers, planting a kiss on her nose.

She looked over at the digital clock. "Wow. That was a long night."

"It was."

She turned her body toward him. "Was it crowded?"

"Yes. Way too many folks."

"Too many?" She ran her fingers through her hair. "Since when is that a bad thing?"

"Let's just say one too many."

"What do you mean?" she asked, giving him a look. She sat up and scooted herself all the way back against the headboard.

"It was Colette. Colette came in tonight with a couple of her friends."

Sequoia frowned instantly. "I thought you'd asked the bouncers not to let her back in after all the crap she pulled years ago."

"I did. But that was a long time ago. I've got new guys, and a new cashier. I'd forgotten about it, actually. I just never thought she'd have the nerve to come back in there."

Sequoia began massaging her temples. "Anyway, I'm not surprised." Her voice grew deeper. "Did she at least behave, Torino?"

"In a way."

"What does that mean?"

"Colette wants child support."

Her eyes bugged. "Child support? She wants you to pay child support for Kyle's son?"

"She's still insisting I'm that boy's father."

"Oh, please. I thought after she showed up in Mason's backyard threatening to stab herself in the stomach when she was pregnant, she'd go away and live her tripped out, wacky life and focus on her so-called modeling career. Now, all of a sudden out of the blue she wants child support. That's just crazy."

"Honestly, I think they're having problems. For her to come up with this now, she's obviously suddenly worried about money. And, she said she wants something else."

30

"What?" She braced herself.

"She wants to give Kyle Jr. the Wilson name."

Sequoia paused and took a moment to breath. She looked at Torino like he was just as crazy as his ex. "Kyle Jr., would be a Wilson." She shook her head. "I've heard it all now." She fidgeted with her wedding ring, twisting is back and forth while looking into nowhere.

"Makes no sense to me, either." He sat up.

"Torino, I've never brought this up before, but I'm going to tell you something. Venus and Mercedes talked to me about the fact that Kyle Jr. has your eyes, your face and your skin tone. Not Kyle's, but yours. And Colette, well she looks like a busted Vanessa Williams. That child looks just like you. Actually, he looks just like TJ."

Torino simply said, "I know."

She titled her head. "You know?"

"I've thought about it more and more the older he gets. I saw him and Kyle at Starbucks last month."

"Oh you did? And you stood there watching him with a kid who could be your own son? And then you go back and live your life like that's just gonna go away." She scooted over to face him, turning her torso his way. "Don't you think it's kinda fucked up that Kyle's playing house without really knowing it?"

"First of all, like I've told you, I don't know how I could be the father. I just can't be. Either Kyle's the father and the light skin, light eyes skipped a generation, or someone else is the father. But I am not. And second of all, I couldn't care less about Kyle."

"And why is that, Torino? Because he slept with Colette on the night you two argued after the club? Right before you and I hooked up? Have you ever gotten over that mess?"

"I left Kyle in charge of the VIP passes for the club and he was charging people cash money before they ever hit the door. Cash just for adding their names to the VIP comp list. Kyle's a thief. And yes, I'm over that."

"Oh, so you still despise him for only that reason and nothing else?"

"Like I said, I don't give a damn."

"Looks like that thief stole your son."

"Sequoia." Torino turned to face her.

"Look, I'm going to try and be cool through this." She took a deep breath. "One thing I know for sure is you need to take a paternity test. That woman could end up with half of everything you've worked so hard for, everything *we* have, and she's just the type to do it. Not to mention the fact that her little boy needs to know for sure who his real father is. Is he a junior to Kyle or not? The name Torino Jr. is already taken." She fluffed her pillow to lie back down, securing herself under the covers.

"Sequoia, like you said, there's only one Torino Jr. and he's in the next room sleeping."

"I'm just telling you to handle your business. Don't allow this to get us off track after all these years. It's long overdue for you to handle this and get a paternity test."

"I've got this. Don't worry." He lay down, as well, and got under the covers facing her, hugging her around her waist.

"Torino, are you sure you wore a condom every time you slept with her before we started dating?"

"I'm absolutely sure I did."

She sighed.

"Look, baby, we'll get through this. Come here." He placed his hand on her thigh and began rubbing between her legs, aiming his middle finger toward her middle split.

Her voice was bored. "Good night, Torino." She moved his hand. "You know I've gotta get up early in the morning and take TJ to the doctor to get his *brown eyes* checked." Her sarcasm reeked.

He looked at her like *no you did not.*

"Good night."

He said, "I love you."

"Turn off the light." She sounded bossy.

He twisted himself around, reaching over and turning off the light, lying down again.

She faced him. Eyes closed. Silent.

He faced her. Eyes open. Silent.

She looked at him briefly, almost through him and turned to face the other way, scooting to the far side of the bed, assuming the fetal position. She eased into the comfort of the mattress with the covers to her chin. "I love you, too," she said barely.

Then he said, "You should know. Colette said she impregnated herself with sperm from my condom."

4

Mercedes

"Are you cheating on Dad . . ."

On a bright Monday morning, the second day of August, Mercedes rushed off to work.

Her office was in a high-rise in Century City on Century Park West that overlooked Beverly Hills, Hollywood, and Downtown L.A. She owned Simpson Models. Simpson was her maiden name and the name of the business she inherited.

The work space was designer quality, mainly chrome and off-white with two large offices and eight cubicles. Black and white photos of the many models she represented and shows she had produced lined the hallway entrance that led to the desk of her long-time assistant, Vicky.

"How's it going?" Mercedes asked, dressed in a black double breasted with wide leg pants, briefcase in one hand, fuchsia shoulder bag hanging along her arm.

"Good. I see you're not answering your phone," Vicky said to her boss, sporting a Madonna tee shirt, vintage jeans, and black and white checkered Vans.

"I heard it ringing when I got out of the elevator, I just couldn't find it." She held up her purse. "It's lost amongst all of the useless clutter I've got in here."

"Well, Star is on line one. We've both been trying to reach you."

She walked fast, saying, "Oh, okay. She never calls here. Thanks. Did you send me photos of the new shoe line for next week?"

"I did. I emailed it to you a minute ago."

"Cool." Moving a mile a minute, she tossed her purse onto the guest chair, and slid her briefcase under her desk. She sat in her leather executive chair and pressed line one and powered up her computer. Her many rows of framed family pictures stared at her. "Hi, Star. Sorry I didn't answer my cell. I've been rushing trying to get up here. I have an open call soon. How are you?"

Without delay, Star said, "Mom, you know my friend out here in Atlanta named Trinity? I think you've heard me talk about her. Her mom remarried about ten years ago and I was telling you how Trinity was estranged from her dad and I called you to tell you how much I appreciated you and dad being together, raising us."

"I think so, yeah."

"Trinity's last name is Todd, but that's her step-father's name. Her real dad's last name is Germany."

"I see." Mercedes signed on to her computer.

"And, well, she's not estranged from him anymore. She reunited with him a few months back, and she was in L.A. visiting him recently. His name is Ryan Germany."

Pop!

"Ryan Germany?" Mercedes turned her chair away from her desk and faced toward the window view, thinking, *small ass world.*

"Yes." Star kind of waited.

"Okay. So what's up?"

"What's up is that he's a member of the city council there in Los Angeles."

"I know that."

"You do?"

35

"Yes." Mercedes sighed. "Star, get to the point."

"Trinity was at his house when she came in town. She overheard him tell a friend that he met Mason Wilson's wife in Vegas."

"Oh really?" Mercedes crossed her legs and bounced her foot.

"That's what she heard him say. I mean you would know. Anyway, she heard him say that he wished you weren't married. That you and him spent time together. That he didn't go into detail but Trinity knew from what she heard that he was attracted to Mercedes Wilson. You. My mom."

"Well, first of all, I know my name. And second of all, that's really interesting, but I can't tell you that I know what that was about."

"You can't? You said you know him."

"No, I heard of him. I can't remember meeting anyone like that."

"But you were in Vegas last month, right?"

"Star, I will tell you one thing. I won't sit here and let you beat around the bush like some detective, tossing me pieces of a story about some *he said she said* like this. I am your mother, not some boyfriend of yours you're trying to bust because you think he's being unfaithful."

"I didn't use the word unfaithful."

"You might as well. You're saying he said he spent time with me. That's just ridiculous. I'm happily married and wouldn't do that and you know it." She turned back toward her desk and began clicking the mouse, logging in to her email.

"Mom, I'm just asking."

"No. You're not asking, you're telling, Star. You're suggesting with a titillating build up of a story and I'm not having it. Just get to the point if you want to ask me something."

"Are you cheating on Dad with Ryan Germany?"

Mercedes looked up at the ceiling, cut her eyes to the window, and then looked back at the computer screen. "No."

"Then you won't mind if I tell Dad then, right?"

"No. I don't."

"Okay. Fine."

"Fine."

Star continued though her tone had abated. "This is embarrassing. She overhears something knowing the conversation was about her friend's mom."

"If he said he was in Vegas, and I was in Vegas too, maybe we did meet. But your friend can't jump to conclusions anymore than you can."

"It just sounds weird, Mom."

Mercedes fiddled with her braided gold necklace with one hand, the other hand on the mouse. "Then maybe she should ask her dad what's up to get clarification, versus her eavesdropping on him. She should ask him to tell her what he's talking about, and then maybe you can tell me, and your dad. You know me better than that."

"I do? Okay. Whatever." Star could be heard clicking her tongue.

"What does 'whatever' mean?"

"I've got rehearsal in a few minutes. Bye." Star shoved her mother with her words and clicked her off with the push of a button.

"Bye," Mercedes said out loud to no one as she slammed down the phone. "Shit!"

She fought to shift her focus from the thunderstorm she heard approaching, wanting to head back home and get back in bed and wake up again, retrying the day in case it was all a dream.

Vicky sent her an IM. *Hope you're okay. Your nine o'clock open model call is ready to go.*

But Mercedes couldn't go back to bed.

And she couldn't go back to Sin City to undo her sins.

She prayed Star's words were only a reactionary bluff.

She got up and mumbled, "Maybe she's on her damn period." And then she said loudly to her assistant, "Here I come."

5

<u>Venus</u>

"Mom, what's his problem?"

It was a week later.

Venus arrived home from work just before six-thirty in the evening.

She did not need to pick up Skyy from pre-K because Claude had taken the day off, but she did stop at Ralph's in the Ladera Center to pick up a few things for dinner. Tonight she planned to make her family their favorite dish, shrimp and chicken fettuccini.

"Welcome home," Claude said, sitting on the recliner in the family room doing work on his MacBook.

"Hello, man of leisure."

"Hardly." He looked over at her as she closed the door with her foot, hands full. "You need help?"

"No, I've got it. Just a couple of bags. Where's Skyy?"

He refocused. "She's next door playing with Faith. Faith's mom asked if they could play together. Her mom even offered to help out if we ever need back-up during the day."

"I know. She told me that, too."

"Yep."

"You're really serious about me being a stay at home mom again, aren't you?"

"I am." He glossed over the topic. "How was your day?"

"Busy." Venus, wearing an olive green pantsuit, had even pulled out the emerald earrings and matching heart-shaped ring Claude bought her while they were in Italy for their anniversary last year. "Our talent team got Steve Harvey to let one of our kids come on his radio show and guest host for ten minutes next month. The girl is HIV positive. Those ten minutes aren't only going to make her day, they'll make her life."

"That was nice of him. Congratulations." He looked over at her again. "You look nice, by the way. I'm feeling that jewelry. Where'd ya get it?"

She winked. "My man bought it for me."

"Oh really. He must really love you."

"Oh, he does."

Claude grinned.

"And your day? How was it?" she asked.

"I picked up Skyy from school and took her to McDonalds. She played most of the time. Barely ate."

"I'm not at all surprised. I'm sure she was excited." She took the groceries from the bags and put them on the sink. "Give me about forty-five minutes. I'm making your pasta."

"That's what I'm talking about." He pressed the keys on his laptop. "So, you think maybe you'll be able to pick her up one day next week?"

"I'll see." She slipped off her shoes near the kitchen table.

"Venus, dear, what about if you just tell them you need time off?"

"I have to fit it in."

"Fit your daughter in?"

She took a large skillet from the cabinet. "Claude, leaving early is gonna be tough. It depends on meetings."

"You're a director."

"Yes, I am. And?" She watched his fingers work while he talked. She frowned. "And what are you working on, anyway? You're affixed to that laptop."

He spoke while reading. "I just got this email from Attorney Sampson. He's still working on getting Cameron's issues cleared up. Cameron will be home tonight. For now, it looks like the school is holding steady about his expulsion. It's gonna be a damn fight."

"That's crazy."

"Turns out there's a girl who searched that mess for him on the Internet. Basically did his work for him. Cameron says he didn't know she copied it from a website. But when the school interviewed her, she admitted it. It's his girlfriend."

"Not Candy."

"Yes."

She took the almond milk and shrimp from the refrigerator. "Actually, I guess I'm not surprised. Damn, those two. First they got in trouble for joyriding in someone's car. Then, she pawned stolen merchandise to buy him an iPhone for his birthday. And now this. She's a mess."

"He needs to cut her loose. She's crooked as a question mark and messy as a soup sandwich, if you ask me. She's gotta go."

"I agree."

"Hey, Pops," Cameron said, coming in through the kitchen door. He wasn't alone.

"Hey, Cameron." Claude turned around looking very reserved.

"Hi, Mom."

Venus said, "Hi, Cam." Then she saw his girl behind him, closing the door. "Hello, Candy." Cameron dwarfed her petite frame, even with her trendy high heels.

"Hi there, Mrs. Wilson. Love your shoes. And your ring is beautiful."

"Thanks." Venus examined Candy's mature figure. She had the porcelain face of a twenty year-old and the sexy body of an Atlanta stripper.

"Hello, Mr. Wilson."

Claude leaned forward and placed the laptop on the table. He turned toward the kitchen. He tried not to look at Candy. "Son, come here for a minute."

Cameron, tall and thin, walked into the family room. "Yes."

"Looks like you've got some mess going on."

"Yeah."

"This could mean you don't return to Berkley. You know that?"

Candy stood next to Cameron. "If he doesn't go back, I won't either."

In his mind Claude shook his head. He cut his eyes to her. "Candy, does your dad know what happened?"

"Yes, Sir."

"And. What did he say?"

"He knows I found the information online. I didn't copy it word for word though."

"But the school's Honor Council found that three distinct paragraphs of Cameron's research paper were plagiarized from a Wikipedia article. Basically a copy and paste. They found him guilty. But did you get kicked out, too?"

"No."

"And why not?"

Cameron said, "Dad, it wasn't her homework. It was my responsibility."

Claude looked at his son with impatience. "See, this crap has taken valuable time out of my days. This thing is costing me money."

"Then don't put any more time into it. I'm cool. Even if I have to go somewhere else."

"Then you can pay for that 'somewhere else.' And tell me, what will you do if you find that the majority of your classes aren't even transferable?"

"Why wouldn't they be?"

"That's just how it goes." He looked at Candy but spoke to Cameron. "Why don't you have her check the Internet to find out? But I'm not paying for your last year of school. That's on you."

"School can wait a little while. I'm ready to work full-time anyway."

"Waiting is guaranteed to mean you'll never finish."

Candy said, "Mr. Wilson, I'm sorry." Her eyes were downcast like a sad puppy.

Claude stood and then walked to the front door, opening it, "Candy, would you mind? We need some family time before I go get my daughter."

"Dad, she was coming up to my room."

Venus just watched from the kitchen, pulling rotisserie chicken from the bone.

Claude shook his head, holding on to the nickel doorknob. "No. Not right now."

Candy said, "It's okay." She gave Cameron a kiss on his cheek. "I'll talk to you later." She walked to the door, switching in her four inch gladiator heels.

"I'll be by," Cameron said back to her.

She exited.

Claude closed the door. "No you won't. What you're gonna do is put some work into this. The work you didn't put into that research paper. I'm done. And if you stay here I want rent." He cut his eyes and walked in the kitchen. "Actually, Venus, we need to make a decision on moving to Laguna. My new office will be open soon."

"New office?" asked Cameron.

She said, "Your dad is opening a second real estate office. It's in Laguna Hills."

Claude looked serious. "I'm ready to move up and move on before our past catches up with us."

"What past?" Venus asked.

"Venus, we need a change and you know it."

She said, "Honey, I'm fine with that, but for me, my only concern would be my commute to work."

He interjected as though certain, "Not if you quit. And as far as schools for Skyy, Parent Elementary out here is cool, but there's an elementary school called Valencia I hear is excellent. I sent you a link to the school site."

"I know. I opened it at work but didn't get a chance to check it out like I wanted to. I do think we need to do some serious research and go out there, too."

"I agree. But overall I think the schools out there are better. Less crowded. Plus, Cameron, you can go to school and work out there." He looked at Cameron. "Get you away from that fast-ass girl."

Cameron looked at his dad like he wanted to say something but he didn't. He just stood in place.

"The new office will be open next month. I already have a list of houses lined up for us. Plus, I feel some mess is about to blow up. I just know it." Claude walked away and took his cell as it vibrated from his pocket, holding it to his ear. "Hello?" He headed toward the back of the house.

Cameron walked over to Venus in the kitchen. "What's his problem? I swear Dad is going through *man-o-pause*."

She fought off a laugh and turned on the water to wash her hands. "Sheesh. You know how he is. But you must admit you messed up. You violated the school contract. He's disappointed."

"That contract applies to situations I knew about. I didn't know it was plagiarized. They didn't even give me

44

a fair chance. They could have suspended me but they expelled me. That's not fair, especially since it's my first offense."

She dried off her hands with a paper towel. "Bottom line, Cam, you knew you turned in work you didn't write."

He shook his head. "Okay, I did." He looked frustrated. "Anyway, Mom, please tell me you're not gonna quit your job."

"I don't know."

"Dad's trippin, if you ask me."

"He's not. He just tired of B.S." Venus walked out of the kitchen and toward the front door, turning her head to talk loudly toward the back of the house. "Claude, I'm gonna go ahead and get Skyy."

"I'll go with you," Cameron said right away.

Claude yelled back, "Yeah, you do that. And check the mail while you're at it. Might be some more mail in there for you. And Cameron, don't you bring Candy back up in here. Candy ain't always sweet, you hear me?"

Venus looked forward and opened the door.

"Yes, Sir." He rolled his eyes, sighed, and then said to Venus as he followed her out of the door, "I'll check the mail. *Adios Mio*," he said, insinuating *Good Lord*, in Spanish for only Venus to hear. The Spanish she had taught him through the years.

"*No, lo conseguiré*," she replied, letting him know she would get it herself.

He closed the door behind them.

Both of them had a moment of much needed fresh air all to themselves.

45

6

Sequoia

"That would be a hot mess."

The house in Baldwin Hills on Coliseum Street where Sequoia grew up was a remodeled, tri-level monster, with rust stucco and green shutters. It had many large rooms and floor-to-ceiling windows. Sequoia's mother, Ruby Smith, had since passed on, but years earlier she had lost the property to foreclosure. Sequoia moved her mother in with her in Culver City before she got married to Torino. But recently, Sequoia was proud that she had the means to buy the house for nostalgic reasons when it came on the market. She turned it into her own catering location.

She had transformed the kitchen into a restaurant-style chef's dream, complete with commercial appliances and a ten-by-ten island with copper cookware hanging from stainless steel pot racks. Having learned how to cook from her grandmother, Sequoia and two of her employees, her cook and her young assistant, were hard at work that Thursday, getting ready for a weekend event at a businesswoman's home in Brentwood.

Sequoia sat on the upholstered chair in the formal dining room across from her sister-in-law, Mercedes. The sound of pots clanging and a low volume hip-hip radio station played. The smell of something hearty was coming from the kitchen.

"So, Mason's serious. I mean, about running for city council?"

"He seems to be." Mercedes looked relaxed, sipping from her glass of ice-water.

Sequoia looked over some invoices and asked, "What would he have to do in order to run?"

"From what he tells me, since there's a vacancy and it's not actually election time, he wouldn't run. He'd need to get appointed to the post by the council members. Looks like the council is about to interview candidates. Not sure if he officially applied, though. I think it'd be temporary until the election in a couple of years. It would take a while to find out."

"Interesting. But he met with someone already?"

"He met with Eric Garcetti. And someone else." Mercedes picked up her phone from the table as it rang, reading the name on the screen. "Oh Lord," she said to Sequoia, "Excuse me." She greeted the caller. "Hello? Hi, Colette." She raised her brows, mouthing to Sequoia, "What the hell?"

Sequoia's mouth flopped open. Her eyes were stuck on Mercedes.

Mercedes continued, "Yes, it has been a long time . . . Everyone's okay, thanks. How've you been? . . . Uh-huh . . . He's that old already? . . . You did? I'll bet he is . . . So you waited all this time to try and get child support? . . . No. I know you tried to tell him. Well, why don't you wait until the lab results come in and go from there? . . . True. Listen, it's good hearing from you." She looked at Sequoia like she would rather slit her wrists than talk. "Keep the faith. It'll all work out for everyone . . . Excuse me . . . Huh? Oh, I'm sorry, Colette, but I can't get you any work. I have very few shows coming up and too many models. Not a lot of requests to book outside of my Simpson Models productions, either. You understand . . . Okay. Well . . . I'm sorry about that. Listen, you take care. Bye." She hung up and put the phone back on the table, looking relieved to be done.

Sequoia finally closed her mouth. "Oh, no she didn't."

"Yes, she did. I dang near hung up on her. Almost didn't answer, but I wanted to know what the hell she was up to."

"She's talking to you about her filing for child support from Torino?"

"Yep."

Sequoia looked through her papers again, shaking her head. "That woman. Why is she so desperate after all this time? It's like she has a motive that just popped up out of the blue."

"I agree. When it comes to her, who knows?" Mercedes sipped more of her water.

"And she actually had the nerve to ask you for work?"

"She did. She does sound desperate, you're right."

"Oh well. I don't know what's up with Kyle's income, but you can't depend on some back-child support scheme to live off of." Goosebumps formed on Sequoia's skin and she shivered. "Umph. Her name makes my skin crawl. If Torino is the dad, that chick will be in my life for the rest of my life. That would be one hot mess."

Mercedes said, "The most important thing is that Kyle Jr. knows who his birth father is. Nothing else."

"Well, when we saw that boy years ago at the restaurant, I think he was barely two, we asked ourselves then why he didn't get his parents' eyes."

"Yeah, but you know, brown eyes are dominate, even if both parents have light eyes."

"That boy looked like Torino, light eyes, brown eyes, purple eyes," Sequoia said, as though sure. "Actually, Torino Jr. looked like that when he was younger. I've thought about that all this time."

"I guess we'll know soon enough, won't we? Maybe it's good we're finally getting everything straightened out."

"I guess so. Torino got served. There'll be a hearing for the paternity and child support."

"How's Torino handling it?"

"One minute he says the boy might be his. Then he says he couldn't be. But then, and this is what I wanted to tell you . . . " Sequoia leaned toward her friend and spoke lower, "when Colette came into the club the other night, she told Torino she used sperm from a condom he'd tossed." She nodded for emphasis. "Yes she did."

"Ewww. No she did not." Mercedes turned up her nose.

"Did. And knowing her, I'm sure she did that more than one time. That's so Colette."

"Oh Lord." Mercedes fanned her hands through the air. "That's so nasty, is what it is."

"Yeah, well, there you have it. Crazy Colette. And hell, I say we need to check Torino's crazy level, too. I mean he hit that repeatedly, even after he knew she was special."

"She is that."

Sequoia's assistant approached. "Mrs. Wilson. Do you need me to hostess the event, or will you?"

"Oh, I'll do it. Just have everything there and ready to go. It won't be a big party, so I'm fine."

"Okay. We've got the main course in the freezer, the meatballs and Shepherd's pie. And we'll come back tomorrow to do desserts and vegetables. And those cheese biscuits."

Mercedes licked her lips, acting like her mouth was watering. Her hand was to her chin. "Dang that sounds good."

Sequoia told Mercedes, "I'll save you some." She then told her assistant, "Okay good. Thanks."

"Sure." Her assistant walked away.

"So, where's TJ?" Mercedes asked.

Sequoia looked at her watch and gathered her things. "Actually, I'm about to run off and get him. He gets out of pre-school in about thirty minutes." She got up.

"Okay." Mercedes stood with her purse in hand.

"I love you, girl. Thanks for coming over."

"No problem." They hugged. "But, hey, cheer up. You know you can expect some roller coaster rides with these Wilson men."

"Seems Mason's good. He's behaving."

"He is."

"He's not tripping about Vegas?" Sequoia looked like she intended to make a joke.

"No. You're the only one tripping about Vegas. Let it go."

As they walked to the front door, Sequoia looked at Mercedes with a side angle. "Is something up?"

"No. Stop."

"Okay," Sequoia said. "I know you."

"Actually, I thought you did, but obviously you don't." Mercedes stepped over to her white CLS that was parked in the driveway next to Sequoia's white Range Rover.

"I guess if I don't by now I never will."

"Then you never will. I'm good." Mercedes put on her burgundy shades. "I'm headed back to the office. Kiss TJ for me."

"Will do. *Ciao*, Sis." Sequoia smiled, but still knew in her heart, though not in her head, that her sister-in-law cheated on her husband.

7

Mercedes

"What was that about?"

That evening, Mercedes was back at home spending time with her mother-in-law, Mattie. Mattie's hair was thick and long and wavy just like Star's. It had always been the texture of an Indian's hair, dark with a few platinum strands. It was down her back past her backside. These days, however, it was fully gray and always cornrowed, flowing down into a long braided ponytail by either Star or Mercedes or Lucinda. If Mattie touched the top of her hair and it felt like it was undone, she would point to whomever and put them to work. She swore by Camay and always smelled of White Shoulders. She was one who always had it together. An original diva.

Today, like the other days, the smell of White Shoulders was in full effect.

Mattie's room was average size with a queen bed against one wall and a big dresser with a wide mirror along another wall, positioned perfectly so Mattie could see herself. There was a rocking chair and a large television, and also a beautiful shelf that had family pictures ranging from when she first got married to Jesse, to a photo of blue-eyed Nadia. There was a glass vase full of white tulips along her nightstand. Mason would make sure to bring her fresh flowers every week.

The décor was green. Always green. From the chair, to the dresser, to the bedding, to the carpet. Hunter, jade, moss, it didn't matter. The only splash of color other than green was a big, red, framed photo of a heart, and the bold word, LOVE.

Mercedes, barefoot in a short cotton robe, dialed Mason's number and he answered, but just as he greeted her through the phone, she also heard him answer from behind her in the hallway. She turned around at the same time that he walked in. She hung up looking surprised. "Where're you coming from?"

"Starbucks."

"No, I mean, you were down the hall?"

"Yeah. Looking for Lucinda. I thought Mom was with her."

"Mom's always in this room."

"No. Lucinda has her in the wheelchair at the front window of her room so she can look outside at the street. Mom was just in her room last week."

Mattie grunted. Her weathered face told on her years.

"Anyway," Mason said, coming over to stand at Mattie's bedside. "Hey Mom." He kissed the soft, red-clay skin of her cheek.

Mattie gave another grunt and turned her head toward Mercedes.

Mercedes remarked, "She's saying stop messing with me."

He talked to Mattie even though she still looked at Mercedes. "Mom, she's the one who asked me where I'm coming from in my own house."

"Whatever. Mom knows."

"What she knows is, you still don't trust me."

"Oh, please. Whatever, man." Mercedes put up her hand.

"Next subject. Mom, you look pretty." He looked down at her hand. "Got your nails all done up. Can I get some of that manicure treatment?" He extended his left hand toward her.

Mattie looked at his hand and turned up her chiseled nose.

Mercedes smiled. "She looked at you like, not with those claws."

Mason looked at his own hands. "What's wrong with my hands?"

"You need to cut your nails, Mason."

"They're fine."

"They're long is what they are. Huh, Mamma?"

Mattie winked, reaching for Mercedes's hand.

"Case closed." Mercedes chuckled. "Sit down, spend some time."

His phone rang, "I will. Hold up."

Mercedes said, "Hey. How come I didn't hear your phone ring when I just called you?"

"I was on the phone and clicked over. Dang."

"Dang, nothing. Always on that phone."

He answered the call giving Mercedes a stare of warning. "Hey there, what's up shining Star?"

Mattie groaned and tried to lift her head.

Mason asked, "How's my girl?" He noticed Mattie's reaction and put the phone on speaker.

"Fine." Star's tone was bland.

Mercedes said, "Hi, Star. We're here with Mamma."

Star's voice beamed. "Hi, Grammy. Miss you. Love you. You're my pretty girl."

Mattie's arms shook, and she opened her mouth like she was preparing to be spoon fed.

"You should see her. She's so excited," Mercedes said.

"My pretty girl," Star said. "I'm excited, too."

"How's it going?" Mercedes asked her daughter.

Her tone became lower. "Good. Dad, can you take me off speaker, please?"

"Sure. Hey. What's up?" he asked, walking out of the room, holding up one finger to Mercedes as if asking for a minute.

Ten minutes later, Mercedes sat in a chair at the foot of the bed, rubbing vanilla lotion on Mattie's feet. "I'll paint your toes this red color called Hot Sauce. You do look hot, my hot girl."

Mattie gave a green light smile.

Mason said from behind Mercedes, "That is a hot red, I'll say that. Nice color." He put his phone in his pants pocket.

Mercedes asked right away, "What was that about?"

"Nothing," he replied, only looking at Mattie.

"She's doing okay?"

"Yep."

"She couldn't talk so we could all hear?"

Mason darted his eyes at Mercedes and then back to Mattie, raising an eyebrow.

"Oh. Okay. I guess you'll tell me," she said.

"It's no biggie. She just needs money as usual."

"Okay. I can put money in her Bank of America account. How much does she need?"

"I've got it." He again gave Mercedes a look like she should drop it. "I'm going downstairs to write." He stood at the side of Mattie's bed again. "See you later, Mom."

Mercedes asked, "So soon?"

Instead of replying, Mason leaned down to kiss his mom. She frowned but puckered her lips. He gave her a loud smack on the cheek and she smiled. "No that's what I'm talking about."

"How sweet. Still don't know why you can't spend more time."

He headed to the door then turned around and said, "Actually, come here for a second."

"Okay." Mercedes stood up. "I'll be right outside the door, Mamma."

Mattie gave a tiny nod.

Mercedes went out into the hallway and he stepped out too, then he closed the door.

He said, "Listen. What's up with you and this Vegas trip you took last month?"

"What do you mean?"

"What's up? Someone saw you with some guy." He looked anxious.

"No they didn't."

He spoke fast. "They did."

"They who?" She put her hands on her hips.

"I'm asking the questions. Tell me what happened."

She looked back at Mattie's door and stepped further down the hall.

He followed.

"I was with Sequoia, and only Sequoia. After the fashion show we went to this club inside of the Mirage. I think it's called Jet. Really, no biggie."

"I would think people would know Sequoia is not a guy. What went on? With a guy."

"I danced once. No big deal."

"I'll tell you if it's a big deal or not. With who in particular?"

"This guy."

"This guy, huh?" He looked away and leaned against the banister, crossing his arms. "You let me sit up the other day and tell you I had a meeting with Ryan Germany. Was he the guy?"

Mercedes aimed her sights anywhere but on her husband. "Yes."

He looked nowhere else but at her.

"But it was just one dance," she said.

He said fast and deep, "Stop it." His frown was major.

She now looked right at him. "Mason."

He stepped a foot closer to her and spoke like he was fighting to keep it down. "Tell me right now, and cut out all the bullshit. What happened?"

She put her hand up. "Okay. There was a guy named Ryan, and he asked me to dance and I did. I had no idea he was with the city council until he told me."

"When did he tell you?"

"After we danced."

"So you spent time with him?"

"He bought us champagne. Mason, there were a lot of people who went out after the show. Actually, he was in the show. He was one of the celebrity models."

He shook his head. "See, you're making me put pieces of the puzzle together. You've got me working too hard." His jaw was tight. "You're about to piss me off. Where was Sequoia?"

"She was right there. It was the three of us talking."

"Cedes. He wishes you were single?"

Mercedes shrugged her shoulders. "I suppose so. I know Star told you he's her friend's dad. I can't be responsible for what he wishes. I definitely told him I'm married. Very happily married."

"He flirted?"

"He did."

"You flirted?"

"No."

"Were you attracted?"

"Mason, I'm married."

He asked again, almost twice as loud as the first time. "Were you attracted?"

"Yes." Mercedes spoke, though in her head holding her breath. "But nothing happened."

Mason froze and stared. His eyes said, *screw you*, and his body said, *good riddance*. He turned and stormed off, down the stairs to the front door. He slammed it as he left. The enormous house shook.

Mercedes took one step in his direction. Her heart said to run after him and calm him down, assure him she was innocent. Yet her head said for her to hold up.

Innocent?

So she let him go.

Half dizzy, she took slow, long steps to Mattie's door and then a deep breath, adjusting her shoulders and concentrating on holding her head up high. She opened the door and smiled only for Mattie, walking over to the bed.

Mercedes had a tear in her eye that was stuck there from the moment Mason walked out of the house. It stayed where it was while Mattie looked up at her. Mattie's hands began to shake. She opened her mouth. Mercedes kissed her on her forehead, and this time it was Mattie who made the sound of a smack.

"Mamma. I love you," Mercedes said with a voice that was about to break. She closed her eyes and the stubborn tear fell.

Mattie reached up toward her face and wiped the track of her daughter-in-law's tear.

Mattie's eyes began to well up.

Still, they just embraced.

Mason arrived back home at nearly one in the morning and woke Mercedes with a kiss on the lips.

She was only half asleep, having kept close watch on the clock, seeming to awake every thirty minutes.

Without saying a word, he pulled back the covers and got in bed, but instead of turning over to go to sleep, he climbed atop of her, using one hand to lift her pink nightie and pull down her panties.

Surprised and relieved, she immediately pulled them down and off in submission, assuming the missionary position to make love to her husband. He inserted himself and she moaned, louder than normal, sinking her nails into his back, and hugging him tight.

Her mind wandered with lust.

Pop!

She fantasized.

His face was buried into her neck, and then his pace sped up as he lifted his head, looking up toward the headboard.

She closed her eyes and allowed her emotions to race. The passion and heat of his hurt could be felt. His heartbeat was fast and hers was faster. She could feel the reverberation of both. Again, his face found its way to her neck and his lips were to her ear just as Mercedes felt herself about to release her worry and tension, when he whispered, "This will be our last time together."

Mercedes froze while he kept up his thrusts. On her end, all was in pause-mode, even her heart, as though it stopped. Mouth wide open, she looked over to connect with his eyes and tried to push him upward by pressing her hand against his chest. He leaned up for a minute, yet kept making love to her.

"Why?" Her one word was bated and complicated.

His response sounded simple, matter-of-fact and sure. "Because, you slept with another man."

And Mason climaxed.

8

Venus

"You told Dad where I was?"

The next afternoon, Friday the 13th around four-thirty, Venus was just leaving a conference in Beverly Hills, headed toward the door when she answered her phone.

"Yes, honey?"

"Are you still at the Screen Actors Guild event?"

"Yes. The volunteerism conference." She detected a rush in his voice. "What's going on?"

"The alarm went off at the house."

"What?"

"The alarm company just called. I thought you were there already. Where's Cameron?"

"I don't know. You think maybe he set it off?"

"I don't know. You call him. I'm headed home. Call me if you find out anything."

"I'm leaving here now."

"Bye." He clicked off.

Venus immediately switched over to dial Cameron. "Cam, are you home?"

"No." Loud music played in the background.

"Where are you?"

"I'm at a friend's house. Why?"

She spoke louder. "The house alarm went off. Your dad's headed there now, and so am I."

"Oh, no. I don't know what happened." He paused and said to someone, "Turn that down, I'm talking to my mom." He then said, "I left early this morning, right after you guys left. I set it and headed out."

She said, "I'm sure it's just a false alarm."

The music was lower. "Yeah, it happened once before last year while I was there. It just went off by itself."

"Okay, listen, I'm headed home now. I should be there in like thirty minutes or so."

"I'll go by there, too."

"No. Let your dad go first."

"Okay."

She just had to ask. "Are you at Candy's house?"

"Yes," he replied slowly, as though maybe he should not have.

As she rushed to her car and pressed the button on her key, she said, "Anyway, I'll call you back."

Cameron said, "Later."

While Venus was a couple of minutes from home, Claude called again. "What was it?" she asked without even saying hello.

"The police are here."

"Okay." She waited for more.

"Someone did break in. The front door was wide open. They took every television we had. And, it looks like they have our jewelry that was on the dressers in the silver jewelry boxes."

"Oh, shit! What about the safe?"

"The safe was untouched. Or at least maybe they couldn't crack the code. And they didn't take any computers, thank God."

"Oh my. I can't believe this."

"See, I'm telling you. It's time to move."

"Claude, I'm sure this was completely random. These things happen everywhere."

"Well, if I had to guess, I'd say that Candy girl had something to do with it. Most times when flat screens are taken, it's because someone came into your house and dropped a dime. I don't trust her. I've just got a funny feeling."

"I'm sure we'll find out. Once the police do their job, we'll know."

"I'll be outside when you pull up. And I'm telling you, tomorrow, we're taking the day off and heading out to Laguna to find a place. I printed out some listings this morning. I can't believe this."

"I'm pulling up now. Hanging up." She saw two police cars and an unmarked car in front of the house, one parked next to Claude's car in the driveway, which was his second car, a black Audi A8. She parked in front of the house next door and got out, running up to Claude who had just come outside. "Oh my, God. I still can't believe it."

He hugged her. "I know. Where was Cameron?"

"He's at a friend's house." She stood next to him, watching another police car pull up.

"Candy's house?" Claude's arm was around her waist.

"I don't know."

He removed his arm and turned to face her. "Venus, where is he?"

"Yeah, he's at her house. He's been there since this morning."

He looked like he wanted to say something, but instead he said, "I've gotta pick up Skyy."

The police officer who pulled up approached with his partner. "Are you the homeowner, Sir?"

"Yes. I'm Claude Wilson. You two can go on in."

"Thanks." He looked at Venus. "Ma'am."

"Hello."

Venus heard the officer say to his partner, "That's Mason Wilson's brother."

The other officer looked back.

"Claude, I'll go get Skyy."

"Here. Take my car. I think they parked too close to you. You're blocked in."

"Okay. Be right back." She took the keys from Claude and walked to the driver's side, getting in his Audi. Right away, Venus saw Claude's briefcase on the floor of the passenger side. Something inside told her not to. But as soon as she backed up and pulled off, waving to Claude as he went back in the house, at the very first stop sign she leaned over and simply clicked it open, noticing file folders and a few envelopes. She flipped through the letters, some looked like the ones from the mailbox that day, and there it was. The letter Owen sent her. Only it was just the envelope. Empty. The letter he had written Venus about her so-called freaky past and real intentions, was missing.

Later, Venus had taken Skyy next door to their neighbor's house until the investigators and alarm company representatives left.

Venus was at home, looking around to see what all was missing, thinking about the violating creepiness of knowing someone had been in their house to burglarize them. And also thinking about where Claude could have put that letter, as it was obvious now that he read it.

She heard her phone ringing. It was on the kitchen table next to her purse. She ran to it, picking it up. "Yes, Cam."

Cameron's voice was mad. "You told Dad where I was?"

"Calm down. He asked. I had to."

"Man." Cameron reacted sighing.

"Cam, don't worry about that. I think we're gonna go ahead and move to Laguna Hills. And, I'm seriously thinking about working from home, doing something else so I can be home with Skyy. You can work and go to school out there. This could be a blessing in disguise. Let's all take this and turn it into something positive. We've been through too much, coming so far since the days after I married your dad when you and I had such a hard time. We've got to focus on our family."

"All I know is I need my own place. I just need enough money to get in a place and then I can move on. Maybe I'll ask Uncle Mason if I can live in the spot where Grandma and Grandpa lived that he owns. You know, their old condo in Fox Hills."

"Cam, I don't think you should live anywhere other than home. And Mason's kept that place for sentimental reasons, but I actually heard he might sell it. The first thing you need to do is make your own money. Your dad and I can't loan you any money. For your own good, you need to get a job."

Cameron sounded distracted. "Hold on. Wait. Mom, I'll call you right back."

"Okay."

She heard him say with irritation, "What?" The call ended.

Venus watched Claude wrap things up with the alarm guy who reset the codes. She noticed Claude now had his briefcase in hand.

She headed upstairs and into their bedroom, placing her cell on the bed and then examining the top of the dresser, inside some of her drawers, purses, and other items.

Right away, she thought to look for the black velvet ring box that she kept in the back of her lingerie drawer.

"Dammit," she screamed, frantically rummaging through her panties, baby dolls, and teddies.

It was gone.

The box that she kept her heart-shaped emerald ring in was missing.

She let out a high-pitched wail. "Claude!" just as her phone rang.

"What?" he replied boisterously from downstairs.

She hurried to the bed to pick up her phone and pressed the screen. "Cam," she yelled just as loud.

"Mom. Candy just admitted it to me. It was her. She had someone break in. I'm sorry."

It was truly Friday the 13th at Claude and Venus Wilson's home.

9

Sequoia

"... her husband having had sex with Colette."

The Friday morning air was dry and hot, although it was barely eight o'clock.

It was a week later.

August 20th.

A court date.

Torino, wearing a gray suit and maroon tie, was behind the wheel, and Sequoia, wearing a little black dress with pumps and a blazer, sat in the passenger seat as they headed downtown. He took the exit from the 110 Freeway, and though few words were spoken along the way, he spoke up, out of the blue, sounding just as blue. The topic was an obvious one.

"We were unmarried. That boy is not my son." He kept his eyes on the road.

"Lighten up. You sound like you're rehearsing for the witness stand."

He said nothing.

"Look at it this way. This is just way overdue. It's a shame you and her couldn't do this on your own without the courts."

"It's okay. I'm actually relieved to be able to prove I'm not the father."

Sequoia turned and looked at him. "Torino. This is not the Maury Povich show."

"Funny." He didn't laugh.

"Kyle Jr. needs to know."

Torino just looked straight ahead.

"With Colette, anything is possible."

"I know. I'm just going with what I believe will be the best case scenario for Kyle Jr. For him to be with the mother and father he's known. And honestly, what would be the best case scenario for us, too, is to move on and get this behind us, for our sake, and for TJ's sake."

"I'm still amazed that any woman would do something so desperate to keep a man, to have a child just to get him to stay."

"It didn't work. Even if she did tilt her ass back on the toilet and insert some sperm. Still doesn't mean it's my child."

"True." Sequoia looked out of the passenger window and could see the parking lot for the courthouse. "So what happens after today? I mean so, you go in and deny that you're the father and they order a paternity test?"

"That's what Attorney Phillips tells me."

"And Colette's given them all of your information? Like, how would she know all that? Your income and everything."

"They'll request it, I guess."

"I still say she's in dire straits. And Kyle's mighty quiet."

"He has been for years. What would he be saying right about now?"

"I was wondering about that. What man is gonna be okay with his son's mom, his woman, suddenly just deciding to seek child support from someone, when he thought he's been the father all along?"

"What makes you think he believes he's Kyle's biological dad? He might have his own doubts. No telling who the father is."

"Yeah, but who else was she seeing? You never mentioned that Colette was cheating before that night she ran to Kyle after you two argued at the club." Sequoia waited. "Oops, can't believe I just asked that. Duh."

"Yeah. I don't put anything past her." Torino's phone rang. He put it on speakerphone. "Yeah."

"Good morning, Torino. It's Attorney Phillips."

"Good morning."

"You almost here?"

"Yes, we are. My wife and I are parking now."

"Good. Come up to the seventh floor and I'll be in the hallway just as you come off the elevators."

Torino said, "Got it. See you in a minute."

The courtroom was full. Every seat was taken and a few stood in the back. It was a large room with the judge's bench, bailiff, stenographer, and the judge's assistant, who handed him file after file, keeping the cases moving along.

Sequoia was in the seat right next to her husband. She wore just enough sexy as though it were her intention to mess with Torino's ex. More than a few times, she had looked over at the plaintiff, Colette Berry, from the other side of the room, taking in the rare view of the woman who had caused so much trouble.

The older male judge said, "Case number 2164C2010. Berry versus Wilson. Are all parties in the courtroom today?" The brass nameplate before him read, THE HONORABLE JUDGE STEVEN GARRETT.

"Yes, Your Honor. I'm attorney Royal Phillips representing Torino Jesse Wilson." The attorney and Torino stood.

"Yes, Sir. My name is Colette Berry." Colette was unrepresented. She stood as well, all two hundred plus pounds of her. And a prematurely graying Kyle Brewer, Sr. was right by her side. His eyes were as hazel as ever.

As Colette stood tall, Sequoia gave a quick sigh of relief. It was almost as though the fact that Colette no longer looked like the quintessential model brought Sequoia pleasure. She wondered how Mercedes could have possibly put Colette to work nowadays anyway. She just couldn't stop staring, no matter how hard she tried.

"You may come up to the respective microphones before me," the judge announced.

Torino and his attorney approached and stood side-by-side.

The way six foot-tall Colette began to walk, you would have thought it was one of Mercedes's fashion shows because even though she was thicker than a Snicker, she wore a tight crème colored pantsuit and worked it like she was back on the runway in 2004, wearing high, spectator pumps, excusing herself all ladylike as she stepped past each person seated in her row, approaching the microphone like she was about to do a fancy Tyra Banks spin move, flinging her golden, flat ironed hair from side-to-side. She held on to a file folder and a white leather satchel. Her caramel eyes matched her skin. She managed a quick look back at Sequoia.

Sequoia still stared whether Colette looked or not. She imagined her husband having had sex with Colette. And knowing that she herself was not the only one in the room who did made her stomach ache.

Torino only looked straight ahead.

The judge said, "Attorney Phillips. Your client has been named in a child support case. The petitioner, Ms. Berry, has asked for assistance from the court in establishing paternity." He wrote as he spoke. "We will grant Ms. Berry's request as part of the requirement that paternity be determined prior to moving on to the custody phase of this case."

Colette spoke up as though she was asked to. Her voice was high-pitched and she spoke fast. "Your Honor, I've also asked that my only child, my son, Kyle Jr.'s, name be changed."

The judge looked at her with a stern face. "Ms. Berry, I understand that you do not have the benefit of a lawyer, although I do suggest that you obtain one. I won't assume that affordability is an issue for you, but there are *pro-bono* attorneys whom you can seek out and retain.

"Now, here's how it works in this courtroom. You will not speak unless a question has been asked of you, or unless I inquire as to whether or not you have anything you'd like to add, is that clear Ms. Berry?"

"Yes, Sir." She looked down at her file folder, covered her mouth and gave a short cough. She sorted through papers using her fingertips, with her long, pink-and-white French nails.

The judge continued, "We will not jump the gun and move ahead to consider anything, including last name, custody, or support until we establish paternity as required by law." He looked at Torino. "Mr. Wilson, for the record, you are denying paternity of Kyle Chad Brewer, Jr. Is that correct?"

Torino replied. "Yes, Your Honor."

"I am therefore ordering you to a laboratory, to be chosen by you from a list we will provide, to obtain testing through a DNA buccal swab within the next thirty-days. Ms. Berry, as well, you will need to bring Kyle Brewer, Jr. to a laboratory that is also from that list for testing within the same thirty-day period. The results will be sent to me and I will announce the results on, let's see . . . that will be September 28th. That's a Tuesday, at 8:30 in the morning in this courtroom. From there we will proceed depending upon those findings. If the test is negative, the case will be closed, and if it is positive, and if confirmed that Mr. Wilson is the father, I will proceed to the next phase and order child support, and also issues of custody and name change will be addressed at that time. Is that clear?" He looked at Torino first.

Attorney Phillips whispered in Torino's ear. Then Torino said, "Yes, Your Honor." Torino's head nod accompanied his words.

Then the judge looked at Colette.

"Yes, Sir."

"And I see that back-child support is requested. Is that correct, Ms. Berry?"

"Yes, it is." She tilted her head to the side.

"Has Mr. Wilson paid any monies for this child, or spent time with the child?"

She fingered the strands of her wispy bangs. "No, Sir."

"Is it your claim that the child was conceived in California?"

"Yes, Sir." Colette shifted her weight from her left leg to her right.

"Okay." He began writing again. "Please see the clerk for the list of court approved laboratories, and this case will continue on September 28th. Any questions?"

"No, Your Honor."

"No, Sir. I understand."

"See you back here then." He closed the file and handed it to his assistant, taking another file in hand. "Next case."

As the judge read the names and file number of the case to follow, the attorney walked over to get the list of laboratories from the clerk. Torino stood back, waiting for Colette to gather her papers and step away first. She did slowly with just as much flavor as when she entered. She didn't look at Torino, but simply stepped down the aisle toward the door with Kyle hurrying up to position himself right behind her.

By the time Torino and Sequoia made their way to the door and exited the courtroom, Colette and Kyle were standing right outside the door.

Kyle could be heard saying something to Colette about her forgetting to get the list.

Standing within three feet of them, Torino spoke first. "Hey, Colette."

"Hi." She kept her eyes on Sequoia, head to toe.

"Kyle." Torino said.

Kyle replied. "Hey, man." He looked to Sequoia, "Hi."

Half way between Sequoia greeting Kyle, Colette said as though in a sudden rush, "Come on, Kyle. Let's go."

Kyle gave Mason a head's-up nod and Sequoia waved to Kyle as they headed toward the elevator. Kyle waved back. Colette had her back to them, only looking behind for a second to make sure Kyle right there. He was.

Sequoia continued watching Colette walk.

Attorney Phillips came out and said, "That was quick, huh?"

"It was," said Torino. "Is it usually like that?"

"This was just to order the test. Plus, it looked like they have a lot of cases to get through today. Sometimes the next phase gets more involved. But I'm hoping we won't need to deal with the child support phase. That'll be addressed the next time."

"Okay."

"Here." He handed Torino a paper. "This is the list of laboratories. Go ahead and get that swab done. Don't wait. A month can go by fast. Let me know once you get it done. The results will be sent to the court."

"Will do."

"Bye," the attorney said to Sequoia. He then walked away.

"Good bye," she replied almost a moment too late, seeming preoccupied.

Torino noticed. "You okay?"

"I am. You?"

"I am." He folded the paper and they began to walk. "That was interesting, to say the least."

"It was." His words were brief.

She said, "I'll tell you one thing. Colette and Kyle look stressed."

"I know." Torino took his vibrating phone out of his jacket pocket and worked his way through the screen to read a text message. "I just got a text from him. From Kyle."

"What?"

They stood before the elevator and Sequoia pressed the down button.

"He wants to meet me at TGI Fridays in Ladera. Tomorrow afternoon at two."

"Oh no."

"Oh no, what?"

"I know you're not going. You can't trust him."

"I don't know."

Sequoia crossed her arms. "Uh-oh. You'll go."

"Maybe."

"You just make sure you listen more than you talk."

Torino looked down to read another message. "Says it's important." He began typing, and pressed the screen, putting his phone back in his pocket as the elevator arrived.

"What did you tell him?" Sequoia stepped inside first.

Torino followed. "I told him, yeah, I'll be there."

"I knew it. Just an accident waiting to happen. This whole thing."

And the elevator went down, down, down to the ground floor.

10

<u>Mercedes</u>

"What the hell happened?"

They say a home is not a house and a house is not a home when two are far apart and one has a broken heart.

For Mercedes Wilson to turn her house into a home again would involve the man of the house coming back to it, willingly.

It was August 26th and Mason hadn't spent the night at home in exactly two weeks. Mercedes had talked to him on the phone a few times, but only briefly. Whenever she brought up any conversation that revolved around the two of them personally, or the Vegas incident, he would change the subject and rush off. He had been home only twice to get more of his things, both times while Mercedes was at work.

Mason was staying in the upper unit of a duplex they owned in Leimert Park on Creed. It was the same place his half-sister, Cicely James, who was also co-owner of Foreplay before Torino bought it, lived in, rent free for so long. Cicely is the woman Mercedes swore was Mason's side piece, and she also swore Mason was financing Cicely, being her sugar daddy. But it turns out the woman was not only gay, not into men whatsoever, but she also turned out to be the love child of Jesse Wilson and his mistress. Quiet as it was kept, Mattie knew all about it and wanted nothing to do with Cicely so the Wilson brothers tried to hide the truth for years, but

Mason caved in and told Mercedes after her suspicions became a problem. And eventually, Cicely sold her interest in Foreplay to Torino and moved to New York with her woman to open a nightclub there.

Mercedes sat at the kitchen table flipping through a *Vogue* magazine, turning the pages but not really taking in the content. Mind on her marriage, marriage on her mind.

From the backyard she heard Nadia barking and whining, and then just as Mercedes was about to go check on her, Rashaad came in through the back door, spitting image of his father just a lighter shade of brown. He wore black jeans, a black golf shirt, and a black cap.

Mercedes's hand was over her heart. "Oh. Oh my. Hey, Son. I was wondering what all that commotion was about. I thought you were your dad." She flashed a full smile.

"Nope. It's just me."

"Just you. Please, you look good," she said as he came over to give her a kiss on the cheek. She hugged him tight.

"Thanks. Whatcha got to eat?" he asked, breaking from their embrace and heading straight for the refrigerator.

Mercedes told him, "I made some turkey spaghetti earlier if you want some. Other than that there's some fried chicken from a couple of nights ago."

He looked inside. "Hmmm."

Mercedes said, "No. First of all, I should be asking you, what do you want? I watched you win the U.S. Open while you were in Georgia and talked to you after, but haven't seen you at all this month. So in honor of you being able to come home, you tell me what you'd like to eat, and I'll make it."

He shut the refrigerator door. "Wow. I won't pass that up. Maybe turkey wings and cabbage and those fried pork steaks you always make."

"Can you eat that kind of food now? With that physique you have, I'd think swine and gravy would slow you down."

"Oh, I'll work it off."

"Okay, if you say so. Then that's what I'll make tonight. You are staying the night?" She looked hopeful.

"Not sure. I have to be in Switzerland by the first. I might have to fly out tomorrow."

"You are so on the move. My goodness, I wanted to say, I'm glad you bounced back from that loss in Ireland last month. I know that was tough."

"Yeah, but that was yesterday. Like Dad always says, you're only as good as your last game."

"I guess so."

"Where is he anyway?" Rashaad asked. He leaned against the gray soapstone counter with his hands in his pockets.

She moved her magazine over and leaned forward. "Rashaad, listen. I was going to tell you. Just didn't seem to be the right time. But your dad and I, we've been having some conversations, and we, well, he felt it was best for him to go over to the place in Leimert for a while until we iron things out."

"Iron what out?"

"We've got some issues and he's just taking time to clear his head."

"What?"

"This is best for your dad and for me both. We'll work it out."

"How long has this been going on?" he asked, arms now folded.

"A couple of weeks."

75

"A couple of weeks? I talked to him and he didn't say anything about it. I thought he was here last time I called him."

"I'm sorry."

"That's just not cool. Dad doesn't leave. Why would he leave you, and Grandma? He can clear his head in the guest room if he needs to."

"I don't know."

"Does Star know?"

"She might."

"Did you tell her?"

"No. But your dad may've. If she does know I'm surprised she didn't tell you. You guys talk about everything."

Rashaad said, "Well, Star's kinda upset." He looked to be forcing himself to switch up. "I cheated on Sasha."

"Cheated on Sasha? How does Star know that?"

"Star called the night all this happened because she was gonna go out with me and Sasha while I was in Atlanta for the U.S. Open, but when I told her what went on, she just went off and decided she didn't want to go."

"Well what happened? And Rashaad, don't you act like you can't tell me. Don't you even try it."

"Oh boy." He scratched the back of his head. "I'm still thinking about what you said about you and Dad." He continued. "So, what happened was, this girl asked one of the caddies to introduce her to me, and long story short, she ended up coming to my hotel room in Atlanta. It turns out Sasha flew out early to surprise me and got in a shouting match with the girl in my hotel room. Somebody called the police. It was a mess. Someone said we were disturbing the peace."

"What? Did they press charges?"

"Mom, when the police came, it was like they just turned the other cheek, and then they were basically bold enough to ask me for my autograph."

"Oh, Lord. You're getting the celebrity status perks?"

"It's crazy. So, anyway, Sasha and I went out without Star, and we took my caddy Winton with us. People were crowding all around us like mad. So, anyway, that was it. It all blew over."

"Wow." Mercedes took a second. "I'm not going to preach, Son. But you know you need to be careful. You know women out there will be after you for your fame and money. We've talked about this before. And the lady you're with will surely get all tripped out when she thinks you're letting some of those very women who are after you, get close to you. It's emotions, that's all. So, you and Sasha are okay now?"

He stepped away from the counter and toward the kitchen door. "Yeah, she's fine. But Star got on me more than Sasha did. You'd think I cheated on her, the way she was acting when I told her."

"So are you and Star speaking?"

"We are. Just not as much. Star is devoted to a fault. Anything that happens that goes against what she thinks is fair and just, gets her all riled up."

"I know. That's just how she is. Always has been."

Rashaad walked toward the family room. "Is Grandma up?"

"She was when I went in there about an hour ago."

"I'm going in there to see her. Is Lucinda here?"

"No. She's out until later tonight," Mercedes replied just as the doorbell rang.

"You expecting somebody?"

She got up. "Yeah, that's probably your Aunt Sequoia. She said she was stopping by."

"Okay. I'll come see her in a minute. Be right back. And I was gonna tell you, one day you need to get Skype on your computer. That way we can talk when I'm on the road." He headed up the stairs.

"Skype? I don't know," Mercedes said, going to the front door and opening it. She looked her best friend up and down as soon as she saw her. "Wow, look at you. Looking all sexy."

"Just some cheap skinny jeans. No biggie." Sequoia came inside.

Mercedes looked at her from behind. "All that body you got? And all that booty, it's a biggie all right."

"Look who's talking, Mercedes Kardashian," Sequoia joked.

"Oh, not even. Anyway, how's it going, girl?"

"I'm okay. You know I had to check on you."

"Well, I appreciate it. Rashaad is here, hopefully until tomorrow."

"I saw his big ole Beamer out there. How is he?"

"Good. He's in there with Mamma. He looks good. That boy is such a star. The world is spoiling his ass already."

"He just moved right on into Mason's celebrity spot." She put her purse down on the sofa table.

Mercedes said, "Sequoia, things have changed so much from the days when the kids ran around here, the days when I tried my best to keep up with them. Most times now, this house is quiet. I can't take it sometimes. It's like everyone's gone. Mamma's quiet, and that's hard enough. But now Mason's gone. I was just complaining that having him home was getting on my nerves. Now, it's just me and the dog and Mamma."

Sequoia stepped up and gave her a hug. "My Mercedes."

Mercedes patted her on the back.

Sequoia then asked, taking a step back, "You got any of that lemonade you always have in the fridge?"

"I do."

"Good. I'll be right back. Meet me on the patio," Sequoia said, heading for the kitchen.

"You say so." Mercedes did just that and walked outside from the sliding glass doors. Nadia barked for a second. "Hush, girl. Quiet," she said to Nadia who was on the side of the house.

Mercedes took a seat on one of the hunter green outdoor chairs under the matching umbrella.

The view of the turquoise infinity pool and spa was beautiful. The bright orange Delilah flowers mixed with bold pink impatiens framed the picturesque sight. Palm trees and hydrangea bushes led the way to a handball court and a half basketball court in the very back.

Sequoia, walking barefooted, came outside, holding two tall glasses of lemonade. "So tell me. What the hell happened with Mason?"

"He just left."

Sequoia placed the glasses on the table and went back to close the sliding glass door. "That's what you said on the phone, but what was it? After all this time, what would make him just leave?"

Mercedes picked up her glass. "Thank you. Girl, I really feel like I should ride on over to that duplex in Leimert where he's staying and get him, or call him a zillion times until he brings his ass on home, begging him till I'm blue in the face. But I know Mason. He's hurt. He's got too much pride to make this easy on me. He needs time away."

Sequoia sat across from Mercedes. "I understand that." She looked serious. "I just need you to tell me if this had anything to do with what happened in Vegas

79

with Ryan. You can get mad if you want to, but I know you and him connected. I just know it."

"Why do you say that?" Mercedes drank her lemonade.

"Because, you're human. You've been married for a long, long time. You've been true. I know you've been faithful. But, you're human."

Mercedes looked out along the pool. "True."

"See, I'll tell you. I saw him coming up. Ryan. It was after you and I walked to your room first, and then I went on to my room. When I got in there for a minute, I had a taste for a little bit more of the slot machines. Honestly, I didn't want you to know, because earlier, the only reason I stopped playing was because you told me not to let the casino rob me blind." She smiled.

Mercedes was focused.

"So I went downstairs anyway and when I got off the elevator in the casino, I saw him come around the corner and press the button for the same group of elevators I got off of. He didn't see me. He was looking down at his phone. Or maybe he did, but I never saw him look my way."

Mercedes took another sip. She stared at Sequoia. "Maybe his room was on one of those floors."

"Maybe not. I overheard him tell you he was staying at the Venetian. But that's enough of me talking about what happened. It's your turn, sister."

"Sequoia." Mercedes paused. She placed her glass down and rested her elbow on the table, leaning forward. "My God. I can't believe what a small world it is. First of all, small world meaning that Ryan is someone whose daughter knows Star. And, small world in that Ryan ends up interviewing Mason about the city council seat. For real, Mason hasn't talked about politics since college. I'm telling you, it's like it was just supposed to happen, and supposed to come out."

"Maybe. If something happened, just tell me. If you're worried about me telling Torino, I wouldn't do that. And I'd definitely never tell Mason."

Mercedes said, "So, you know how we talked when we checked into the hotel about how we should just pretend we'd have enough nerve to sin in sin city, you know, acting like we were free and single for a few hours?"

"Yeah. Walking through the casino when we first got there, just excited to be able to get away."

Mercedes looked toward the sliding glass door, and then back at Sequoia. "Well, I did have the nerve. Seeing Ryan come up to me at the fashion show when I signed him in as one of the models. Him flirting with me like that, complimenting me. And then he kissed my hand. I got mad. But, in a way, it was kinda nice." She was talking like she didn't want to admit it.

"I understand. I knew you were feeling him."

"I played it off, I thought."

"You didn't."

"I guess I didn't. But you know how they talk about chemistry. Like something you can't explain, kind of an animal instinct. I'm telling you, he's someone who just got my estrogen going and, Sequoia, after I danced with him at the club, actually it was during the dance, I had to stop before the song was through. I didn't know if it was the alcohol or not. But I felt like it was just so sensual, but so dirty."

"We were buzzed, now."

"We were. When you and I said goodbye in the hallway once I got to my room, I think it was like one in the morning. And then when I got in my room I had a message on my phone. I thought it was Mason so I called him, woke him up actually, and said goodnight. He said he didn't call. So when we hung up I checked my messages, and it was him. It was Ryan telling me he was up, and that he wanted to make sure I made it back to the room. That he wanted to know if I was okay." Her voice became a notch lower. "I listened to his message and then hung up. I was hot. I'm telling you, hearing him just worked me over. I can't remember the last time I masturbated, but I wanted to. But instead, I called his room and he answered. He told me he just made some coffee. I didn't even want any but I told him out of the blue, 'I'll take cream and sugar.' He said okay. Before I knew it he was at my door. I heard him knock. I stood there for a minute. I turned the knob, pulled the door open, and there he was, tall, young, fine, smelling good, and smiling, standing with a cup of coffee in his hand. He stepped in saying nothing. I closed the door and locked it. Twice. And Sequoia . . ."

Nadia barked up a storm.

"Nadia, hush. Nadia," Mercedes said loudly toward the side of the house.

Suddenly, Rashaad slid the door open with a force and bellowed, "Mom, Grandma's acting weird. It's like she won't wake up."

Mercedes sprung to her feet and yelled, "Oh my God!" rushing inside with Sequoia and Rashaad right behind her.

11

Venus

"Claude, you're crazy."

The next day Venus was at work in Westwood. She had planned to leave early and had just returned from a very important meeting with her boss when she noticed a missed call on her cell from her other sister-in-law, Sequoia.

Venus had left her a message the night before, so she took a break, closed her office door, sat down on the tan loveseat across from her desk, and dialed. She already knew what her first question would be after Sequoia greeted her. "Hey, Sequoia. What in the world happened to Mattie? Rashaad told Cameron he was scared to death."

Sequoia replied, sounding as though she was mobile. "She's fine, thank God. I was there when it happened. Mercedes said it's called hypopnea. It's almost like sleep apnea but it's decreased breathing. I think the muscles in the airway relax, but bless Rashaad's heart, he thought she wasn't breathing at all. Mercedes said it happened before so she went in there and pinched the hell out of Mattie and she woke up looking mad as hell, like somebody woke her up from a wet dream."

"No you didn't. You need to stop."

"I know. But I felt so sorry for Rashaad. That boy looked like he was about to have a heart attack all on his own."

Venus said, "I bet he was. So is it similar to under-breathing?"

"Your guess is as good as mine. I'd never heard of it."

"Wow. That's not good. I'll explain it to Claude when he gets home. But still, I'm glad she's okay."

"Me too." Sequoia then asked, "So, you guys are moving out of Ladera?"

"We are."

"You must've made that decision pretty quick."

"We did. You know the house was broken into, right?" Venus queried.

"I did. Mercedes told me."

"Yeah. There's just a lot going on. But besides, Claude's new office in Laguna Hills opens soon. We went ahead and got a great house out there and listed our house for sale."

"How'd you close so fast?"

"Claude handled all that. He paid cash on a great deal. All I know is it was about to go into foreclosure and was listed for over nine-hundred-thousand, but we got it for it for a little over seven. And for that neighborhood in Laguna Hills, it's called Nellie Gail, that's unheard of."

"You are kidding me. In Orange County? I thought those homes were way more expensive than over here."

"They can be. I think you can find some for about the same, but the closer you get to the beach it gets pricier. And there are some estates with panoramic views in Laguna Hills for five-million and more. This house we got originally sold for a million four. You know the market."

"I guess so. I know it's nice. As long as you're happy, that's what matters."

"All I know is we walked in and saw this amazing spiral staircase that splits off to the left and to the right, and there are wood built-ins and shiny wide planked floors. I just about fainted. Skyy's got this pink bedroom next to ours. I'll send you some pictures but you'll have to come by once we get settled in."

"I will. Sounds fancy. I'm just wondering, I thought Orange County was mainly white. There's black folks out there?"

"Not a lot. But a few."

"Just get ready. It won't be anything like Ladera."

"I'm sure. But hey, just hoping they'll be color blind like we are."

"Okay. So what does Cameron think about it? I mean about leaving Ladera."

"He's good. He's been out there at the house for a few days, just being there for us so he can let the cable company folks in, gas company, stuff like that. Plus, he's setting up his room. I hope he'll be able to go to U.C. Irvine or Cal State Fullerton. I guess you heard about his academic situation at Berkeley?"

"Torino told me. I guess Claude talked to him. Claude was pretty upset about it."

"You're telling me. But, it'll all work out. So, how's TJ?"

"He's fine. Just growing fast."

"And how's everything going with you and Torino?" Venus asked.

"He's just working through this custody suit after Colette went ahead and filed after all these years."

"Well, if that child does turn out to be Torino's, we'd need to have a real celebration to welcome him into the family."

"True. I just hope things get decided and die down."

"Me too. For everyone's sake." Venus then said, "Well, girl, I'm about to head out of here. I'm at work. I need to go back home and meet the movers."

"Okay. I'm about to host a function in Long Beach. Let me know if you need anything."

"I will. Talk to you later."

By that evening, the moving company had gotten through the first phase of packing everything up, getting things ready to go. They would return the next day to physically move the contents to the new house.

With the room illuminated only by the glow of the nightlight, Venus sat on Skyy's twin princess bed and leaned over to tuck her in and kiss her on her nose. "Goodnight, sweetie. Sleep tight."

All that was left in the room was the bed, one pink wicker chair, and one small *Hello Kitty* suitcase.

Skyy turned onto her side and gave a tiny yawn, and then asked, "Where's my brother?"

"Cam is at our other house, remember Mommy told you. We'll see him tomorrow."

"Is he in my new room?"

"No, he's in his room. That pretty pink room is only for you."

"Can I sleep there tonight, too?"

"Not just yet. Just one more day."

Skyy then asked, "Where are my dolls?"

"We're taking all of your dolls to the new house. We'll make sure they're just fine."

Skyy's eyelids looked heavy. She asked while pulling the sheet up to her chin. "Can I sleep with you, Mommy?"

"Not tonight, Skyy. Now you be a big girl and go to sleep. Tomorrow's the big day." Venus stood and headed to the door. "Goodnight."

Claude suddenly stood at the door, placing his hand on Venus's shoulder. "Goodnight, pumpkin."

"Goodnight, Daddy."

"Love you."

"Love you, Daddy. Love you, Mommy."

"Love you, too, sweetie. See you in the morning," Venus said, closing the door as Skyy closed her eyes.

Claude and Venus walked down the hall to their bedroom. He entered his new code into the keypad on the wall and set the alarm as Venus plopped down on the bed, falling onto her back and sighing as her head hit the pillow.

"Tired?"

"Heck yes. Plus, I looked around the house today thinking I can't believe we've accumulated all this stuff. We should've had a yard sale."

"Anything you want to leave we can have Goodwill come and pick it up. We just need to get things packed up and out. I have some guys coming to redo the floors and work on the roof soon so this place will sell."

Venus gave him a smile. "You know what? I'm really excited. I didn't think I'd be, but I am. I never thought I'd be able to handle leaving this house. There are so many memories."

"We should've gotten a new house when we got married, anyway. It was time."

Venus reminded herself that it was the same house Fatima lived in before she died. Same bed. Same everything. "Honey, I wanted to tell you. I talked to my boss, Ann Howard, today at work and I gave her my notice."

Claude looked like she had to be kidding. "You what?"

"I did. I resigned."

"Wow. What was it that made you decide? The commute?"

"No. I mean, that would've been a literal trip. But, I just feel like you do so much for us, so much for me and

Skyy, and Cameron. You've worked hard. You handle your business. I don't think it's too much to want your wife to be home to raise your young daughter. I know Cameron is older and he's on his own, or will be soon, but we're pretty well off financially, and I can go back to work once Skyy gets older."

"Well, needless to say I'm happy."

"I am too. We have to count our blessings."

"I understand how much you love what you do over there. Just making sure you're sure."

"I'm sure."

"Then I'm good with it. Thank you." He stood up and leaned over her to plant a kiss.

"Thank you." She kissed him back.

"I'm about to take a shower."

"Oh, okay," she said, still lying on her back.

He said from the doorway of the bathroom, "You care to join me?"

"I'd love to."

The warm bursts of water sprayed them down at the same time. Venus was facing the showerhead with her hands pressed against the limestone shower walls. Claude was right behind her.

The chamomile body wash bubbled up upon her backside and his chest. Her hair was wet, but it didn't matter.

It was their last night of making love in their Ladera home.

And he was inside of her.

Claude had one hand on her hip, one along her back as he bent over ever so slightly, being taken away by the feeling, the sensation, and the elation.

He said in a romantic, deep voice. "So, you know the lady I told you about who works in my office. The one with the child who can't seem to get her hours right?"

"Yeah."

"She told me she and her husband were swingers."

Venus stayed in position but wanted to look back at him. "Swingers?"

"Swingers."

"Honey," she said while grinding back at him, "why are you telling me this?"

"Because she asked if we'd ever done it. I told her no."

"Why would she ask you that?"

"Somebody brought it up at work one night, and she said it was no big deal."

She ceased her grind. "Oh, so then she asked you?"

"Baby, you know how we are. Just like the night we got together with Fatima. It's no big deal."

"Claude, wait a minute." She began to turn around and he pressed on her shoulder as though trying to keep her in position.

"You know what? I think it'd be cool to maybe think about trying a threesome again."

"Claude."

"It's not like we haven't done it. And I know you even did it before that."

"What are you talking about?"

"I just know it wasn't your first time. And you and Fatima definitely weren't mine."

"Good for you. But it was for me."

"Are you sure?"

"Claude, let's just stop."

He leaned in to kiss her back.

She began to cautiously grind back again.

"You know I'd like to see you and another woman, enjoying each other."

"You would?"

"I would."

"What would we do?" She sounded fake.

"You'd kiss and explore. Come on, baby, you'd know what to do. I know you're a freak."

"If you want me to be, I'm game." She tried to play along but her arousal began to subside.

"Good. So, how was Owen? Was he any good?"

"Owen?" Venus turned back and moved her body away from Claude. His penetration was halted. She faced him with the water to her back. "What is your problem?"

Claude just stood there, wet, still with a hard on, angry, talking. "Maybe you can tell me all about it so I can really get to understand just how much of a freak my wife is. Just how hard she tried to get with Owen because Fatima had him first. And how soon it was that you decided to get your hooks in me before Fatima died. I really hope you didn't have anything to do with Owen killing her. Was it to be with him, or to get her out of the way so we could be together?"

She shook her head at him. "Claude, you're crazy."

"Oh, I'm the crazy one, huh? Or is the crazy one in prison whose had both you and Fatima turned out?"

"I'm not listening to this." She pushed the shower door open and rushed out, grabbing her towel. She looked down at his still full attention.

"It's cool though. I'm not mad." He closed the door and continued to wash down his body alone. "Believe me, it's all good."

Venus stepped out of the bathroom with a towel wrapped around her, heart racing, wondering to herself. *Where in the hell do we go from here?*

90

12

Sequoia

"So why's he trying to be your best friend again?"

The tangerine sun was generous but not brutal. The sky was powder blue.

Summer still hung on by its fingertips, knowing Fall was soon to make its debut.

It was a beautiful day, the Friday before Labor Day.

Sequoia and Torino spent the afternoon having lunch near his club Foreplay in Hollywood. The restaurant was called Cravings on Sunset, an Italian Mediterranean restaurant, chic and popular with lush décor. Sequoia and Torino loved the ambiance of the sidewalk seating. Patrons dined outside while sitting on mahogany chairs under large, bright yellow umbrellas. Whenever the weather was nice and Sequoia and Torino had time, they made sure to stop by and enjoy the superb dishes.

Torino was casually dressed in jeans.

Sequoia wore a coral and teal striped dress.

The aroma that wafted outside from inside the restaurant was of garlic and basil. Torino and Sequoia were quick to devour their shared order of calamari, and next were their lunch entrees of almond crusted trout and chicken tarragon.

Taking a big sip of her lemon drop cocktail, Sequoia brought up the subject she had been wanting to talk about. "Okay, so I know you kept postponing meeting with Kyle. Did you get to do it today?"

"We did. We talked," Torino replied.

"And?" Sequoia asked, then taking a small bite of her mashed potatoes.

"You and I were right. Colette is struggling and trying to make money. He made it clear to her that she's got to carry her own weight. Well, I guess that's an understatement."

"You're referring to her having gained weight."

"Yeah. Don't act like you didn't notice."

"Well, she is tall."

"Sequoia, please. Colette is fat." Torino drank from his water glass, making playful eyes.

"She's big. So, go on."

Torino poked a piece of chicken with his fork and left it there. "Kyle's coming up on twenty-three years with the fire department."

"Okay, I know that's how you two met, right, when you tried out?"

"Yeah, and I didn't make it, thanks for reminding me."

She smiled. "And so . . ."

Torino jumped in to explain. "He's about to retire and I guess he's tired of financing Colette. Seems she's not booking any modeling jobs anymore and she doesn't have any other skills. She's complaining no one will hire her. I guess she made up some bogus resume but no bites."

"I know. She called Mercedes about working in one of her shows." She dabbed her mouth with the linen napkin.

"So, that's what's up. Pointing the finger at me, saying I'm Kyle Jr.'s father is more beneficial to her right now if she can get child support."

"So why'd he tell you that? Why would he share that with you now?" Sequoia asked before she resumed eating her fish.

"I think first of all he wanted to say he messed up. You know, him getting caught selling VIP passes and pocketing the money. He did say he was sorry. He said he played me because he was mad. And Colette played him because she was mad at me. And so I guess they both got played. He fell into that, being weak, and thinking with his dick. All these years later, after he played house for so long, it sounds like he's a little bit more humble now. Especially since, get this . . . Colette is kicking his ass." He took a small bite.

"No way. Colette is swinging on Kyle?"

He paused while chewing and then swallowed. He then took another sip of water. "Let's just say she's trying. He keeps defending himself but he said the last time it happened, he was ready to knock her ass out. So, he told me he's ready to pack up his things and leave. He's going to file a restraining order on her this afternoon. He said they fight every night. He, himself, said she's crazy."

"Damn. Took him long enough to realize that."

Torino ate more of his lunch, talking with his mouth half-full. "He knew all along. He's just bonded to his son. He raised him for so long. And now I'm quite sure that Colette has figured out that Kyle is about sick of her, so now she gets desperate, can't control him, and so she starts swinging. Shoot, she swung at me once and only once. I threw her on the ground and pressed my knee to her chest until she begged me to let her up. It never happened again. I told him he needed to deck her ass one time and show her he's not the one."

"Please, if he hit Collette's crazy ass, she'd call 911 so fast."

The waiter walked up and asked, "Is everything okay? Can I get you something else to drink?"

"No, I'm fine," said Sequoia. She then looked across at Torino. "You okay?"

"I'm good. Thanks."

"Sure. Enjoy," he said, heading off to another table.

Torino continued looking at Sequoia and then casually at the people and cars that passed by along Sunset Boulevard. He leaned back and folded his arms, saying, "Yeah, from what Kyle says, she's the one who calls 911, even when she's the one tagging him. But I guess the cops always look at the guy. So, when they kept giving him the third degree like they'd take him in, Kyle said he decided to forget it. He told me he thinks it's best for him to leave her altogether."

"So why's he trying to be your best friend again?" She took a final sip of her cocktail.

"He needed to give me the one-up. If you ask me, I think it's messing him up, messing with his ego. I mean, like you said there he is raising a boy with his name. Then the mother comes up with a scheme to get back-child support from her ex-boyfriend, claiming he's the father, wanting to change the name to the ex's name. Any man would snap after that. I'm surprised he's kept his cool this long."

"Damn," Sequoia said, looking bothered. "And she has the nerve to try and take you to court when she's got all that going on? She can't possibly think she'd be awarded custody and get child support."

"That's why Kyle and I talked. He's ready to leave but wants to keep an eye on Kyle Jr." Torino dipped his bread into the last of the cream sauce left on his plate.

"You really think she'd hurt Kyle Jr.?"

"He thinks so."

"And?"

"And, honestly, he told me flat-out he thinks Kyle Jr. is my son. Just like she was saying when she got pregnant, and then she changed her tune."

"Oh wow. Well, even if you are, Kyle still deserves custody, don't you think?"

Torino bit into the bread and shook his head, chewing.

"He doesn't want custody?" Sequoia asked. "How could he not? He's been raising him all this time."

Torino said, "He said he wants to do what he can to make sure I, uh, you and I, get Kyle Jr."

"But why? And what makes him think we'd want him?"

"He asked me if we did. I told him I couldn't answer that. Told him I'd talk to you."

Sequoia shook her head. "I'm sorry, but I just think he'd regret that. Leaving her ass or not, that is his son. Blood or not."

"He'd be involved, he said. What he wants to do is get Kyle away from her first, and as soon as possible."

"How?"

"We came up with a way to do it, if you're cool. Are you down with the possibility of raising Kyle Jr.? Living our lives with him and TJ under the same roof as brothers?" He ate his last bite of bread and then sipped his water, tossing his lap napkin onto his empty plate.

"I don't know. Like I said, I'm not sure Kyle can just walk away like he thinks he can. Plus, it would be a lot harder on us to have him full-time, and her or him not sharing custody or having visitation rights. Plus, you think she's crazy now? She'd flip out even more if that happened. Our lives would be a living hell. And, Torino, the question still remains, is he your son?"

"As far as that, what Kyle and I talked about was I wouldn't take the DNA test."

"And why not?"

He leaned forward, placing his arms along the table. "Because, what I can do right away is just change my answer to her summons from contested to uncontested. I can stop denying I'm the father and that way, there would be no paternity test. Admitting that I'm the father moves it right into the custody phase, and that's when her issues will come into play with proof that the police came to their house. Also with the restraining order Kyle's going to file today, there's no way the judge would grant her full custody."

Sequoia put her fork down. "I don't know. You two sound like you've got it all figured out, but you can't be so sure Kyle could really handle this. And you can't be too sure the judge would allow you to not take the DNA test that he's already ordered, and also, that he wouldn't award her custody and back-child support. It's her word against his as to who's hitting who."

"I say it's worth a try."

"I say you should go ahead and do the test. You have to want to know, right?"

"I do."

"Plus, I think all this should be on Kyle, not you. He's been with her this long. He can't come running to you now. He got himself into this."

"True. But again, what if I am the father and he's just been playing dad?"

She said, "First of all, didn't he sign the declaration on the birth certificate when Kyle was born?"

"He said he didn't."

"Damn."

"I know this is complicated. A lot of what-ifs."

"Torino, I hear what you're saying. But as far as the paternity of that child, you may not want to know, but I sure as hell do."

"Then we'll find out on our own once all of this is done. We'll take a test on our own. First things first. I'm not gonna fight her right now."

"Have you thought about the fact that maybe her sneaky ass put him up to this to keep you from doing the DNA test on time, and he never ends up filing a restraining order? That they made this whole thing up about her being abusive? How can you trust him after what he did, out of your life for this long, and now he's suddenly in your corner? You need to be careful, Torino. That's all I'm saying."

"I thought about that. But what I think we need to do is wait for Kyle to file his complaint today. He said he'd email me copies of the paperwork, including the police reports. In the meantime, I'll talk to Attorney Phillips, okay?" He examined her face. He pulled her eyes to his. "Just tell me you're with me."

She blinked fast. "It just sounds way too messy. But, you got into this, you get this handled." She gave him a stern look. "And I'm telling you, I want to know if he's your child, Kyle's child, Bobby Brown's child, somebody's kid. I'm not playing on that."

"You will. Thanks."

Sequoia scooped up her last bite of potatoes. "You and Kyle talking again. Ain't that a trip?" She ate it and looked away.

"That's life. You just never know."

Sequoia rolled her eyes. "Oh, I *know*. It's some out and out bullshit is what it is."

13

Mercedes

"Ten minutes later he was gone."

That following day was a Saturday.

Lucinda was home with Mattie while Mercedes decided to simply ride around, just driving, not concerned about a destination or the high price of gas. Just driving.

A call came in from Venus. And she ignored it.

A call came in from Sequoia. And she ignored it.

A call came in from her assistant. And she ignored it.

Unless she saw the name Lucinda or Mason on her caller I.D., the calls would go to voicemail. And it was okay.

After driving north on 405, to the 5, and straight up the 14 Freeway almost to Palmdale, she exited and got back on, and then drove back south for miles and miles, past the Centinela exit and down toward the bay area, driving, even without the radio or iPod. She didn't want to play Brian McKnight, or Joe, or Mary J., for fear that some old love song would come on and encourage her tears to reappear. The tears that accompanied her until she finally fell asleep the night before.

All she did was drive and think.

And then she exited once again and got back on the freeway, headed northbound again. Suddenly, in the blink of an eye, she let out a scream so piercing that it made her ears ring. She shook her head and banged on the steering wheel, hollering repeatedly, "Shit! Shit! Shit!"

It was at that moment when she pressed the button and said, "Call Mason."

She could hear the phone dialing and ringing once, twice, three times, and a voice, her missing husband's voice that said, "Hello?"

"Mason." She struggled to make her verbal tone the complete opposite of her mental state.

"Yeah."

"Just checking to see if you want to come home and barbeque Monday, Labor Day."

"No."

"Okay. Well, it was good seeing you the other day. The night you came by because Mamma had the scare with her breathing."

"Just glad Mom is okay."

"And I'm glad you got to spend a little time with Rashaad before he left."

"What's up?" His tone was as though he would rather stick needles in his eyes than talk to her.

"Why are you sounding like that?"

"Like what?"

"Like you're so rushed."

"I've got a meeting."

"Where?"

"What's up?" he asked again.

"I need to talk to you. We need you here, Mamma and I. And the kids need to know we're cool. Come home."

"Those kids are grown. They'll live."

"I know they're grown, but still. And by the way, to top it off, Star's avoiding all my calls."

His voice was a bit kinder. "You haven't talked to her?"

"I've tried. Haven't heard back. I left a message and a couple of emails."

"Are you ready to tell her what happened?"

"I'm more interested in telling you what happened."

"Really?"

"Yes."

"You snuck off and got caught up in your attraction to another man. What more do I need to know?"

"You need to know the truth. Not what you only imagine happened, or what you suspect happened. I need to talk to you. Please. Make time for this. For us. This is important."

He skipped over her sentence. "I'm trying to work it out so that Mom can be with me. Both her and Lucinda."

"What? Her and Lucinda. Mamma's fine here. And you're not over there permanently, you're just getting some space."

"I didn't tell you that."

"Maybe I assumed since you won't talk to me." She geared up. "How can you be so cruel as to leave and then say you're gonna cut me off from Mamma, too? I dealt with everything when I found out you were sleeping with the red-headed woman, repeatedly. And not because you told me, but because I had to play detective after seeing her hair everywhere and realizing you were cheating on me. You two even had phone sex. Come on. I know you're not serious about not coming home."

"See, when all of that happened you went through your pain, eventually saying if it ever happened again you'd take the kids and leave. And now when I have to deal with the reality of what you did, you act like I owe you a free cheating ticket. Well, I don't."

"I didn't cheat. I need you to hear me. Please, Mason."

"Go ahead." He waited like she should spit it out.

"No. Not while you're rushing off to a meeting, and not over the phone. Meet me later at our spot at the beach in Palisades about six. Say yes because I'm telling you I can't live like this."

"If you're one minute late, I'm pulling off."

"I'll be there. Love you. Thanks."

Click.

It was 5:30 and Mercedes pulled up perpendicular to the lifeguard tower in the parking lot along Pacific Coast Highway near Temescal Canyon Road.

She sat, making sure her words were together, making sure to keep it real, making sure not to stumble or seem deceitful when really the night in question was a blur. She had practiced how to say it. Say what happened that one night in Vegas. The city that never sleeps where what happens is suppose to stay there. Only being that the world is so small, a young girl named Trinity who knew another young girl named Star spread the word and so it was. Mercedes found herself in Mason's shoes wishing things had not gotten out, because suddenly the whole notion of *what you don't know won't hurt you* made complete and total sense.

At 5:59 Mason drove up in his 2010 red Corvette with darker than legal tinted windows. He pulled up beside her and turned off the ignition. He stayed inside, and she could barely make out his face. She got out of her SUV and walked to his passenger side, opened the door and got in. His dashboard resembled a cockpit. His flashy sports car told on his mid-life crisis, showing the world that he no longer had small kids whom he needed a backseat for.

The skin on the back of Mercedes's heated thighs pressed again the coolness of the tan leather seats. Her heart thumped so hard she swore he could hear it.

He smelled like the cedar and orange zest of his regular I Am King cologne by Sean John. It was so him. She was addicted to the scent. She was hormonally bonded.

She inhaled him and sighed big, saying, "Thanks for coming."

"Talk." Wearing all black, he leaned his elbow against the middle console and rested his hand under his chin. He leaned his seat back and looked out toward the vastness of the ocean.

Mercedes, wearing all white, just went for it. "Sequoia and I checked into the Planet Hollywood Towers just after one o'clock. The fashion show I did for the designer, Armani, was at eight that evening at The Cosmopolitan.

"By the time we got our room keys and walked through the casino, I called you and left you a message. I knew you were writing. I think Sequoia and I had played slots for a minute, maybe some blackjack . . ."

"Get to it."

Mercedes spoke to the side of his face. "The first time I saw him was when I was checking in all of the male models. I knew we had celebrity models but honestly, I'd never heard of him before. I sent him over to wardrobe. He tried to flirt and I knew it. I wanted him to know it wasn't cool. That was after he tried to hold my hand, I think. I think I told him to never touch me again."

"LOL."

"So, anyway, a few people and Sequoia and I went to this bar called Jet. It was maybe eleven or twelve that night. He came up to us and asked me to dance. At first I told him no, but then a song came on, I can't even remember what it was. I just said yes, thinking one dance was okay."

"Slow song or fast?"

"Slow."

He finally looked to his right, eyes meeting hers. "And you don't remember the song?"

"I don't. I promise you. I was a little buzzed . . . "

"Next." He looked straight ahead again.

"About halfway through the song I told him I was going back to the bar where my sister-in-law was, and we stopped dancing. He walked me back. I told him goodbye and he continued to talk. I had a quick conversation with him, showing him my wedding ring and telling him I was married, and that I wasn't interested. He said he meant no disrespect."

Mason cleared his throat.

"He walked away and then sent some champagne over to me and Sequoia."

He gave a quick laugh. "And you drank it?"

She answered, "We both did. I only saw him maybe two more times dancing or standing around and then we left. Me and Sequoia."

"And?"

"And we took a cab from the club back to the tower at Planet Hollywood. Went up to the 24th floor where our rooms were. I think it was maybe one in the morning by then and our flight left that morning. Sequoia went on down the hall to her room, and I went in my room. I called you. You do remember when we talked? I did that because I saw that I had a message on the hotel room phone. At first I thought it was you, but you said you didn't call. After we talked I checked it. It was him."

"How did he know where you were staying?" Mason asked in a monotone voice.

"I don't know. Most of my staff stayed at the same hotel."

"And he knew your name?"

"From the show, I'm sure."

"Get to it."

103

"The message was, *This is Ryan. Hope you don't mind that I called. Just making sure you got back okay. If you can't sleep give me a call. I'm at the Venetian*, and he gave his room number. Said he wasn't ready to call it a night. I just, before I knew it, well I just called him and he offered me coffee, and I'd say within thirty minutes he was at my door." She took a breath and swallowed hard.

"Coffee. At one in the morning?"

"Mason, I know it makes no sense, but my head was spinning and I just opened the door and then he came in, and then handed me the coffee and then he sat on the sofa. Then I sat on the other end. I never drank the coffee."

Mason took his shades from the sunglass holder near the visor. He put them on and slumped down further in his seat.

"I think I was flattered. He was younger. Honestly, I'd felt like my days of ever turning heads was over. I knew it was wrong having him there. I at least felt I kind of knew him from the show, as opposed to someone on the street. I know that makes no sense. I know none of this does."

"You need to nail the ending in three sentences or less." He started up the car, looking like his ego was holding its breath.

"We talked. He sat closer to me, and he kissed me. A few minutes later he was gone. Nothing else happened."

"That was four." Mason paused. Then it was like his words escaped him. After a few breaths he sat up. "Get the fuck out of my car before I come around and yank your ass out."

Mercedes made a move toward touching his arm. "Mason."

He grabbed his door knob and pulled on it, appearing ready to step out.

Mercedes beat him to it, opening the passenger door and hopping to a stance. Before she could close the door all the way he backed up and sped off, leaving her standing there in her own insecure, unfaithful wonder.

The truth had been told, yet she felt like a murderer more than a cheater.

She felt like she had just admitted to killing their twenty four year-old marriage with one simple kiss.

14

Venus

". . . with her fit body and strong legs."

Seven o'clock in the evening.

A warm, slightly windy night in Laguna Hills, part of the land known as Rancho Niguel in Orange County proper.

The lush hills, breathtaking beaches and rich vegetation, as well as the Spanish and traditional architecture, make Laguna Hills a great place to live.

Claude Wilson had seized the opportunity to lease an office building on Los Alisos Boulevard. It was located in a strip mall with enough space to accommodate twelve realtors.

It was the first day of business for Wilson Realty of Orange County, September 17th, a Friday.

Venus was less than three blocks away, having driven from Ladera after picking up Skyy from Parent Elementary. Though she only enrolled a month ago, it was her last day. Venus took a call. "Hello?"

Claude asked, "Are you on your way?"

"Yes, me and Skyy."

"Good. And Cameron?"

"I called him and left a message."

"Okay, I'll buzz him."

"Honey, he knows about your grand opening. I'm sure he'll stop by. I'm not far away."

"Cool. Park in the front. The valet guys have spots reserved for you and Cameron. Just tell them who you are."

"Okay. Thanks." Just as she hung up, her phone rang again. "Hey."

"Hey, Mom."

"Cam, where are you? Your dad just asked about you."

"I got your message. I'm down the street."

"Down the street from where?"

"Down the street from the new house. I'm helping someone move some things from her garage into her house."

"Who?"

"One of our neighbors. I was jogging this afternoon and she asked me to help."

"Oh really? You be careful."

"Mom. I'm fine. We're almost done."

"How old is this neighbor? And where is her man?"

"I don't know."

"How old is she?"

"Mid-forties, maybe. Why?"

Her mind filled with doubt. "All right now. Come on over as soon as you can. You know how important this is to your dad." She pulled into the parking lot.

"Okay."

"See you in a minute." She hung up and rolled down her window as she pulled up. "Hi, I'm Mrs. Wilson." The surname on the large black and white sign above the office matched hers. *Wilson Realty*.

"Yes, ma'am. You can just leave your car right here," the valet said.

As she turned off the ignition, he opened the door.

"Thank you. I need to get my daughter." She stepped out wearing peep-toe platforms and a peach pleated skirt with a boyfriend blazer.

"Okay, sure." He opened the back door.

She leaned into the backseat. "Come on, Skyy. Wake up. We're going to see Daddy's new office. Sweetie, come on."

Skyy barely opened her eyes, turning her head back and forth, rubbing her nose. "Is my brother here?" she asked, squinting as she looked around, acting like the sun was her enemy. She wore pink with bubble-gum pink fingernails.

"He'll be here in just a few minutes. Come on." Venus unstrapped Skyy and picked her up, allowing her to hold on tight. Skyy rested her head on Venus's shoulder. Venus walked up to the office door as the valet closed the car door. She stepped inside, looking around at the beautiful new office with gray cubicle walls. "Skyy, this is your daddy's new office. Isn't it nice?"

"Uh-huh," Skyy said, speaking slowly while again closing her eyes.

"Hello, Mrs. Wilson," said Claude's assistant, Tina. "You're looking beautiful. And hi, Skyy. My God, she's a big girl. Look how long her legs are." Her voice was perky and fast.

"Yes, she is. She fell asleep in the car." Venus looked at Skyy. "Today was her last day at her school in Ladera. She starts her new school out here on Monday. Kindergarten."

"Really? Oh, that's going to be fun, meeting new people."

A short woman walked up. Cute face. Slim waist. Big hips. Big lips. Dark skin. Dark eyes. Wearing a red wrap dress and red suede pumps. "Hello, there. You must be Mrs. Wilson."

"I am."

Tina said, "Yes, this is Venus. Venus, this is Mary Phillips. Mary's one of the realtors here."

"Hello." Venus gave a greeting that was distracted by deep thought.

"Hi, Mrs. Wilson."

"You can call me Venus."

Mary kind of bowed. "Venus, nice to meet you, and your pretty little girl." She looked at Skyy and touched her leg. "Hi there."

Skyy gave a brief wave.

Venus asked, "Didn't you work at the Ladera office?"

"Yes, I did. I haven't been with the company long. I moved here to Orange County a few weeks ago. My parents live in Irvine and my son and I are staying with them. He goes to Valencia Elementary and I understand Skyy will be going there, too."

Venus said with caution. "Yes."

"I separated recently. Claude was kind enough to let me transfer, and that'll allow me to work more hours since my mom and dad are helping out now."

Venus filed away every word Mary spoke. "Oh, I'm sorry about the separation. But, like you said, it's good that you have help now. That means a lot." She saw Claude approaching. "Nice to meet you."

"You, too."

Venus turned away quickly, eager to be face-to-face with her husband.

Tina still stood there, next to Mary.

Claude was loud. "Hey, there she is. Hey, baby." He kissed Venus on the lips. He wore brown from head to toe.

"Hi." Venus spoke dryly.

"Hello, Skyy. Here, let me have her. She's been sleeping?" He reached out for Skyy.

"Yes," Venus said as she handed Skyy off to Claude. She switched her hobo bag from her left shoulder to her right, then folded her arms, just watching.

"Hi, Daddy," Skyy said, hugging him and kissing him on the cheek.

"Here, she can stand up," he said, putting her down. "She's a big girl. I've got some people I want you to meet. You know Tina."

Tina said, "Yes. She's gonna be tall, Claude."

"Like her dad." He then asked Skyy, "And did you meet Mary?"

Mary said, "Yes, she's adorable."

Claude asked Mary, "Where's little Billy? You could've brought him."

She smiled, showing a slight dimple. "I know you said it was family time, but my parents are watching him. And besides, I've got a lot of work to do tonight. Actually, I need to make a quick call." She looked at Venus and Tina. "Will you excuse me please?"

Tina said, "Sure."

Claude added, "Just know you need to shut that off in a minute. This is a night of celebration with family and friends."

"Got it," she said, walking away.

Claude took Skyy by the hand and headed off as he spotted his top realtor. "Come with my Skyy. Hey Jamal, have you met my daughter?"

Venus didn't watch Claude and Skyy walk away, but she did watch Mary walk away with her fit body and strong legs.

Tina asked, "So, can I get you anything? We've got appetizers and champagne. Or juice, water, whatever you'd like."

"A glass of champagne would be great, thanks." Venus looked at Tina, forcing a smile.

"No problem. And we'll have lasagna soon. I'll be right back."

Mercedes turned toward the window and looked outside. She thought and thought.

After a minute or so, Claude said from behind her. "Hey, baby. You look nice." He placed his hand on her back.

Venus turned around. "Where's Skyy?"

"She's sitting on Mary's lap in her cubicle. Mary's got some pictures of her son, Billy. Skyy's looking at them on the computer."

Venus asked fast, a notch above a whisper, "Really, Claude? Is that the Mary you told me about while we were in the shower the other night?"

"Oh, yeah." He chuckled. "I was just playing."

"You were just playing that she and her husband are swingers. Isn't that what you said?"

He spoke from the side of his mouth. "Venus. Not now."

"Why not now?" Her tone got louder. "I'm in my husband's office with the woman who he brought up while we had sex the other night. If she weren't here, I wouldn't have brought it up. But since she is here with my daughter sitting on her lap, I think this is the perfect time."

He stepped aside and took her by the arm. "Listen. She and her husband did do that. Like I said, she told that to a few people in the office one night when Tina read an article about all of the swingers in L.A. We all said we had no idea. And when Tina mentioned a place in Ladera, some house on Springpark where people go, we were all shocked. Everyone but her."

"I see. So when you said she and her husband, this was what, before they broke up?"

"I don't know."

"What don't you know? She's now footloose and fancy-free and just happens to be living in Orange County. I thought we were moving away from drama and leaving the shit behind. Looks like you ran right to it. Don't let me find out our move was on purpose for that short bitch."

"You need to keep it down. That's the last time I'm gonna say that." He turned his back to the office. "She's not in my life. Not in my personal life. She's an employee."

Venus aimed her fingertip right at his nose. "She's an employee who you brought up while we were having sex, Claude. Don't make me go off up in here."

"You wouldn't do that tonight." He looked back to see if anyone noticed them and he took her by the arm to guide her outside but she pulled away. He shook his head and said, "Not tonight of all nights."

"Try me."

"Venus, what's up with you? This isn't even like you. You're not one who has a problem with things like this. You're not the insecure type. That woman's got nothing on you."

"What she's got is your attention. So much so that you couldn't even leave her name at the office. You brought her home and that's what pisses me the hell off. You just don't get it, do you?"

"I was just trying to spice things up."

"No you weren't. It was you making a point because you found the letter Owen wrote. That's the bottom line. You and your usual passive-aggressive games. Instead of coming to me and asking about the letter you read, you made me sweat like you did and dropped hints like that while your dick was inside of me." She looked around, too, checking to see who overheard. "I knew you had the letter."

"Then you should've asked me about it yourself. Don't think I don't know what's going on either."

"Whatever. But this isn't really about Owen. There's an elephant in the room that I think got in the way before the letter was ever sent. That elephant is sitting over there in a red dress. And whether we live in Ladera or Laguna, I don't think it's going anywhere soon." She clutched her chest as Claude stared at her. Her heart begged for air. She spoke again. "What you need to do is go and get my daughter from that swinging ass elephant, before I embarrass you like you can't even begin to imagine." Venus noticed Mary approaching. Skyy was holding her hand. A fire in Venus's belly hissed.

Mary said, "Here he is, Skyy." She looked in his direction. "Claude, she was asking about her daddy."

Skyy looked up at her dad. "Daddy, can we go to her house so I can see Billy, please?"

Venus spoke forcefully. "No, we can't. Tonight we're celebrating at your dad's new office. Come here." She took Skyy's hand away from Mary's and said to Claude, "On second thought, we're going home so she can eat and get some rest. She's got a big week coming up and I've still got some things to do at the new house." She picked her up.

Claude told Venus while looking at Skyy, "She's wide awake now. I can bring her home."

"Nope, I've got her." Venus turned to walk to the door.

Mary walked away, almost tiptoeing.

Claude stood still.

And then suddenly, Cameron walked in. "Hey, Mom."

"Hi," Venus said, blandly.

Skyy said melodically, "Brother!" She immediately reached for him.

He leaned in to kiss her, taking her from Venus. "Hi, Sister." He grinned big and looked at Claude. "Hi, Dad."

"Hey, Son." Claude looked excited to see Cameron but sounded just as lackluster as Venus.

A woman was with Cameron.

Venus spoke first. "Hi, I'm Cam's mother."

Cameron gave a look like he totally forgot. "Oh, sorry. Dad. Mom. This is Penny. Penny Heinz."

"Hello," Claude said. He seemed to have a glimmer of energy. "Heinz, as in *the* Heinz?"

Penny gave a giggle. "Yes. And hello to you both. And you too," she said to Skyy.

Skyy smiled.

Penny continued. "Nice to meet you, Claude. Your son told me about your grand opening and that he was coming by. I asked if I could come with him. I hope you don't mind." She had ashen skin, jet black shoulder length hair and a major bust. Her tight, hot pink button-up sweater contrasted her tight white jeans.

Venus asked, totally avoiding eye contact with Claude, "Are you the neighbor my son helped move some things from the garage?"

"Yes, I am." She said to Claude, "Actually, I came because I'm looking for some property in San Diego. And I have a house in El Toro I'm looking to sell, too. So, this is perfect timing."

Claude said, "Okay. I'm sure we can help. Let me introduce you around." And with that Claude walked away with Penny, leaving Venus and Cameron and Skyy behind.

Venus still didn't look at him. "You have fun, Cam. I'll see you at home." She reached for Skyy.

Cameron handed his sister back to Venus. "You leaving already?"

"We are."

Skyy asked, "Mommy, can I stay with my brother?"

"No. Now stop, Skyy." she replied as if in no mood.

"What's wrong with you? Why aren't you staying?"

"Well, to tell you the truth if I wasn't so pissed off I would stay just so I could keep an eye on that one over there in the red dress named Mary whose got her sights on your father. And also, I'd stay because that one you just walked in with I guarantee you has her sights set on you. I can't believe you brought her over here." She frowned.

"Mom, she's a neighbor. And if she's looking to buy or sell that's a sale for Dad."

"Money, we've got. One less sale won't break us. But I'm telling you, Cam, don't you hook up with her."

"Mom, please." He looked as if he wouldn't dare.

"That's all I'm gonna say. I'm taking Skyy home."

Just as Venus took one step toward the door, Tina walked up holding a glass of champagne. "Here you go, Mrs. Wilson. You're leaving already?"

"I am, but I'll see you later. Thanks, Tina. Maybe my son wants it."

Cameron took the glass. "Thanks."

"Sure," Tina replied.

"Tina, you know Cameron," Venus said.

"Yes. Hello." Tina's smile and stare lingered.

"Hi." Cameron's didn't.

"Well, we'll see you later. Drive safely." Tina walked away but turned to specifically say, "Bye, Cameron."

"Bye." Cameron did not look back.

"That's the kind of girl you need to be with. A nice girl, your own flippin' age, with a job."

All Cameron could say was, "Mom, you know you're gonna hear about this later from Dad."

"I don't care." They both walked out the door.

"You need to be in here supporting him."

"Goodbye, Cam."

"Goodbye. Bye, Skyy." Cameron stepped back as the valet opened Venus's front and back door.

Skyy waved as Venus put her in the backseat.

Cameron went back inside, sipping his champagne.

Venus got in and started up the car as the valet closed her door.

She looked toward the front door and saw Claude standing there looking at her. Alone. His face was upset.

She sped off.

Her face was his twin.

15

Sequoia

"... please don't go telling Mercedes ..."

Some call it the hottest catch action spot in Ladera. It's Starbucks in the Ladera Heights Shopping Center, bordering L.A. and Inglewood, where people spend hours playing chess, smoking cigars, chatting, writing, and plain old chilling, enjoying the lovely scenery.

Once a car pulls up, the patrons have already spotted the driver and all of its passengers, braced and ready to witness their stride inside, ready to score them as though voting on a reality show.

Some of the customers really do come in for coffee, but the ambiance and feel of the place make it an undeniable hot spot. It is, by its own right, a character. A person, place, and thing.

This day, a busy Monday, three of the patrons were very familiar to the other patrons. Actually, the three of them were family. All Wilsons. And all turning heads.

Sequoia strolled into the coffee house, looking sexy in curve contouring leggings and with a polka-dot sleeveless blouse and lace ankle boots.

A few minutes later, she walked out after getting her brew. She put back on her tortoise shades and walked up to one of the tables that had been unoccupied when she had gone in. Her figure was the focus of attention. Even to her own husband, who stood as he said, "Hey, you. I thought you had a meeting with a client?"

Sequoia replied, "I did."

Mason also stood, as Torino hugged and kissed his wife.

She continued, "We had it at The Custom Hotel on Lincoln and it only lasted about an hour. I was on my way back home when I realized I was having a sugar-free soy vanilla latte craving." She giggled as they broke from their embrace.

"They use extra addiction juice. They know what they're doing," Torino said in agreement.

Still standing, Mason added, "They bank on it."

She stepped over to hug him, as well. "I know that's right." She went back over next to Torino. "Don't mean to interrupt."

"No, you just come on and sit down," Torino said emphatically. "We just got here. We haven't even gone inside yet. I didn't see your truck."

She looked a few rows over and said, "Right there."

He watched where her eyes pointed. "Oh, okay. Well, have a seat."

She did, adjusting herself to get comfortable, placing her leopard purse along her lap and her cup on the table. Large umbrellas shielded them from the peek-a-boo afternoon sun.

"How've you been Sequoia?" Mason asked, sitting down only after she sat.

"Good. Just trying to keep these catering jobs in order, drumming up as much business as I can."

"That's the way. Get that word of mouth going. You got any business cards? I can pass them out to some of my golf buddies."

"Okay, cool. I think I have some." She reached into the side pocket of her purse. "Here. That's nice of you."

He took the cards, placing them in his dress-shirt pocket. "No problem. I got you."

"I see that," she said.

A group of men walked by looking at Mason. One of them pointed. "What up, Chief?" the guy said, nodding and looking like he saw Michael Jordan.

"Not much." Mason just smiled. He then asked, Sequoia, "I know Cedes told you I moved out, right?"

"She did. I'm sorry. I hope you guys work things out."

"Well, it's funny you should be here, because actually I don't want to get you in the middle but I just have to ask, I mean, when you were in Vegas. What was up with Ryan Germany coming into the picture? I thought you two went there to work." He looked at his brother. "Torino, I'm not saying anything happened on Sequoia's part."

"Oh, I know that." Torino looked certain.

Mason said, "Yeah, I know that's right. You went to your room, right?"

Sequoia took hold of her cup with both hands. "Actually, I did, and then I went back down and lost about five hundred dollars in ten minutes, so I went back up."

Torino just listened.

Mason said, "Torino, don't act like you don't know what happened."

"Man, my wife and I talk about everything. I knew how much she lost, and I know what she did, and didn't do."

"Okay, then." Mason looked serious.

Out of the blue, a couple came up and stood before Mason. A petite woman said, "Excuse us. My husband won't ask you, but he plays golf and absolutely idolizes you. Do you mind if we have your autograph, please?" She placed a napkin and ink pen on the table. "I'm so sorry to bother you," she said to Torino and Sequoia.

"It's okay," Torino said.

Sequoia drank her latte and looked on.

119

"Okay, sure." Mason looked at the lady's husband, taking the pen in hand. "Hey brotha, what's up? What's your name?"

The man was heavyset, and older than his wife. "My name is Jesse."

"Oh, okay. That's my dad's name." Mason wrote him a note and signed it. He handed the napkin and pen to the man. "Here you go."

The man took it and grinned. "Thanks so much. Bye."

"Take care."

They walked away fast, reading what Mason wrote. The man looked back and gave Mason a high-five with his eyes.

Mason gave one back, and said loud enough for the man to hear, "All right now, Jesse."

"That was nice of you," Sequoia said.

"It just goes with the territory." Mason shrugged it off. "You've been around long enough to know that."

"True." She then said, "So, Mason. Back to what you were asking me."

"What I'm asking is if you and Cedes talked about what she was doing like, you know, before it came to him coming to her room. Did you ask her what was up?"

Torino interjected, "Man, don't you think that's putting my wife in one hell of a position?"

Sequoia placed her hand on his thigh. "Honey, it's okay. I mean, as far as I know, nothing happened."

"For real?" Mason looked skeptical.

She continued, "We talked about it, but all I know is what she told me, and nothing was up. I know nothing seemed inappropriate when we were out. And as far as I know, once we got back to our rooms she went to sleep."

"Well, then you don't know, because that's not how it happened."

"What'd she tell you?" Sequoia asked, placing her cup back down.

He sighed. "She told me she let him in. She told me they kissed."

Torino said, "Man, I don't believe that."

"I'm sure you don't, hell, it's not your wife we're talking about. But not only do I believe it, I believe there was more to it than that. But hey, you know, I'm not getting you two involved anymore. But I'm just saying, Sequoia, you're my brother's wife. I know you and Cedes have been close since forever, so even if you did know something, with all due respect, I wouldn't think you'd tell me anyway. But, I'm gonna leave it at that."

Sequoia picked up her cup again and nodded.

Torino said, "You two need to work that out. Bottom line, you guys have been through a whole lot in all this time, raising kids and getting to this point in life. I mean to live under two separate roofs is crazy. Work it out at home, man."

"All I know is, I can't even look her in the face. Actually, I want Mattie with me. I was gonna talk to you and Claude about this. I just think it's messed up for me to leave Mom there."

Torino asked, "Have you moved out and taken all of your stuff?"

"No. Not yet." Mason crossed his legs.

"Are you going to?" Sequoia asked.

"I don't know." He took his phone from the table and scrolled through it. "But anyway, that's my little corner of the world drama." He put his phone back on the table and had a look on his face like he had regrouped. "I know you two have enough to deal with, having Colette all up your butts again. I wish you the best with that madness. That's enough trouble right there. Torino was telling me about Kyle saying Colette is punching him out. That doesn't surprise me at all."

Sequoia replied, "Yeah, that's what he said."

"If it is true, getting that boy from her should be just a matter of proving her to be an unfit mother. Kyle stepping up like that is all right with me, especially after all that happened." Mason eyed a top-heavy woman who walked up. He then looked away. The woman opened the door to go inside and kept looking back at him.

"You say so," said Sequoia. She noticed him notice.

Mason asked Sequoia, "So, how are you dealing with all that baby-momma drama?"

"Not good. A little anxious. But, we've just gotta get through it." She scooted her chair back and took a long sip. "Listen, I'm gonna get going. By the way, I know you have a book signing later tonight. I heard you on the radio this morning. I'll be home with TJ. Torino, you're still going, right?"

"No, I can't. I thought I could go in later but we've got a security meeting tonight. I need to be there."

"It's cool. Handle your business."

Sequoia said to Mason, "Good luck."

"Thanks."

She stood and Torino stood. They hugged and had a prolonged kiss. He popped her on the backside, looking like he had it like that.

She blushed. "By the way, you two need to get in there and order something before they charge you rent for these front row seats."

Torino asked Mason, "Yeah, man you want the Macchiato, right?"

Mason stood as well. "Yeah. That'll work."

Sequoia walked over and hugged him goodbye.

He said, "You be careful. Don't be causin' no accidents walkin' up outta here."

"Yeah, right."

Torino said, heading to the door to go inside, "Yeah, you. I'll see you at home."

"Okay. And since this is Club Starbucks, I'm gonna tell you both," she looked at one and then the other, "don't let the eye candy up in here blind your asses."

Mason said, "I don't know what you're talking about. What's she talking about, man?" he yelled toward Torino.

"Bye," was all Torino said as he went inside.

Sequoia told Mason as she walked away, "Oh, and good luck with your plans to run for city council."

"If I can't clean up this mess, you best believe that won't be happening."

"Oh, you'll be fine. I can just see it. See you later."

"Bye, family."

Sequoia smiled and walked to her car, looking back for a second to see the top-heavy woman who went in before, now headed for Mason's table. Sequoia took her phone out of her purse and dialed. After four rings, she heard Mercedes's voice and then a beep. "Hey, girl. Wanted you to know I just left Starbucks. Mason and Torino are here. We talked for a minute. Mason brought up Vegas. Sounds like there's something he knows that I don't know. Call me when you can."

As soon as she hung up, a text sounded that read, *Babe, now please don't go telling Mercedes what Mason said. C u later.*

Sequoia got in her car and then replied, *Ok.*

16

Mercedes

". . . sneaking a kiss upon Mattie's nose."

The place was abuzz at seven o'clock in the evening. It was standing room only for Mason's signing at the corner book store in Inglewood. As Mason and the owner walked in, readers had their cameras and cell phones in hand and snapped picture after picture of the superstar. There was a signing table with stacks and stacks of books and a huge poster of Mason.

Mason sat at the table while the owner spoke to the excited crowd. "Thanks for coming out tonight. As you all know, our own local resident, former golf pro, Mason Wilson is now an author. He's written _Shadow on the Green_, and his second title, _Grip it and Rip It_, comes out next summer. We had him here before but there were so many people, we couldn't accommodate everyone, so we scheduled this as a part-two a while ago. So, he's here with us now." People clapped again.

"He basically needs no introduction, though you all know he's been ranked as one of the most successful golfers of all time. A former number one, he's won ten majors, fifty PGA tour titles, and was honored seven times as player of the year. In 2007, he was listed as one of _Forbes's_ highest paid sports figure in the world. And now his son Rashaad Wilson is making his way as a pro, following in his dad's footsteps, being sponsored by Nike. He has won national tours and had six top ten finishes this year already. He's the youngest person to win a PGA sanctioned event. Surely because of this man who introduced Rashaad to golf at a very early age. So, without further adieu, please welcome Mason Jeremiah Wilson."

The audience stood and applauded, and a couple even screamed. Mason stood, shook hands with the owner, and then took the microphone.

His charm and politician-like presence were on high. "Oh, I'm telling you now, whoever told you my middle name is in trouble." The audience laughed.

The owner joked, "Actually, your son Rashaad called earlier today and asked us to throw that in."

"I'm gonna get him. I'm telling you, talk about grip it and rip it, he's in big trouble. Though I will say I've gotta have some respect for him. I mean as of last week, already in his young career, he has more birdies in one round than me. He has seven. So, I might need to let him slide on this one. He's just better than me, and I guess I just have to live with it." The ladies in the front row smiled and he smiled back.

"Thanks for coming out. *Shadow on the Green* is a book I felt strongly about writing because some, not all, of my experiences on the green involved racism. Mostly during the time I played the game it was color blind. But behind the scenes I felt there were times I was labeled too black if I supported certain organizations, like the Congressional Black Caucus, Urban League, or NAACP. Also, I was confronted by someone claiming to want to manage my career, and take me to the next level, a 'white level' as he called it, if I would just seem a little less black. If I just moved away from Ladera Heights and found a place in Beverly Hills, or some other city where I would be among fewer people who looked like me. That person went to some pretty interesting ends to try and blackmail me, but, I held my ground and I'm glad I did. I still live in Ladera and I'm just as black as I was when I first picked up a golf club, shadow or not."

The audience applauded.

"But, this book is about more than what happened to me in golf. The message in this book can be correlated into any aspect of life, and I wrote it with that mission in mind. A mission to show how standing your ground can work in your favor. My father always told me that champions aren't those who never fail; they're those who never quit. Champions fail sometimes but are never failures, because failure is an event, not a person. Don't be afraid to dream in life and be brave. Don't take the least line of resistance. There are great *blessings* from those *stressings*. The message in *Shadow on the Green* is don't stop, dream big, and never give up, even against all odds. Thank you."

The readers stood and put their hands together as Mason gave the microphone back to the owner.

His eyes made their way to the back of the room, and in the very corner, standing behind a Hispanic man, peering over his shoulder, was Mercedes. Nodding. And applauding.

After a forty-five minute question and answer period, it was time for Mason to sign his books. He was seated at the table while the owner and his wife had everyone line up by the number that was written on their receipts.

A half hour later, with the line about thirty deep, Mercedes's phone rang. She quickly turned it to silent and stepped back, facing the wall, trying to look incognito.

"Hi, Lucinda," she whispered.

Lucinda spoke with her Puerto Rican accent. "Ah, Mrs. Wilson, I was just wondering when you'd be back. I need to get home so I can go out with my friends. I need to be there in about an hour." She rolled the last letter of her last word.

"Oh, I forgot. I'm sorry. I'll leave right now."

"*Gracias,* Mrs. Wilson. *Adios.*"

Mercedes watched her popular husband greeting, signing, talking, laughing, and taking pictures. She pulled herself away, sneaking out, at least satisfied that he had seen her, but not satisfied in knowing he made a point to pretend that he did not.

A while later, Mercedes arrived home and Lucinda left.

Twenty minutes after that, Nadia began barking from the backyard like she heard a siren, just as Mercedes walked in Mattie's room. She tiptoed up to her bed, sneaking a kiss upon Mattie's nose. Mattie's nose twitched and she turned her face away. And then, Mattie began coughing.

Mattie opened her eyes and looked up at Mercedes, gave a smile and coughed again. And again.

"Are you okay? Do you need some water?"

Mattie still smiled but Mercedes noticed that her skin seemed to darken. The veins of her neck protruded, and her mouth remained open. It looked like she was choking.

"Mamma!" Mercedes screamed, pulling Mattie up by her shoulders and then crawling in the bed behind her, leaning her forward and grabbing her along her chest, using the palm of one hand making a fist with the other, squeezing intermittently. She gave quick movements inward and upward just below her ribcage. "Cough it out. Cough it out, Mamma."

But Mattie didn't. She began to gag and her head slumped to her left. Mercedes squeezed again and again, and then propped two pillows under Mattie's head while aligning herself to face her. She opened Mattie's mouth and pressed on her tongue, reaching back with two fingers. Nothing was in her airway. She then straddled her, pressing the palms of her hands onto her chest. She noticed Mattie was turning purple.

"Mamma! No, Mamma, cough for me. Breathe. Please breathe. Oh my God. No, Mamma!" Her frantic words were the foreground to the background noise of Nadia barking frantically.

Mattie's eyes closed.

Mercedes hurriedly climbed off of Mattie and grabbed the cordless landline, dialing 911 and pleading as they answered. "I need an ambulance. My mother is choking. She can't breathe. Please come here quick. On Ladera Crest. Please hurry!"

The operator said, "Yes, ma'am. Did you try the Heimlich?"

"Yes."

"Did you check her throat to see if she's choking on her tongue?"

"I did."

"Is she breathing at all?"

"No."

"Is she on the floor?"

"No. She's on the bed."

"Ma'am. Lay her flat on her back on the floor."

Mercedes dropped the phone and with all of her might she scooped Mattie up, stepping back and placing her along the carpet. She took hold of the phone again. "Okay," she said, waiting for instructions.

"Now, put your hand on her wrist and check her pulse."

Mercedes said, "I can't feel it."

"Do CPR. Do you know CPR?"

"Yes. Wait." Mercedes put the phone on speaker and placed it down on the floor next to Mattie's head. "Okay."

"Kneel next to her and put your hands against the middle of her abdomen. Push down on the center of her chest, pump hard and then tilt her head back. Lift her chin, pinch her nose and cover her mouth with yours. Blow until you see her chest rise. Give two breaths. Then go back to pumping against her chest. Do it again and again."

Mercedes did. She was sweating and her skirt had risen up to her waist. She still tried.

She heard the woman say from the phone, "Hello?"

"She's not breathing."

"Keep doing it, we're on the way. They're pulling up now. Do you hear them?"

"No." Mercedes began to shake, and then she answered, focusing on listening for the sirens, "Okay. I hear them. Hurry!"

"They're there. You're doing fine. Just keep it up."

No words from Mercedes.

Nadia barked as though hit by a car.

The lady said, "They're at the door. Let them in." There were three loud knocks, and repeated ringing of the doorbell.

Mercedes still said nothing. She just pressed on Mattie's chest.

"Ma'am, are you letting them in?"

Mercedes grabbed the phone and hopped up and ran down the stairs to the front door, opening it. The paramedics rushed in and followed Mercedes upstairs. They entered the room and scrambled to attend to Mattie along the floor. Mercedes couldn't see her mother–in–law from the width of three burly men before her.

Mercedes still had the phone in her hand. "Hello?" she said, sounding scared to death.

"Okay, ma'am. You did great."

Mercedes said, "Bye," as though in a daze and simply hung up, standing before the door to Mattie's room.

She stood there trembling, and actually pinched her arm, hard, without looking down. And again she pinched herself. She felt the pain and took a deep breath, realizing this was not a dream. She instantly used the landline to call Mason. It went directly to voicemail. Her voice was piercing. "Mason! Mason, call me right back. It's an emergency!"

Struggling to remember her brother-in-law's number, she called Torino and he answered. She hollered with all of her might, watching the paramedics work on Mattie. "Torino, Mamma stopped breathing. I can't reach Mason. The ambulance is here at the house. Come quick, please!" she begged in terror. "Hurry!"

It was then that Mercedes began to sob, crying a river in the name of her mother-in-law.

Nadia joined her, howling as though tormented by an unimaginable, gut-wrenching pain.

But, it was no one's imagination.

It was real.

17

<u>The Wilsons</u>

"... beyond the rainbow why, oh why, can't I?"

Adark Saturday. Fall had fallen. Hearts had broken. The sky was gray and the autumn leaves were brown. A tribute to a matriarch's life had been planned.

Front row, the Wilson family.

All dressed in black.

Edwardian dresses with large satin bows.

Organza suits with white Peter Pan collars.

Velvet tiered skirts with ebony blazers.

Six button double-breasted suits with solid silk ties.

Three piece pinstripe with French-cuff dress shirts.

The fashions were classic and rich.

Their faces were dark and sorrowful.

Yet Star smiled.

Her lace pinafore pleated dress had a wide silk sash.

The smile, and the outfit were for her Grammy.

Her Grammy whose body lay before them in the silver metal casket.

The viewings had already taken place.

The enormous stained glass windowed sanctuary in Playa Del Rey called the Angel City Worship Center was packed, almost as packed as it would have been for a regular Sunday morning service. The rows of red velvet seats were full. The cathedral ceiling was adorned by soft water color paintings of blue skies and white cottony clouds with soaring angels. It was a day to celebrate a queen angel gone home to her king. A day the Wilson family had long dreaded.

The salt-and-pepper haired, well dressed reverend who the Wilsons had known for decades and who they called the Rev, had already spoken with vigor and passion for about thirty minutes about the meaning of life and the amazing life of Mattie Wilson, his church member and friend who died of complications from Alzheimer's.

He spoke from the altar. "I met the classy couple, Jesse and Mattie Wilson, when their youngest son, Torino, was a teenager." He looked toward Torino and then back at the audience. "In the beginning after they moved from Houston the Wilsons would always bring all three boys to early service, all well dressed in suits and ties, very well-mannered. And of course Mattie, who was truly the original diva, wore a fancy hat and tailored suit, looking like Michelle Obama, and they'd sit in the front row. I wasn't the pastor back then. My dad was. But I'd notice that at the end of every service when some people would wait around to meet and greet my dad, the Wilsons would always wait patiently in line, standing with their sons. They would step up and shake his hand, each paying their individual respects. Not once did they look impatient or did they rush.

"They came to church together and worshiped together. Their father Jesse would even usher the Thursday evening services. And then one day their oldest son who you all know, Mason Wilson," he said while looking directly at Mason and nodding, "headed off on tour to embark upon his record-breaking pro-golf career, and whose own son Rashaad, by the way, is now following in his footsteps. So though at one time it would be the five Wilsons each week, then there were four, three, and eventually two as the young men attended less and less frequently, each having their own lives but nonetheless they came, even eventually bringing their new family members."

He stepped from behind the podium. "The family that prays together stays together, and Jesse and Mattie Wilson were married for forty-two years before Jesse went home to be with the Lord. A lifetime of loving each other, two souls have now been reunited eternally. What a blessing. No longer suffering. No longer in pain. Let us not be selfish and mourn for ourselves as though we feel we'll never see them again, only focusing on our own sense of loss. You will meet again.

"Let us rejoice and be thankful. John 14, verses one through four, *Let not your hearts be troubled. Believe in God, believe also in me. In my Father's house there are many rooms; if it were not so, would I have told you that I go to prepare a place for you? And when I go to prepare a place for you, I will come again and will take you to myself, that where I am you may be also. And you know the way to the place where I am going.* And John 14:28, *If you loved me you would be glad that I am going to the Father, for the Father is greater than I.*

"Psalm 51, verse seven, *Cleanse me with hyssop, and I shall be clean; wash me and I will be whiter than snow.* If anyone had a clean heart and a steadfast spirit of joy of His salvation, Mattie Belafonte Wilson had it. She was loving and she endured. Born in 1931, she had a life some wouldn't call easy, growing up an only-child in Mississippi. Raised by a single mother who would work three jobs just to keep on the lights while Mattie would often stay home alone making her own way, barely a teen.

"She married her childhood sweetheart named Jesse Wilson. When they earned their college degrees they married and had their three boys who later took care of their mother after their father passed away. They kept her home, even when the signs of her failing health were obvious. When the Lord called her home she was just shy of turning eighty. But when it was time you can trust and believe that Mattie Wilson closed her eyes and held out her hands, saying, 'Thank you, Lord, for this amazing life. I'm ready. I'm coming home.' Here's a video portrait of the many phases and stages of the life of, Mattie Belafonte Wilson."

The instrumental version of the song, "Home," by Stephanie Mills played through the speakers and a large projector screen appeared. The pictures began to scroll along, one by one.

There were shots of Mattie pregnant with Mason - one of her with Torino as a baby - one with Claude hugging her - a shot of Jesse Wilson holding Rashaad in the hospital the day he was born - a family portrait of all three sons, along with Rashaad, Star, and Mercedes just before Jesse passed away - and a photo of Mattie with Nadia when they first brought her home. Also, there was a picture of a three year-old Star, sitting in her grandmother's lap at the piano, playing away with just one finger. The presentation ended.

"A beautiful life. A job well done, Mattie Wilson. You lived the time between your birth and your passing with purpose and left much to show for it. The people here today honor you, cherish you, acknowledge you, and love you, for the lives you have touched are many. We celebrate that beautiful life you lived, and your talented granddaughter, Star Elizabeth Wilson, has selected a song she'd like to play on the piano, just for you." He looked at Star and offered a large smile. "Star." He motioned with his hand for her to approach, and he stepped aside, taking a seat next to his wife near the pulpit.

Sitting next to her brother Rashaad, Star stood as those in attendance applauded. Wearing black ballet slippers, she walked over to the white baby-grand piano while the musicians put down their instruments and allowed her full reign. She held her head high and positioned herself smack dab in the middle of the shiny bench. She cracked her long, slender fingers and positioned her feet over the pedals, then placed her hands into position, took a deep breath and began to play. With blue-gray painted nails, her trained fingers worked with precision.

With every keystroke she gave a subtle shoulder sway, moving along to the melody. The notes signaled a familiar song. She stared straight ahead at the casket before her, then down at the keyboard, and then toward the audience, and said with volume, "This is the song my Grammy liked. We'd watch *"The Wizard of Oz"* all the time together. No matter how she felt, she'd focus on nothing but the television screen when we'd watch it. I'd crawl into bed with her and we'd just watch. Her favorite song of the entire movie, the one she'd sing along with and eventually hum along to was "Over the Rainbow."

Star continued to play, sharing her gift from God - the gift that had landed her scholarships and recognition and led her toward her bright future, all inspired by her grandmother who had taught Star to play when she was only three.

But this time at the age of twenty-two, words accompanied the notes and Star began to sing – sing from a place deep down in her soul, a place that only her grandmother knew about before now. "Somewhere over the rainbow, way up high, there's a land that I heard of, once in a lullaby." She belted out the words, continuing to sing about troubles melting like lemon drops, away above the chimney tops, and then sang, "That's where I'll find you," changing the words a bit with a twinkle in her eyes. It was a soulful and powerful rendition.

Mason, who had been holding it all together on the outside allowed his insides to show and a tear rolled down his cheek and into his mouth. He swallowed and coughed. Then another tear followed, this time making it to his chin, which he dabbed away.

Mercedes was way ahead of him. She wiped her mascara-laced eyes with a white handkerchief, sniffled and then squinted her eyes shut only to reopen them releasing more tears. She was moved by the sight and the sound of her daughter paying tribute to a grandmother she had grown to love in a way she would never love anyone else. She was also in shock that her baby girl could even carry a tune, let alone do it very well. She looked at Mason who only looked straight forward, so she did as well.

Torino held Sequoia just a little bit tighter, and Sequoia squeezed little TJ's hand.

As the song went on, Claude, who was seated in-between his wife and daughter, placed his hand on Venus's thigh just as Skyy snuggled in closer to him, tucking her legs underneath her. He kissed the top of her head and wept.

Cameron and Rashaad sat next to each other, both with their mouths wide open. Rashaad wiped his eye and played it off as if something was in it. Cameron looked over at him and nodded to say, *it's okay*. Rashaad nodded back.

Mattie's caregiver, Lucinda Ramirez, was next to Rashaad along with her family. She cried like a baby having told Mercedes she was mad at herself for not staying over the night Mattie died.

Extended family members filled the remaining reserved rows.

Meanwhile, Star continued to show that she was given the perfect name. She shined so bright that it was blinding. A beam of light shone through the stained-glass windowpanes that aimed itself directly upon the piano and its pianist. The rays had met their intended target who ended her song, singing, "If happy little bluebirds fly beyond the rainbow why, oh why, can't I?" Then Star held the last note, pressing the keys even harder, giving strong pitch and tone. Her efforts were all for her grandmother, every ounce of breath and every intense facial expression she could muster. She pounded the last set of keys to signal the final note and sat straight up, tearless, and said before anyone could applaud, "Grammy always had a lot of sayings, like 'do it right the first time,' and 'it's not what you say, it's how you say it,' and 'God don't like ugly,' and 'the early bird gets the worm.'"

Mercedes looked at Mason. He looked at her and winked.

Some people smiled and some laughed.

Star smiled. "One special thing my Grammy always said when preparing me for life out in the world, that I could have sworn I heard her whisper to me this morning when I looked out of her bedroom window was, 'A lady always knows when to leave.'"

With that, Star got up. It was then that everyone stood and clapped while she headed for her grandmother's open casket again. She stood over Mattie's body. Mattie was dressed in green with her silver gray hair in cornrows by Mercedes. Star leaned down, hair in cornrows as well, and planted a kiss on the coolness of Mattie's cheek. She removed a note from her pocket and placed it on Mattie's stiff hands, leaving it there. The front of it read, *Pretty Girl*.

Star stood tall, turning back around toward the still standing crowd and walked over to take her seat. Her brother sat as well, hugging her tightly. Mercedes hurried over and sat next to Star. She put her arm around Star and checked for tears, rocking her back and forth. Mercedes wept for the both of them.

As they left the service a little while later, all family members proceeded to the awaiting cars that would proceed to Holy Cross Cemetery. The lead car was the one that carried Mattie's body.

Star looked up in the sky before she ducked her head to get inside of the limousine. The day's grayness had managed to morph into blueness. And Star saw . . . a rainbow.

She smiled a colorful smile.

A smile that was stronger than her anxious, frowning tears.

18

Venus

"Don't let pride do that to you."

Later that day, Venus and Claude had everyone out to their new home in Laguna Hills for the repast. The kitchen had an octagon-shaped island. It was roomy yet cozy.

Mason stood in the kitchen leaning back against the island. Claude and Venus stood before him.

"Man, you okay?" Claude asked.

Mason's eyes were reddened from tears. "I should've brought her with me."

"Don't do that to yourself. None of us should. We didn't know when she'd pass away. It would've happened no matter who she lived with. It was her time."

Mason only looked at the floor. "I'd just told Torino I was going to bring her with me." He looked at his brother. "Man, Mom's gone." Mason's face was pained.

"I know. But Mom lived a long, good life." Claude sounded positive.

Venus spoke up. "Mattie wasn't living the quality of life she would've wanted. Before, she was so independent, and yet over the last years she was bed ridden and couldn't speak. Her non-ambulatory state was tough on her. And on us. Like Claude said, it was just her time."

Claude said, "It is hard to face the fact that she's really gone. She's no longer in pain, though. Bottom line."

"I just wanted to be home more so I could spend time with her."

"And you did. You did fine. We did fine," Venus said.

Claude told his brother, "Mason. One thing I know is you need to go home. After today you need to remind yourself not to let more time go by without being with your family, man. Come on. Don't let your pride do that to you."

"Pride?" Mason looked like he fought not to react. "You're actually right. I should've been home. Home with my family when this happened. I shouldn't have had to leave my own house to deal with what my wife did."

Venus said to him, "I know you and Mercedes have some things to work out. But remember no one came closer to loving Mattie like she was their own flesh and blood than Mercedes. Mattie had taken the place of Mercedes's own mom. No matter what, she was there for her. I'll give her that. No one blames her."

Claude added, "I can't imagine what that's done to her. Mason, go home."

"Hi, everybody." Mercedes came into the kitchen and stood by the other end of the island.

"Hi," Venus and Claude said together.

She asked, "Mason, you still haven't eaten?"

"No."

Mercedes headed toward the dining room. "Let me go and get you a plate. You've got to eat something. The food is excellent. Sequoia did a great job."

Venus said, "She sure did."

"I'm good," Mason said.

Mercedes stopped and walked back to them. She looked reserved.

"Mercedes, how are you? Are you okay?" Venus asked.

140

She sort of replied, saying, "I'm about to go home, actually. I'm tired. I need to take Rashaad back so he can catch a flight later on tonight." She asked Mason, "Honey, are you coming?"

"No."

"You sure?" she asked.

"I'm sure." He took a step away from the island. "Where's Rashaad?"

Mercedes said, "Oh, he's in the living room with Cameron."

"I'll be right back." Mason stepped up to Mercedes and leaned in, kissing her on the cheek.

"Okay," she said, blinking fast, looking flushed.

Mason walked out.

Claude followed.

Venus told Mercedes, "He loves you. You know that."

"I do. He's just so damn stubborn." Her eyes looked misty.

Venus told Mercedes, "I don't know the details but I do know you two have been together too long. Something like this just goes to show, you never know when in an instant, life can be taken away. It's just way too short."

"I agree."

"And I'm sorry you went through what you did that night. Thanks for doing all you could to revive Mattie."

Mercedes remained solemn.

Venus said, "I can imagine it was hell. It was just her time."

Mercedes said, "Thanks for having the repast here. The house is beautiful. I'll talk to you later." Just as she finished her sentence, Star walked in. Mercedes said, "Hey, honey."

"Hey." Star looked at Venus. "Hi, Auntie." She walked over to the kitchen sink, looking out the window.

"Hi there."

Mercedes said, "Rashaad and I are going."

Star kept her back to them. "He told me. I just took Skyy and TJ in there with him and the guys."

"Okay. I'll talk to you later. You did a great job today. Proud of you."

"Bye."

Mercedes started to walk out. "You coming back to the house later?"

Star replied, "No. I'm staying with Dad tonight."

"Good. Glad he won't be alone. You either. I'll talk to you all later. Bye Venus."

"Bye. Call you later."

Mercedes exited the kitchen.

Star turned to face Venus. "I like your new house, Auntie."

"Thanks. We're still getting settled in. Honey, I want you to keep your head up. Grammy loved you. You've got an angel now."

"I know. I loved her. Funny thing is she was like my friend even though she was almost four times my age. I could tell her anything. She was my second mother, and then she started being like a little girl. The older I got it was like the younger she got. She needed me to keep her calm and make her feel like she still had all the answers, even if she couldn't remember our names." Star shook her head. Venus came to her and hugged her tight. "I hate Alzheimer's. I'm gonna miss her, Auntie." Star broke down, shaking, trembling, and finally crying. Sobbing in her aunt's arms.

"Let it out. You need to. You have to."

"It's so hard."

"I know. I understand."

"I'm sorry," Star said, letting go of Venus and wiping her eyes. It was like she was forcing herself not to totally lose it. She sniffled and tried to regroup. "I'll be right back. I'm going to the bathroom for some tissue." She stepped away.

"Love you."

"Love you, too," Star said as she headed out at the same time Claude walked back in. Star looked down while covering her eyes.

Claude said to Venus as he stood next to her, "Well. Speaking of love, I love you."

"I love you."

He put his arm around her waist.

She said, "Sorry about Mom. Sorry about everything. About the other day at your office. Everything."

"Me, too," he said as they kissed.

Troubles seemed to have melted.

At least for the time being.

19

Sequoia

". . . ever hit or verbally abused your son . . ."

So, Mr. Wilson, I see you've changed your reply to the child support claim and you're no longer contesting paternity. Is that correct?"

It was the custody hearing date, September 28th.

Torino, the respondent, was present and accounted for. "Yes, Your Honor," he said, wearing a dark suit and tie.

Sequoia watched, all eyes and ears, dressed in black.

Kyle was absent.

Colette, the petitioner, was front and center. And now she had a female attorney. Attorney Randolph.

The judge said, "I'd ordered a DNA test to be taken and it appears only Ms. Berry has done that for Kyle Brewer, Jr. Is that right?"

Attorney Phillips replied for his client, saying, "Yes, Sir. Mr. Wilson is admitting he is the father."

The judge looked at Colette. "Well, Ms. Berry, it looks like we'll move right on into the custody and child support portion of this case since Mr. Wilson is now admitting paternity, and therefore is jointly responsible for the health, well being and care of the son the two of you have together."

He spoke to Torino's attorney, saying, "Now, I see you've submitted paperwork to support Mr. Wilson's apparent claims that Ms. Berry is unfit, and that she's been accused of violence against her former live-in boyfriend." He flipped through the paperwork. "I see that the police were called about three times for claims of domestic violence. Each time Mr. Brewer was the one who called. Yet when police came out it was Ms. Berry who complained that he was the one who hit her and that she reacted in self defense." He looked at Attorney Phillips.

"Yes, Your Honor. And, we have documents here to verify that Mr. Brewer filed a restraining order only three weeks ago and has not seen or talked to Ms. Berry since. He is very concerned about the emotional welfare of the child."

"Does Mr. Brewer see the child? I would think not with a restraining order on the child's mother."

Attorney Phillips said, "He moved out and left the child with Ms. Berry."

The judge asked, "Ms. Berry, have you ever been abusive to Mr. Kyle Brewer verbally or physically, striking him or harassing him?"

"No, Sir."

"And have you ever hit or verbally abused your son, Kyle Brewer, Jr.?"

"No, Sir."

"Now, Attorney Randolph, we have the police reports, but no charges were brought against your client or the other party. Because there were no charges, these have no bearing on whether or not Kyle Jr. is in danger. I'm going to take these into due consideration, however. I'm going to award Ms. Berry, and Mr. Wilson, joint custody."

Colette looked displeased.

Torino looked surprised.

"As far child support, Mr. Wilson, how long have you been aware that Kyle Brewer, Jr. is your biological son?"

"Just since Ms. Berry came to my place of business right before all of this, warning me of this child support claim and informing me that she used my sperm to impregnate herself."

The judge looked perplexed. "Is this true, Ms. Berry?"

"No, Sir," she said plainly.

"Did you go to his place of business?"

"Yes, Sir."

"Did you impregnate yourself?"

"No. I never said that. Sir."

"When did you inform Mr. Wilson that he was the father?"

"While I was pregnant."

The judge's eyes moved to Torino. "And Mr. Wilson, you didn't believe her?"

"No. I knew it was impossible because I always used protection, but based on her claim when she came to my place of business as to what she did, I have concluded that he is my son."

"Based upon that, huh? Okay. Ms. Berry, the period of time that Mr. Wilson did not know he was the father cannot count as time considered in back-child support. I will issue an order of support," he began writing, "for two-thousand dollars per month, starting the day Mr. Wilson filed the answer acknowledging that the paternity was uncontested. You are both ordered to work out a custody arrangement plan with the family court mediator immediately following this decision to work out holidays, frequency, etcetera."

Colette looked like she wanted to speak, but didn't.

Attorney Randolph spoke for her. "Your Honor, my client is seeking attorney's fees and court costs, as well as five-thousand per month, which is a small fraction of Mr. Wilson's seven-hundred-thousand dollar income. A great deal of the money Ms. Berry receives will be spent making a home for Kyle, Jr. Ms. Berry would like the opportunity to give their son a comfortable and equal lifestyle when he is not with his father."

The judge replied, "Attorney Randolph, the plaintiff and respondent were never married. That's first of all. Second of all, I have not awarded Ms. Berry full custody, with Mr. Wilson having visitation rights. In that case she may have gotten more support, however, two-thousand is more than enough. Also, one person's lifestyle does not entitle the other parent who makes less income to garner the difference through child support. There is no alimony, as I said they were never man and wife. And the amount awarded is sufficient to provide for a seven year-old. The medical insurance is to be provided by Mr. Wilson, so that won't be an issue for Ms. Berry. If he goes to a private school, there's enough for food, clothing and other necessities. This child can live quite nicely. Some parents don't make that per month for an entire household. Ms. Berry is expected to make a living for herself, and her son actually. Is that clear?"

"Yes, Sir," Colette replied, looking let down.

"Yes, Your Honor," Attorney Randolph answered.

"I will, however, grant fees and court costs to Ms. Berry."

Colette gave a slight sigh of relief.

"Now, as far as the name change petition, Attorney Phillips, does your client have a problem with the request?"

"Your Honor, I think Kyle Brewer gave Kyle Jr. his name long ago and has been standing in as the father. We see no reason to change it."

"Ms. Berry, why would it matter at this point? Mr. Wilson has admitted he is the father."

Colette looked certain. "Because my son is a Wilson. He has a half-brother who's a Wilson, named after the father my son will never be named after. I don't think Mr. Wilson would want two sons named, Torino Jr., but I have seen it done before. Mr. Brewer and I are not together and he won't be in this child's life. Mr. Wilson will. Sir."

The judge said, "Ms. Berry, your petition is granted. Kyle Jamal Brewer, Jr.'s name change is ordered, his name now being Kyle Jamal Wilson, dropping the junior, obviously. Ms. Berry, you'll need to get a copy of this order and present it to the Social Security Administration and then when you get his new social security card, take care of his school and medical records."

"Yes, Sir."

"Now unless there are any further questions, these matters are closed."

"None, Your Honor," said Torino.

"None. Sir," said Colette.

The judge looked between the two of them. "I hate to see this. For the sake of this child, get it together. Put him first. Next case, Thomas versus Jarvis."

Minutes later, Torino asked his attorney while standing in the hallway, "So, that's it?"

Sequoia stood at his side holding his hand.

"Yes."

Colette and her attorney had already walked down the hall. She and Sequoia barely gave each other a glance.

"Now what?" asked Torino.

"We go into the conference room with the petitioner and the mediator to arrange custody parameters."

"And then?"

"And then, depending upon which date it's agreed to, Kyle Wilson comes home to spend time with his father. It could be pretty quick."

"Okay." Torino nodded. He released his hand from Sequoia's and adjusted his tie.

"Excuse me for one moment," Torino's attorney said, and then he walked away.

"Sure."

Sequoia said, "Wow. Guess you can't refer to him as Jr., huh?"

"Guess not."

"Even though he might really be."

"I'm calling him Kyle," said Torino.

"So, you're satisfied?" she asked.

"Not really. She didn't lose custody altogether."

"No. I guess we're sharing a child fifty-fifty with *her*," she said as if Colette was the devil herself. "A child we still don't even know is yours."

"We will, Sequoia. We will." He held her hand again.

His attorney stepped up. "Mr. and Mrs. Wilson, right this way, please."

20

<u>Mercedes</u>

"Hang up or I'm leaving."

The next Saturday evening, Mercedes lay on the white sofa in the living room under a chenille throw, half asleep. The television was muted. The only light in the room was illuminating from the screen.

Since Mattie's passing, Mercedes made it a habit to bring Nadia into the house at night just to keep her company. And when it was time for Mercedes to go to bed in her room, Nadia would head straight to Mattie's room and sleep by the side of Mattie's bed.

Mercedes heard the sound of a key in the door and the door opening. Then she heard, "Hi."

"Hey," Mercedes said, realizing it was her husband coming through the front door. She sat up slowly, struggling to focus, squinting as Mason closed the door and turned on the living room light. She stretched her arms in an effort to force out the kinks, glancing over at the huge wrought-iron clock on the wall.

Nadia, who Mercedes thought was by the sofa, came running downstairs wagging her tail and circling Mason. She seemed more excited to see him than she had ever been when Mason lived at home.

He bent down to pet Nadia, giving off a few chuckles. "Hey there. Look at you. Calm down, girl."

Nadia savored the attention and followed Mason's steps as he walked toward the recliner, placing his keys and some mail on the cushion.

Nadia sat next to where he stood.

Mercedes wiped the corners of her eyes. "Are you coming home, or just coming by?" She rubbed the soles of her bare feet together.

"Coming by for a minute just to check the mail and get more of my things. I called but you didn't answer."

"Okay." Mercedes elongated the one word as though his reply was not what she wanted to hear. She picked up the remote and turned off the television.

"You've been sleeping all day?"

"I have." Her hair was mussed up and the mascara on her eyes was smudged. She was in need of a waxing, a pedicure, a fill, and a toothbrush.

"Where's Lucinda?"

Mercedes folded the throw neatly and placed it on her lap. "I let her go. I told her we didn't need her. She was a nurse."

"Thought maybe she could stay on as housekeeper."

"I'm good. Not much going on here that needs to be kept, really. Other than me."

"I'm sure Lucinda's taking this hard, too."

"She is."

He said, "She was Mattie's caregiver as well as nurse." He headed upstairs.

Mercedes looked up toward the landing and noticed Mason heading toward Mattie's room, not theirs, with Nadia right behind him. She then heard her husband walk to the other side of the house into their bedroom.

Within ten minutes, Mercedes had turned the television back on and leaned upon the sofa cushions simply scrolling through the channels, still with the sound off.

Mason came back down with a Nike shoulder bag.

Nadia stayed upstairs.

Mercedes looked over at Mason. "Did you go in her room?"

"I did."

"It's like time stood still in there."

"I see that. Here. Your phone was by the bed." Mason extended his hand and offered Mercedes her cell.

She took it, placing it on the coffee table. "Thanks."

"I noticed an RG in your contact list. Is that . . ."

She jumped on his words. "Oh, you noticed, huh?"

"Is it?"

"Yes." She looked on edge.

So did he. "You exchanged numbers?"

"No. He put his in. I forgot about it."

"Forgot?"

"Yes, I forgot." Mercedes took a breath and transferred the topic. "You talk to Star?"

He looked like he would only allow her evasion for about ten quick seconds. "Yes. You?"

"For a minute. I wanted her to know she didn't do anything wrong by telling you."

"I think she believes you're the one who's mad."

"Why?"

"For telling me."

"She didn't say that to me. Honestly, instead of her thinking I'm mad, I'm the one who thinks she's still mad. She's distant."

"Really?" He just stared at Mercedes.

She saw the look on his face and nervously smoothed her hair, and wiped under her eyes. She kept the topic where it was. "Years ago, she was the one who resented you for being famous and being gone. She even took your old Porsche for a joy ride and crashed it into a tree to get your attention. She's always been almost angry because of your fame. But you learned how to show her you care, even when you didn't have time to spend with her. You bought her cards and made her feel special, and you've taken the time to visit her in D.C. and Atlanta. You really have shown her that she matters. It's like somewhere along the way things went from being mommy's little girl, to being daddy's little girl. I never noticed it until that phone call that day. But, I can honestly say I probably would've done the same thing in her position."

"She's a rebel."

"Don't mess with her Grammy, and her daddy." Mercedes managed a snicker.

"I guess so." He again stared. "So, you changed the subject. Why do you have his number?"

She began to frown. "Mason, you know what? I think I have it because, well no, I know I have it so I can call him right now and let him tell you what happened. Hold up. Here." She snatched her phone from the table.

Mason's eyes flashed a stop sign. "No. Don't dial his number. Hang up."

She pressed *RG*. "Oh, yes I am because you're standing before me with a duffle bag full of your clothes to take out of here and start a life without me and that's more than I can take." The phone rang. "You're spending your days and nights away from me because you think I had sex with this man, and I did not. I did not. I did not. Actually, I wish I never met him." The phone continued to ring. "Now, maybe if he tells you that himself you'll believe him, because you surely don't believe me."

"Calm down."

"I can't be calm. This is my life."

He demanded, "Hang up or I'm leaving."

There was an answer. "Hello?"

"Ryan. This is Mercedes from Vegas." She kept her eyes on Mason, who kept his eyes on her. "The owner of Simpson Models. Well, I need you to do me a favor."

Mason looked like he could stab her as he took his keys and mail from the seat of the recliner and simply left, slamming the front door closed.

A few seconds went by.

She continued anyway. "Listen, I need you to know I made a big mistake. I'm a married woman. And I think you know by now that I'm Mason Wilson's wife. Those few moments we had together have ruined my marriage."

"I don't want any mess. I can't have any."

"Then maybe you shouldn't have come on to a married woman. And no, I shouldn't have responded, either. I wish I could go back and never have given you any attention. My whole life is different now. So much has happened. Why did you call me and leave that message at my hotel? And why did I call you back?"

His voice was deep. "First of all, you're a beautiful woman. I'm sorry about what's going on. I wish things were different."

"I'll tell you now, I wish things were the same as they were before I met you."

He maintained a clam tone. "Your husband seems to be a reasonable man. Surely he knows what he has." He paused. "You're right. We made a mistake. But it was only a kiss."

"You're single. For you it was only a kiss. For me it was infidelity. Goodbye."

"Goodbye. And I hope to see your husband around in these arenas. He'd be great."

Mercedes hung up without further reply.

She called her husband but he didn't answer.

Her voicemail message was, "Please call me. I love you. It's too damn quiet. Come home."

Mercedes fought back the tears and went upstairs. She ended up in Mattie's room. She sat on the bed, and asked out loud. "Mamma. Why?"

She looked to the side on the nightstand and saw a plaque with a figure of an angel. A plaque that Mason must have left.

It read: *John 14:1 Let not your hearts be troubled.* Mercedes nodded that's right.

She held the plaque tight and laid down, giving in to the mattress. She snuggled up to the jade blanket and sniffed it. It still contained the scent of Mattie's White Shoulders perfume.

She dozed off in the safety-kiss of the room's essence.

Nadia lay at the side of the bed, safe as well.

Both broken hearts praying for mending.

In time.

21

Venus

"... I'm not his real mom."

Claude had only been home for a little while after a long day of driving from Laguna to the Ladera office. He had stopped by the old house and back to the new office. He looked drained.

Though it was nearly seventy degrees outside, the fireplace was lit for pure ambiance. It was a quiet moment after enjoying the soulful ox-tails and green beans and rice that Venus made for dinner. She now had time to cook and be the housewife they agreed she would be.

It was a night of Claude and Venus enjoying their new home. Just being. Even if only for a few minutes. Especially since Skyy was around the corner visiting a friend from her new school whose mom promised to bring her back by nine. It was eight-thirty.

They were in the family room curled up together on the sectional, legs intertwined, talking. On the oversized oak coffee table before them, two rum-mojito cocktails awaited their respective sippage.

Claude asked no questions about Owen.

Venus asked no questions about Mary.

"I really do love this place," Venus said, looking up at the marigold and white trey ceilings. "Even the city. This was a great idea."

"I agree. I'm glad you approve."

"Are you okay dealing with all that's happened? With Mattie I mean."

Claude said, "I'm still trying to adjust. For years I've tried to brace myself for the reality of living life without her. I still can't believe it. Like this morning when I was driving into L.A., I thought about stopping by Mason's house to see her and then I realized that won't happen anymore."

"It does seem like a dream." She snuggled closer. "But, it was great having everyone over for the repast. We've gotta have the family over again, but next time it needs to be for a positive celebration. We need to make sure we take time to get together like we used to."

"Agreed."

"Maybe even for your birthday in November."

"Maybe." Claude leaned over to take his glass in hand. "You want your drink?"

"No. I'm fine. Thanks."

He took a big sip and placed the glass back on the table. "So, where's Cameron? I noticed his car was gone."

Venus said, "Honey, you know where he is." She watched his facial expression.

He looked bothered. "Does he even come home anymore? What's he doing with his life? He's supposed to be looking for work and going to school." At that moment, Claude's cell rang from the end table. He untangled himself from Venus and sat up, putting it on speaker. "Hey. We were just talking about you. What's up?"

"Not much."

"When are you coming home?" Claude asked, looking at Venus who listened intently.

"In the morning," Cameron replied and then said, "Hold up, Dad. I called because Penny wants to talk to you." There was the sound of a muffled handoff.

Claude looked like he was in no mood.

"Hi, Claude. How are you?" Penny asked, sounding cheery.

"Penny. I'm good."

"I wanted to tell you I found a few properties in Newport Beach. Do you know that area?"

"I do."

"You think if I email you the links today you can make arrangements for me to see them this weekend? Well, Cameron, too."

"I don't see why not."

"Good."

He pressed mute then looked at Venus. "I want to tell her so bad."

She agreed with him, giving an approving glance.

He released mute and resumed by saying, "Penny."

"Yes," she replied.

"Put my son on the phone."

"Sure. Hold on. Talk to you later."

"Bye."

Cameron took the phone back. "Hello?"

"Listen. I don't want to embarrass you, but we need to talk. You're headed down a path where you're so into these women that you're wasting your time."

"Dad." Cameron sounded like he dreaded his dad's next words.

"Son, you just lost your grandmother. She would want you to make something out of your life. It's time you come home and set some serious goals. Get your resume together. Look up schools you can apply to and get your BA, finally. You're less than a year away. We talked about this before we moved and you agreed, but I don't see you trying. It turns out Berkeley is sealing the issue of the violation of policy because my attorney kept pushing them, but that's the best I could do. There's no getting back in there."

"That's cool," Cameron replied.

"It's not cool with me. It's still time wasted. That money I paid the attorney went straight down the drain. And I'm still the one doing all of this follow-up." Claude said, "It's like I care more about your situation than you do. All you're doing is screwing some woman who's old enough to be your mother, Cameron. This has to stop."

Cameron was quiet.

"And also, just so you know. It's true that Candy admitted to her involvement in the break-in, but today she was arrested as an accessory. It's not her first offense so chances are, she'll do some time."

Venus just listened. It was all news to her.

"Oh man. Okay."

"They found everything that was taken during the burglary between her and two guys. Even your mom's ring. And also, Cal Berkley decided to kick her butt out for writing your paper."

"Good."

Claude raised his eyebrows. "So few words from you. I guess you're just like, on to the next one, huh?"

"Well, I can't really talk."

"Oh really? Man, Cameron, come on." His voice was intense. "I move us to Orange County and in two-point-two seconds you latch on to this woman with money, and you remain in neutral. I'm telling you now I'm not having it. I'm at my wits end."

Venus sat up and took hold of her cocktail, sipping from the glass, holding on to it with both hands.

"Dad," Cameron said, lowering his voice. "I'll be home tonight."

"We'll see. All I know is by the time I get home from work tomorrow I want to hear about your progress with your future plans."

"Agreed. Bye." A voice in the background was heard. Cameron quickly told his dad, "Penny says, bye."

"Tell her bye."

"I will."

Claude shook his head as he hung up and reached in his pants pocket. He pulled out Venus's emerald ring. "Anyway, I stopped by and identified the jewelry. I had this cleaned. The rest we'll need to have delivered."

"Oh my." Venus set her drink down and took the ring from Claude and placed it on her right middle finger. "Thank you." She planted a kiss on his lips. "I'm so glad to have it back."

"Not sure what happened to the box it was in. Most of the jewelry boxes are missing because a lot of that stuff was pawned. But, everything was recovered, so, that's that." He picked up his drink.

"I'm glad. You really did have a full day today, didn't you?"

"I did," he said, taking a sip as the doorbell sounded. "Is that the lady bringing Skyy home?"

"Probably." Venus held out her hand in front of herself and looked at the ring that shined as she got up. "It's beautiful as ever." She walked toward the front door, lowering her voice. "Oh, I was gonna say, I think that because Cam lost his mom so violently, it's coming back to haunt him. I mean, after all, you're not his real dad and I'm not his real mom." She spoke softer. "And the man who is his real father is in jail for killing his mom. That's a lot, honey. Maybe that's why he's so attached to certain women. Seems he lets them do things for him. You ever think about that?"

Claude replied, looking doubtful, "No. He's still a man. Therefore he needs to act like a man and handle his business. I've tried to show him that. No more excuses. You take what life has dished out to you and instead of blaming the *curse*, you make your own *course*."

She stood before the door with her hand on the knob. The doorbell rang again. "Well, I just might be right. I mean for once maybe. Ya think?"

Claude took his last sip and swallowed, and said with a half-grin, "Open the damn door."

22

Sequoia

"... up to her old tricks again."

W hen is Kyle Jr. coming?" Mercedes asked Sequoia while Sequoia drove toward Santa Monica. It was a Thursday afternoon around four o'clock.

Mercedes was at home relaxing, having just worked out at the gym.

Sequoia said, "Torino and I talked about calling Kyle Jr. KJ since he's a Wilson now and not really a junior to Kyle Brewer. Actually, we pick him up from school next Friday and we'll keep him over the weekend, then drop him off at school on Monday."

"I see. Is that so you guys don't have to see her?" asked Mercedes. "I mean most guys pick their kids up from the mom's house."

"That's what she requested, not us. I'm sure there'll be times we'll have to go by each other's homes and drop off, pick up. It should be interesting."

"This has got to be tough on everyone."

"There's no getting around it."

"True. So, I'll have a new nephew. And you'll have another son."

"Yes." Sequoia made the turn from Santa Monica Boulevard to Lincoln.

Mercedes asked, "Have you thought that maybe it would've been nice if Mamma could've met him?"

"I didn't mention it to Torino, but yeah, I did think about that."

"Actually, this is kind of exciting. Are you okay with it?"

"I think so. That is if he is Torino's son." Sequoia watched the street signs.

"He said you'll do the test first thing though, right?"

"He did. But, the fact remains that he and I have got a KJ and a TJ. That's all I know."

"True. It'll be interesting to see how the boys get along, how he relates to the two of you, and just what it is that he knows."

Sequoia said, "You know how kids are. He and TJ will hit it off. Kids know no strangers."

"I know that's right. Where're you headed?"

"To a client's house. They're throwing an engagement party for their daughter. It's over here in Santa Monica. Should be pretty nice. My assistant is already there. How about you? I know you've been working out trying to lose some weight."

"To lose weight, yes. But also, I have to do something other than work, or else I'm gonna lose my mind."

"You hanging in there?" Sequoia asked.

"Trying. Mason came and got some more of his things. After that visit he stopped taking my calls. I've been wanting to tell you that. I called Ryan so Mason could talk to him. It backfired. He's even more pissed at the fact that I even had his number."

Sequoia sounded surprised. "I'm sure he was."

Mercedes's voice sped up. "Girl, he went searching through my phone and came up to me asking why I had the number, so I just dialed it."

"Oh, now see, he's not done. How could he really be done if he gives a damn about whose number you have in your phone?"

"You never know with Mason. He could've been looking for something to start some more mess about. Like looking for an excuse," Mercedes said.

"Oh, I doubt it. It's just his pride. You know how men are. Have the kids been home since the funeral?"

"No. Rashaad has a tournament coming up. I'm driving down to San Diego to watch him. It's been a while since I've done that. I'm not sure if Mason is going or not."

"Good. Glad you're getting to see him play. Listen, I'll call you later. I'm here now."

"Okay."

Sequoia parked along the curb a few houses down and looked at the random people who walked toward the house at the end of the cul-de-sac, her destination. She said, "Mercedes, you know what? I can't believe it. I see Kyle walking up. And he's not alone."

"What? I just know he's not with Colette."

"No. But he is with an Asian chick."

"Damn, he moved on fast."

"I guess so. Unless she's just a friend," Sequoia said, turning off the ignition.

"Maybe."

"But they are hand-in-hand."

"Hmmm. Small world. You gonna talk to him about Kyle Jr., I mean KJ?"

"No. I'll let Torino do that." She grabbed her iPad and handbag. "Listen, you have a good day."

"You too. Good luck with the event."

Sequoia got out of her car. "Thanks." She hung up and proceeded down the street and up the walkway to the ranch style house. The front door was open and the owner stood before her. She said, "Hi, Mr. Brown."

"Hi, Sequoia. This is my wife, Irene." He looked to his wife. "Irene, this is the caterer who was referred to us a few months ago."

Sequoia said, "Nice to meet you."

They shook hands.

His wife said, "Sequoia. Some of your team is already in there setting up, working very hard. They've been passing around hors d'oeuvres and serving beverages. They're doing a great job."

"Well good. Is the kitchen that way?" she asked, pointing past the dining room.

"Yes, right through there," said Mr. Brown, pointing as well.

"If you'll excuse me, I'll head on into the kitchen. Please let me know if you need anything. I'll check back with you."

"We will. Thanks."

Not even twenty minutes later as Sequoia made her way from the small house, into the huge, tropical style backyard, she was greeted with a tap on the shoulder. "Hello, Sequoia."

She turned around. "Hi, Kyle. How are you?"

"I'm good, thanks. And you?"

"Good." She looked at the slender, pretty young woman with Kyle. Her hair was jet black and so long it looked as though she could sit on it. Her lashes looked like they could reach out and touch someone. "Hi, I'm Sequoia." Sequoia nodded.

"I'm Yasmin." Yasmin nodded.

Kyle said, "Yasmin is a former firefighter. We used to work together. I've known her for years."

"Oh, really? I find that interesting. Are there a lot of female firefighters?" Sequoia asked, looking to get a conversation started.

"Not that many," Yasmin said, sounding as if she could not have cared less.

"You enjoy it?" Sequoia asked, looking her up and down, noticing her St. John suit and gold Jimmy Choo wedge sandals.

"I do." Yasmin looked at the people next to them, the people behind Sequoia, and then at the people sitting at a patio table nearby.

"Good." Sequoia looked at her like she was trying to figure her out.

Kyle said, "So, I understand from Torino that things didn't quite go as planned."

Sequoia was ready to talk about anything other than trying to talk to Yasmin again. "Not quite. But we're ready."

"Good."

"I'll be right back. Excuse me." Yasmin walked away toward Mrs. Brown and they hugged.

Sequoia watched. "She knows the Browns, or you do?"

"Her cousin is actually marrying my brother. I introduced them."

"Oh, I see. So you and her are like, dating?"

"We are. All of a sudden we just clicked."

"Really? She doesn't look like a firefighter."

"She was. Take all that glamour off of her and she's pretty athletic."

Sequoia took one last look at her. "I see. Well, you deserve to be happy."

"I hope to be." He then asked, "You're catering this party?"

"Yeah. It should be a small group and just take a few hours. They're nice people."

"They are."

"So, you have a brother, huh?" she asked.

166

"I do. I have two brothers. Just like Torino."

"Nice."

They stood and a few more moments passed.

Sequoia asked, "Kyle, I have to ask you. How are you dealing with not seeing Kyle Jr.?"

"I'm not. It's tough."

"Then how are you gonna handle it long term? I mean, did you and Torino talk about you seeing Kyle Jr. while we have him?"

"I don't think that's gonna fly with Colette. She's pretty mad at me right now. But I had to do what I had to do."

"You're just letting go?" she asked, looking as though she didn't quite get it.

"No. But I didn't bet on the judge awarding joint custody, either."

"Yeah." She said, "Kyle, I'm sorry. Really, I shouldn't have said anything. I'll let you and Torino deal with this."

"No, it's fine. You're Kyle Jr.'s stepmother now. You should be involved."

"Yes, I am that."

"And by the way, I'm sorry for all those years I was upset with Torino. That was some stupid, unnecessary mess."

"Hey, that's life."

"I must say I'm glad you and Torino got together after all those years of being Mercedes's friend. You and him were like oil and water years ago. I never would've guessed you'd end up together. You guys are down for each other like four flat tires. Bonnie and Clyde."

She snickered. "Believe me, we didn't predict it either." A server walked by with an empty tray and Sequoia saw someone trying to flag him down for a drink. "Kyle, I'm gonna finish seeing to everything here.

You enjoy yourself." She then saw Yasmin coming over. "And, I see your date is coming back."

"Okay."

Sequoia gave it one last shot. "Nice meeting you, Yasmin."

"You too." Brief eye contact. No smile. No nothing.

"Bye." Sequoia just stepped away and handled her business.

Hours went by and Sequoia kept an eye on the setup, main course of squash quiche, scallops, ginger beef sticks, and salmon spinach salad. The Sonoma Brut champagne and sparkling water flowed.

The engaged couple, him tall, though dark, unlike Kyle, but with but with the same eyes, and her, a biracial beauty with a short pixie cut and brown eyes, danced along with the guests, celebrating their upcoming nuptials.

Kyle danced as well, but not with his date. He danced with Mrs. Brown and her friends, who were in heaven from his attention. His date watched him from the sidelines.

It was eight o'clock and Sequoia made sure her assistant had everything under control. She said her goodbyes, excused herself and headed out the door while talking on her cell.

"Honey, can you believe Kyle was here with his new girl?"

"What?" Torino said. "He told me something about his brother's engagement party. I had no idea it would be the one you were headed to."

"Well, did you know he had someone already?"

"He told me." Torino sounded unfazed.

"Wow. Okay, listen, I'm headed home. See you soon."

"Okay. TJ's been asking for his mommy."

"Awww. Tell him mommy's on her way."

"See ya."

As Sequoia hung up and walked down the street, she looked down a side street after hearing a door close. She saw a heavyset woman from behind with golden hair walking toward a black SUV. Sequoia still had her eyes on the woman as Sequoia got in her Rover. The woman got inside and started up her truck. She pulled up to the stop sign, turned toward the Brown's house, parked one house down and there she sat.

Sequoia watched her for a minute and called Torino back.

"Your ex is up to her old tricks again. She's sitting outside of my client's house, just watching."

"Watching what? Don't tell me."

She said, "Torino, she's watching for Kyle. I'll tell you one thing. Having her back in our lives is gonna be a stone trip."

23

Mercedes

"... tipping his cap in her honor ..."

I t was a celebrity golf tournament on a bright Saturday at the spectacular eighteen-hole golf course situated atop coastal cliffs that towered above the blue cyan Pacific Ocean. The golf course oasis at Torrey Pines was nestled in the hills with breathtaking views and row upon row of palm trees. It was so impeccably kept and the grass on the fairways was so green, it looked like emerald outdoor carpeting.

It was a sight to see on a beautiful fall day with a whisper of a breeze that blew ever so slightly.

It was the very course in San Diego that Mason played on when Mercedes and Star watched him on TV, noticing a shapely woman with candy-apple red hair in a tight fitting skirt on the day that Mason's infidelity was verified.

Mercedes adjusted the gear of her brain from the past to the present and gave full focus to her young, talented son, Rashaad. He looked just like his dad. He was handsome, athletic, and bowlegged.

He started the day ahead by three strokes into the final round, but he had lost some ground and now, it was his last shot of the final hole.

Mercedes couldn't help but scan the faces in the crowd every now and then to see if perhaps Mason had decided to show up and support his son. It seemed Mason made more trips to visit Star than Rashaad. He said he didn't want his son living in his shadow, following in his footsteps. He wanted him to make his own way. So in an effort to not take away Rashaad's limelight, Mason would watch from the comfort of their family room at home. Today though, Rashaad had invited him personally. And Rashaad invited Mercedes, as well.

Rashaad, wearing blue and white with a white Nike fitted, stood next to his caddy, Winton, his dad's former caddy, and they spoke close to each other's faces, sizing up the next shot. The ball was a short distance, maybe six-feet from the cup. The putt should have been easy. But nothing was ever easy in the game of golf. One shot one minute could change up the next minute. That was the exhilarating part of the game because nothing ever stayed the same.

Winton handed Rashaad the shiny, golden PING putter and gave him a supportive nod, stepping back to move the golf bag away enough for Rashaad to have his space. Then Winton headed to the hole, standing by it just in case.

The crowd was quiet.

Mercedes looked on as if she was holding her breath and fighting to stay calm. Watching her son play always made her a nervous wreck.

Rashaad eyeballed the distance between the ball and the cup, envisioning his stroke and the angle of the ball while imagining the exact trail of the ball necessary to make this a birdie for the win. His fixed, brown eyes looked down toward the ball and then to the cup, down at the ball and again to the cup, over again until he sealed the precise journey in his head.

He then remembered something his dad taught him when he was only eleven. Mason had told Rashaad that the best way to make a putt, the no-nonsense way, was to never look at the hole, and also to close his eyes and listen to the sound of the ball dropping into the cup. He had taught Rashaad to do that as a form of practice, but never in a tournament. Rather he told him that in a tournament, he should keep his eyes down toward the green. But for some reason, today Rashaad was feeling both a little brave and a little nostalgic.

He looked up at the sky and placed a kiss onto his index and middle fingers, aiming his hand up into the air, took his stance positioning himself in line with the flag, gripped the shaft of the club, leaned his torso forward and bent his knees slightly. Then he distributed his weight, relaxed his body, closed his eyes and gave a good solid putt, hitting the ball, all the while keeping his eyes closed.

He listened.

The little white ball rolled with a curve and then cut back toward the exact location of the cup. Winton raised the pin with the blue flag slightly blowing in the subtle wind, and even without touching the circumference, the tiny ball sank right inside the middle of the cup and disappeared. It made a clunk, click, swooshing sound, an old familiar sound to Rashaad's ears. His eyes popped open, lighting up like lanterns even in the glaring sun.

Rashaad's pecan skin looked flushed as he jumped up and down with excitement and vigorously removed his golf cap amongst the roaring cheers of onlookers, tipping his hat to the sky, and then looking over at his mom. He tipped it to her, too, and put it back on. He walked over toward his mother. Standing right behind her without Mercedes even knowing was Mason, stunned, chin to his chest, face beaming.

Rashaad hugged Mercedes who was in disbelief. Her eyes were welled up with tears. He then reached back and put his hand on his father's shoulder.

"I can't believe you remembered that," Mason said, voice shaky.

"I remember everything you taught me. You're the reason. Without you, I wouldn't be in this game. Thank you, Dad."

Mason enthusiastically rubbed the top of Rashaad's head. "Congratulations, Son."

Mercedes turned around toward Mason and they embraced. Then she looked forward and saw Rashaad getting drenched with champagne as he walked like he was a rock star, with a swarm of reporters and fans all around him. He headed toward the tent to receive his trophy and his check for seven-hundred-fifty-thousand dollars, half of which would go to charity. His charity of choice was The Alzheimer's Association. By the time Mercedes turned back around again, Mason was gone.

A brunette, exhilarated female ESPN reporter stuck a microphone in Mercedes's face and asked in an instant, "Mrs. Wilson, you must be thrilled to death that your son was able to pull off this win today, right?"

"I am. I'm in shock." She turned back again to check for Mason once more, and then back toward the reporter. "Um, it was pretty close for a minute. The other celebrity golfers gave him a run for his money, but I'm glad he was able to keep his concentration and pull it off."

"Yes, he did. I wanted to ask you, we've never seen him look up to the sky like that, almost praying. It also looked like he actually closed his eyes while he hit that putt. I've never seen anything like it."

She said, still in awe of the reality of the moment, "You know, Rashaad was just doing his thing. I saw him look up at the sky, and I'm sure it was a tribute to his grandmother who passed away recently. And the closing of his eyes was what his dad, Mason Wilson, taught him

173

to do when Rashaad was little. I just, I mean, I'm so emotional right now, and so thankful. Looking forward to celebrating with my son. Thank you."

"Thank you, Mrs. Wilson. Your husband and son are real pros."

Mercedes tried her best to make it over to Rashaad near the tent when a tournament organizer came over to guide her for the rest of the way. Mercedes stayed one step behind the man, trying to tame her rush of emotions.

She quickly put on her white sunglasses and gave permission for her tears to fall. Not so much from the thrill of the moment with Rashaad winning the tournament in such a beautiful and unique way, but also for the fact that she couldn't even stand next to her husband as a couple and share in the moment as proud parents. She couldn't help but remember that her life, even in the midst of the moment, was falling apart.

It was dinnertime. The lavish A.R. Valentien restaurant on North Torrey Pines Road was known for its fine dining.

Mercedes and Rashaad wore dressy attire in the elegant, private V.I.P. room. They sat at a round table with crystal chandeliers overhead, draped off by ivory chiffon curtains for privacy so they would not be interrupted by Rashaad's adoring fans.

It was a special occasion.

Mercedes said to Rashaad, "I still can't believe what happened out there today." She was done with her meal, having devoured her swordfish and scallops.

Rashaad took his final bite of lobster after dipping it in garlic butter, but still spoke. "It was special. I'm glad you were able to be there. And Dad."

"Where is he?" she asked.

"I invited him." He sipped his iced tea. "And Mom, I told him I wanted you two to talk. That I would go back to my room so you two could have dinner alone together."

She gave him a look like he should not have. "No, this is your night. This is about you, not us."

"That would be what I'd want. You two can't go this many years and then just let things fall apart."

"Rashaad, it's about you right now. I told you, we'll work it out."

"Good. Then you two need to do that tonight. For me. Right here. Now."

Mercedes took a sip of water. "Let's just enjoy our dinner together. You and me, and then when your dad comes, we'll see what happens."

"Sounds good," he said. "But in this family, it takes all of us. Even Star."

"I love you, Rashaad. I can't remember being more proud."

"Thanks. I love you, too, Mom. Thanks for being here."

No more than a half hour later, they left.

No Mason.

Rashaad called his father but he was already on his way home.

He said he had a meeting early in the morning so he went ahead and drove back to L.A.

Rashaad was disappointed.

Mercedes was not surprised one bit.

175

24

Venus

"There's nothing everyday about us."

The late morning air smelled like summer rain, even in the fall. The clouds that filled the sky had not yet shed their precipitation, but it looked like things could change at any moment.

Venus had just walked in the house from the Ralphs grocery store around the corner. It was barely noon. Skyy was still at school and Venus had much to do before picking her up from after-school care.

Cameron had spent the night out again. He did have a long, intense father-son conversation with Claude and promised to be more aggressive in looking for a job. He even applied for admission to U.C. Irvine. Once again he had gone to Penny Heinz's house and wasn't home yet.

Today, Venus planned to head back out to the Home Depot to look for some toffee-colored paint for her and Claude's bedroom, and she had planned to strip down and stain a bookshelf in Skyy's room so that it matched the color of Skyy's new pink walls.

Wearing jeans and a violet cropped sweater, she went back and forth from the bags of groceries she had set on the counter, to the walk-in pantry, and had just put away the pancake mix and box of cereal when her phone rang a few times. She missed it. It was in her purse along the island. It rang again and she grabbed it.

"Hi, Claude."

He jumped right in. "Venus, there's a letter for you."

"What? Where are you? Are you mobile?" She walked back to the counter to gather the empty grocery bags.

"I went by the office and then by the house to pay the guys who worked on the floors. And I checked the mailbox."

"Okay. I'll see it when you get home later."

"It's from the California Men's Colony."

She paused, then gave a breath and asked, "Oh? Why? I mean why does Owen Chambers think he can keep writing me all of a sudden?"

"I guess we'll find out. Find out when we read it together."

She laugh subtly. "I can read it. It's just nonsense anyway."

"We can read it. You got a problem with that?" His tone began to change.

"No. But Claude, I mean we're talking about a letter from a maniac murderer here."

"A maniac murderer writing my wife as if the two have a history together."

She stuffed the bags into the under cabinet. "We don't."

"We'll see."

She said, "No, there's no we'll see. I'm telling you."

"Venus, I'm being cool about this. Don't start acting like this is everyday life for anyone. Not many men have to deal with their wives getting letters from a man serving twenty-five to life in prison."

Venus simply stood in place. "Not very many men dated a woman who cheated on him with a man who'd end up killing her. Not very many men then married the woman's best friend. There's nothing everyday about us."

He said nothing.

177

"Just come home later. We need to get him to stop once and for all." She walked to the sink and turned on the water.

"I plan to."

"See you when you get home."

"Yep," he said with an edge.

Venus just ran the warm water along her hands, turning up the hot water, and stared out of the kitchen window.

A few hours later when Venus returned from more shopping, she pulled up and saw Cameron's car parked in the garage. He still drove his mom Fatima's old Lexus.

She went inside and immediately yelled, "Cam! Can you come down here, please?"

"Yeah!" he yelled back.

Venus put down her keys and purse and went into the formal dining room and took a seat, leaning back against the high back chair. She crossed her legs.

Cameron walked in. "Yes."

"Hi. Sit down please, would you?"

"Sure." He pulled out a chair and sat across from her. "What's going on?" He had on a sky blue Hugo Boss dress shirt and black pants. His shirt was unbuttoned.

"Cam, I wanted to tell you that I set up an interview for you."

"With who?"

"I had a conversation with my old boss at Make-A-Wish."

"You did?"

"Yeah. She knows you studied finance. They need an assistant to the CFO. I'll email you the info but I want you to make sure you give her a call. Her name is Ann Howard."

"Okay."

She checked out his expression. "You look hesitant."

He squinted like he just couldn't see it happening. "It's in Westwood. I don't want to drive that far."

"You don't? You know, sometimes you've gotta sacrifice to get ahead."

"I want to work in Orange County or go to school out here."

"What have you done to make that happen?"

"Oh, no. Not you, too. I already had a job interview today over at an insurance company in Mission Viejo. Penny told me about it."

"That's good. I'm glad. And me asking you to call Ann about the Make-A-Wish job is simply a referral. I want you to follow-up."

"I'll call, but I just don't want to drive sixty-five miles each way. I mean, didn't you quit when we moved out here?"

"I quit because your dad and I agreed that it's better for me to be home with Skyy. That's the only reason."

"Whatever." He put his hands on the table and began playing with his fingernails.

"Okay then, don't call." She watched him begin to shut down. "Cam, what is up with you?"

He looked bored. "I don't know."

"Or the question is, why are you doing this to yourself?"

"I'm fine. I checked out the college website when I talked to Dad. I'm trying. You guys need to give me a minute."

"I just have to ask; don't you want to make your own money as soon as you can?"

"I do. And I will." He came to a stance. "I'll be back on Monday."

"You're going over Penny's again, right?"

"We're going to Santa Barbara for the weekend." He pushed in the chair.

She looked up at him. "On her?"

"Yes."

"Does your Dad know you're going?"

"I'm grown."

"Yes, you are. But based on what you're doing over there with her, you're gonna get kicked out of here."

"Actually, if I do, it's cool." He rubbed the back of his neck and looked over at the wall.

"Cam, you're a man. Where would you go if he kicked you out? I know you wouldn't move in with Penny. Men don't move in with women." Her voice was firm.

"I didn't say I would." He paused like he should not say more, then looked right at Venus. "You know, maybe you guys would be happier if I got a big old house in Brentwood like Rashaad, or if I bought a brand new BMW like Rashaad. I mean, Rashaad is all into the money and everyone's proud of him. And he's too busy to even call me back nowadays. We're not kids anymore. I'm not into the things he's into. I'm not a golfer. I'm tired of being compared to Rashaad, Uncle Mason, Uncle Torino, and Dad. Yeah, Dad and Uncle Mason went to U.S.C. Yeah, Uncle Torino went to Berkley. I didn't even wanna go to college. I went because you two made me."

Venus looked stunned.

He continued, "I'm a Wilson, but I'm really not. Maybe because I don't have a drop of Wilson blood in me. Maybe because I don't know who I am or where I'm from or what the hell happened to my mom. Don't think I don't know the guy who killed her is the same guy she dated when I was young, only back then she called him Bobby. I know his name is Owen Chambers. Don't think I don't remember how much I hated you when you hooked-up with my dad after he adopted me. Don't think

I'm like any of you. Because I'm not." He looked like he could still go one, like more was inside. He dared her to not understand by him not blinking, not even once.

She uncrossed her legs and leaned forward, looking up at him. "Cam. I'm sorry about all of that. But, what is it that you want to know? What is it you need? We've tried to show you that you're family, because you are."

"Who's my real dad? Is it Bobby or Owen, or whatever his name is, or is it the devil? I was there when this guy showed up and shot my mother in the head. The same guy she was seeing while she was with my dad. Oh, but was he my dad? Or was that guy my dad?" His words sounded like he was playing, but his face was not.

Venus forced herself to keep her words to a minimum. "You need to ask your dad all of that."

"Is he or isn't he? You know the truth. Just tell me."

"Ask your dad. He'll be here in a few minutes."

Cameron turned around and headed for the staircase. "When he gets here, tell him I'm not available until Monday. Knowing him, he'll have my things put in storage or out on the porch. But I don't care."

Venus stood and spoke loudly. "Yes you do care, and so do we. This started out as a conversation about a job for you and it's turned into this?"

"Give me ten minutes. I'll be gone." He sprinted up to his room.

She yelled, "Cam, no! Don't leave! *Por favor!*"

He slammed the door.

For Venus, what started out as her wanting to do something good for her stepson, backfired horribly.

By five o'clock, just before Venus was about to leave to go pick up Skyy, Claude came home. He didn't bother greeting her with a kiss, or going upstairs to change clothes, or ask what was for dinner, even though the smell of red wine pot roast and potatoes had taken over the house.

They were in the wide hallway that led from the garage to the kitchen.

He just stood before Venus.

She stood before him holding her keys in one hand, the other hand clutching the leather strap of her purse that hung from her shoulder.

She had just told him that Cameron was gone.

"He what?" Claude asked.

"He left. Actually, they're both gone."

"What happened?"

"I talked to him about the fact that I was able to get Ann from the foundation to interview him. They have an opening."

"How'd that turn into this?"

"We sat down and, it just happened."

"You had like a family meeting with him on your own. Even after I talked to him the other night?"

"I did."

"I thought he had an interview this morning."

"He did. He went."

Claude took a step away and then a step back. "Call him and her. One of 'em."

"I told you, they're gone."

"Where'd they go?"

"He said to Santa Barbara."

"Staying where?"

She said, "I don't know."

He spoke with his hands although holding a few pieces of mail. "That's it?"

"Well, when we talked he had a lot to say. And he asked me if Owen was his dad."

"What'd you say?"

"I told him to ask you."

"Dammit. Here. Open it. Now." Each word was louder than the previous.

Venus took the letter he handed her. It was a white envelope, once again with familiar scribbled, small letters, with the sentences all running together without much punctuation "Okay," she said, opening it.

"Read it." He was so close to her she could feel the heat of his breath.

She saw the first word and said it as though she didn't want to get any further than that. "Venus . . ."

He snatched it and stood just as close to her, talking like she was a mile away. "I'll read it."

Venus Baby How are you You didn't write me back That's okay I just know you're having fun doing what you do So I'm sure I'll hear about this one but here goes Does your husband know you're the one who told me that you and him and Fatima were meeting at the Terranea Resort in Palos Verdes as a ménage birthday present to him And does he know I sat outside of that hotel all night and followed him and Fatima the next morning back to their house and then to Mason's for the lovely family Thanksgiving dinner Hell I'm in here for the rest of my life I don't care but if you ask me I never would've gone over the edge if you hadn't talked Fatima out of going to Vegas with me to get married And if you hadn't told me about the little birthday threesome And if you hadn't told me you wanted Claude all to yourself maybe I wouldn't have allowed you to do just that by me getting rid of her so the way I look at it you're an accessory to murder Don't you agree Who loves you baby OC

Time stopped.

Venus's heart cried.

Her face was blood red.

183

Claude screamed at her as he headed for the door to the garage. "I'm going to get Skyy and by the time I come back I want your sorry ass gone!"

25

Sequoia

"What in the world is going on?"

More than two weeks after the custody court date, the first child support check had already been sent to Colette Berry.

Now it was time for Kyle Jamal Brewer, Jr. a.k.a. Kyle Jamal Wilson, to come home to a house he never knew existed.

Torino walked in through the arched front doors on a Friday at six-o'clock with his new seven year-old son right behind him.

Sequoia had heard them pull up in the driveway. She had been getting ready all day, from what she wore, to what TJ wore, to how the house looked, to what she cooked . . . she was ready. And dinner was ready.

She stood tall as though wanting to make a good first impression. "Hi there." She wore a white blouse with a lace collar and a pair of black pants.

Kyle Jr. replied, looking all around at the large house. "Hi."

Torino closed the door. He was carrying a large shoulder bag. "This is Sequoia. My wife."

"Sequoia?" Kyle Jr. asked.

"Yes. Nice to meet you."

He looked to be in thought.

Torino said, "And this is TJ. Like I told you, and your mom told you, TJ is your little brother."

TJ spoke right up. He wore brown shorts and a bacon and egg happy-face t-shirt. "Hi."

"Hi. What is TJ? Is that your name?"

"It's Torino junior," explained TJ.

They stood next to each other looking like duplicates, TJ tall for his age and Kyle Jr. short for his age. They were the same height. Same everything.

Sequoia and Torino just watched.

"I'm a junior, too. That's why they call me Kyle Jr. My daddy's name is Kyle, too."

TJ's face flashed happy. "Oh, so you're KJ and I'm TJ."

"I'm Kyle Jr."

Sequoia said, "Yes, he is. Kyle Jr. it is then."

"I'm your brother," said TJ.

"But where've you been?"

"I've been here. With my mom and my dad. We live here," TJ told him.

Kyle Jr. said, "My mom is at home. My dad is gone. He was there, but he's gone now."

TJ spoke to his father with a question mark on his face. "But Daddy, you said you're his dad *and* my dad."

"I am," said Torino. "But Kyle Jr. has two dads."

Kyle Jr. looked up at him. "Do I have to call you Dad?"

Torino set the overnight bag down on the living room carpet. "Not if you don't want to."

"Can I call you Torino?" Kyle Jr. asked.

"If you want, that's fine."

"Okay."

TJ said loudly and excitedly, "Here, let me show you your room. It's right next to mine."

They ran off up the stairs and down the hall, Kyle Jr. dragging his army backpack.

Torino walked up to Sequoia and kissed her face. "It smells about as good in here as you look. You made dinner already?"

She embraced him and they walked to the kitchen together. She replied, "Yeah. It's just a pan of enchiladas. We can eat them whenever."

"That'll work."

"I didn't want us to go out to dinner just yet. Thought maybe he could get as much home time as possible this weekend. Just so TJ can bond with his brother more than anything."

Torino walked over to the refrigerator and opened it. "Gonna need to call him Kyle, Jr. I see."

"Looks like it. He is not giving that junior up. No rush."

"I agree," Torino said, grabbing a bottle of green tea and opening it.

The boys reappeared just that fast.

TJ was pumped. "Mom, can we have some Capri Sun and popcorn?"

"You like popcorn, Kyle Jr.?" Sequoia asked.

"Yep. My mom makes it all the time."

Torino reached back in the refrigerator and took out two packages of juice, handing it to each of them.

"Then popcorn it is," Sequoia said. She reached into the pantry and took out the box.

Kyle Jr. looked at Sequoia. "Sequoia, huh? I know you. I think you're like my dad's ex-girlfriend or something."

Sequoia shook her head and gave a laugh. "No, I'm not. What makes you say that?"

"Just heard my mom talk about you like maybe I thought you knew my dad like that." He seemed like he was trying to watch his words. "Just because of some of the things she said."

"Like not good, huh?" asked Sequoia.

"No."

Torino stepped in. "No, Kyle Jr., your dad and Sequoia didn't date." He closed the refrigerator door and walked up behind the boys. "I'll tell you what. One day we'll sit down and explain everything to you. I know it's different, but just focus on enjoying yourself while you're here, and getting to know your little brother."

"Little. How old are you?"

"Five."

"You're big. I'm seven."

It looked like all TJ could do was think of the next thing to do. "Mom, can we play Xbox?"

"Sure."

Kyle Jr. said to TJ, "You have Xbox?"

"Yep. And a Wii."

"Wow. This is gonna be cool." He looked back past the family room and then through the kitchen window to the backyard. "This place is huge."

"You like your room?" asked Torino, as he held his tea.

"I do. At my house I sleep with my mom now. My room is full of junk."

Sequoia put the bag in the microwave and pressed the button. "TJ sleeps with us sometimes. One day, we'll all do a slumber party in our room."

"Okay," he replied.

TJ suggested, "Let's go back to my room."

In an instant they ran off.

Sequoia yelled their way, "I'll bring the popcorn to your room in a second, TJ."

"Okay. Love you."

"Love you, too," she replied loudly to TJ while smiling at Torino.

He said, "Those boys are excited."

"They are."

He just stared at her. "Look at you, taking care of my sons."

"Ah, yeah." She waited for the kernels to stop popping. "And let's not forget to swab the inside of his little, excited mouth. You know I already got the kit."

"I saw it. I've got you."

After a while the bag was done. Sequoia took it out and opened it, emptying it into a red plastic bowl. She headed upstairs.

Torino just watched and sipped his tea, and then said, "Umph, umph, umph. We might need to have our own celebration later on. Damn, I'm glad I took the night off."

"It's about time," she said loud enough for him to hear.

There was the turn of a doorknob and then a tiny knock at Sequoia and Torino's locked bedroom door about two hours after the boys had finally been put to bed.

Sequoia and Torino were deep into a full-on tongue kiss, him lying on top of her, both wearing their nightclothes about ready to consummate the happenings of the day.

They stopped. The knock sounded again.

"Yes," Torino said, hoping off and heading to the door wearing only gingham pajama bottoms.

"The door won't open." It was Kyle Jr. sounding low-key.

"Okay, hold on." Torino opened the double doors and looked down. "What's up?"

Kyle Jr.'s face was miserable. "I want to go home."

"Why?"

"I miss my mommy."

Sequoia stood up in her big tee shirt.

"You do?" Torino took his hand and said, "Come on, let's go back to bed. We can call her in the morning. It's too late to go anywhere tonight. Let's see how you feel in the morning."

"Do you want to sleep with us?" Sequoia asked, heading toward them.

Kyle Jr. didn't budge. "No. I want my mommy."

Torino dropped his hand and walked back toward the nightstand.

Kyle Jr. walked behind him.

"Hold up." Torino took hold of his cell. "I'll call her."

Sequoia stood right next to Kyle Jr. "It's okay, honey. You're safe here."

Torino simply waited while the phone rang and rang. "Let me call again."

Kyle Jr.'s tears began to flow. "I want to go home."

Sequoia said, "Don't cry. I know it's hard getting used to a new house and a new family. We understand."

"Still no answer."

"Can I go home?" he asked Torino.

Sequoia said, "Honey, it's late."

Torino set the phone down. "How about if I come into your room with you? We'll get a book and I'll read it to you, and I'll stay in your room with you tonight. Is that okay?"

Sequoia stepped back and Torino stepped up as Kyle Jr. replied, "Yes." His voice sounded weak.

Torino asked, "Do you want TJ to come in your room, too."

He shook his head.

Torino began to walk out with a frowning Kyle Jr. at his side. "Okay, come on, buddy. Just you and me." He looked back at Sequoia. "See you in the morning, Mrs. Wilson."

"Yes, Mr. Wilson."

She watched them walk down the hall together. Kyle Jr. only held Torino's hand for a second, and then he pulled away. He began to weep.

By five in the morning, Torino's cell rang, startling Sequoia. She jumped up and looked around the dark room, glancing at the alarm clock. She reached over to his side of the bed. The screen on his phone read, *Kyle*.

She answered sounding drowsy. "Hello?"

He was talking fast. "Sequoia, where's Torino?"

"He's in Kyle Jr.'s bedroom. Kyle Jr. was a little homesick and so Torino stayed in there with him."

"I need to talk to him."

"What's going on?" she asked.

"Please, just get him."

Sequoia got up and said, "Hold on."

She put the phone back down and headed fast down the hallway, straight into Kyle Jr.'s room. He was asleep, sprawled out on his back in the middle of his twin bed with his mouth wide open, snoring. Torino was on the floor with a standard sized pillow under his head and a sheet covering his torso, also snoring.

She bent down and shook him. "Torino. Wake up. Telephone," she whispered.

"What?" He opened his eyes and pulled the sheet off of himself.

"It's Kyle. He said it's important."

"What it is?"

"He wouldn't tell me."

"Oh Lord. What time is it?"

"Just after five. Hurry."

"Dang. Where's the phone?"

"In the bedroom."

191

Torino looked half irritated and stood up. He headed to their room and picked up the phone. Sequoia stood near him. "Hey Kyle. What in the hell is going on?. . . She what? . . . Did you believe her? . . . She'd been following you? . . . Yeah. Did you tell her it wasn't you? . . . And then she what? . . . Taking her clothes off? . . . Oh my God. So they called you? . . . Where are you? . . . In Torrance? . . . I thought you were headed to Hawaii for your brother's wedding tomorrow . . . Is she okay? . . . We tried to call her so Kyle Jr. could talk to her but there was no answer. I didn't think anything of it . . . Well, sure. We've got him . . . Yeah, call me back and keep me posted. Actually, I can come over there . . . Are you sure? . . . Okay, we'll keep an eye on him. Sorry, man. Bye."

Sequoia looked stumped. "What in the world is going on?"

"It's Colette. She was calling Kyle, threatening to kill herself because she thought he was getting married this weekend, and then she called him from a railroad track, threatening to drive in front of some train. She got out of her car and ran around, taking all her damn clothes off. Basically, he said she had a nervous breakdown."

"Oh, hell."

Torino took his phone and plugged it into the charger. "She's in some hospital in Torrance on a seventy-two hour hold. Some mental hospital."

"Why am I not surprised? And he's gonna miss the wedding?"

"He actually said he doesn't care about that. Said he's not going anywhere until Colette can go home."

Sequoia titled her head in confusion. "Oh my God. He cannot be serious. You think that man is still in love with her? After all this?"

"I do."

"Damn. He's sprung if you ask me."

"More than he's admitting."

"You just never know."

"Nope." Torino said, "And he's missing his own brother's wedding. I know I wouldn't do it." He began walking back down the hall to Kyle Jr.'s room.

Sequoia walked with him. "I know that's right."

"Plus, the thing is, I just realized he's violating his own restraining order by being around her."

"I forgot about that."

They stood before Kyle Jr.'s door.

Sequoia's arms were folded. "Well, anyway, looks like we might be taking Kyle Jr. to and from school for a minute."

Torino said, "At least for seventy-two hours, I guess."

She gave a soft grin. "You think Colette should get him back even after all this?"

"I don't."

She said, "I think she might lose her fifty-percent custody now. She can't take care of that little boy, let alone herself."

"Well, she got Kyle's attention." Torino spoke lower. "This reminds me of the crap she pulled in Mason's backyard that day she tried to stab herself in the stomach."

She whispered. "You know what they say. Crazy leaves clues. And if that's the case, Kyle is fucking clueless and crazy right along with her. I'm going back to bed. You coming?"

Torino looked back at Kyle Jr. who was still knocked out. "No. I made a promise that I'd be in there when he woke up."

She looked at Kyle Jr., too, still speaking softly. "Poor boy. To have a mom like that."

Torino put his hand on her back. "Good night." He gave her a peck on the lips. "Sorry about all this."

She grinned, eyeing down the definition of his chest. "What's yours is mine."

"That's what I like to hear." He checked her out as she turned. He watched her walk away in her oversized tee shirt with nothing underneath as usual, not even a string. He said, "Wait a minute."

She turned back.

"I say we stay up for another half hour." His look was playful.

She blushed, saying, "Couldn't hurt," and she led the way.

Sequoia got into bed, the scent of her angel-food body oil permeated the sheets.

Torino noticed. "You deserve this."

He stayed at the foot of the bed and took his masterful giver position under the covers and pleased his wife with an oral thank you until her body said, *You're welcome.*

Both were back to sleep, as promised, thirty minutes later.

26

Mercedes

". . . is Cameron really tripping like that?"

The next day Mercedes was at home in her kitchen munching on honey barbeque chips even though she had just come back from working out. She had not noticed any weight falling off because the more she worked out to keep busy, the more she ate her favorite food simply for comfort, to take up the slack of her empty life.

She had a fashion show that Thursday night and though she had been leaving a lot of the bookings and shows to her staff, this was one show she planned to organize because it was for the wife of a top NBA player who was debuting her new clothing line.

Dressed in sweatpants and a crossover sports top, she grabbed more chips and basked in the salty-sweet sensation upon her tongue, preparing to chase it down with strawberry soda when her phone rang from the kitchen table.

She approached it and pressed the screen, smiling as she said, "Hello there."

"Hi, Mom."

"Star, it's good hearing from you. How are things going in Atlanta?"

"Fine. I wanted you to know I have a concert this week, on Thursday night, and Rashaad is coming. He said you might wanna come. I mean both you and Dad."

She darted her eyes upward and said to herself. *Of all the dates.* "Well, he's right. I would like to come."

"Okay."

"Not sure about your dad, though. You'll have to ask him."

Star was very matter-of-fact. "I know. I will. So, do you have a pen?"

"Yeah, I do. Hold on." Mercedes grabbed a notepad and pen from the iron kitchen rack. "Okay."

"It's at the Atlanta Symphony Orchestra, 1280 Peachtree Street Northeast, and the zip is 30309. Right now, flights from Los Angeles to Atlanta are right at three-hundred dollars, so book it soon. But knowing you, you'll want first-class."

"No. That's fine."

Star said, "I guess that's it. Oh, it's at seven in the evening."

"Good. I'm proud of you. I miss talking to you. There's a lot going on, and you know . . ."

"Mom, that's Dad on the other line. I'll see you on Thursday, okay?"

Mercedes paused. "Okay."

"Bye."

Before Mercedes could say goodbye back, Star clicked over.

Mercedes put the phone down and walked out of the kitchen. She went into her office with the slip of paper and logged on to her laptop looking for a flight and hotel. She talked to herself, saying, "I've got to go to this concert. Can't believe both are on the same day. If I don't go, Star would never understand."

When she opened Internet Explorer, a screen popped up and the phone rang from the computer. She looked closer and saw that it was Skype, and the caller was Rashaad Wilson.

She said out loud, "Oh my God. Rashaad. Oh, no, how do I do this?" And then she clicked a box and his video image appeared. He was seated on a sofa, looking like he admired his mom for even trying. She said, "Rashaad?"

"Hi, Mom. You did it." He sounded happy.

Her face lit up and her eyes widened. "I did. How in the world?"

"Mom, I loaded it on your computer when I was home that day we talked about it."

"You are so sneaky. Wow. And I didn't even notice it until now. This is crazy."

"You have to click where it says that you can allow me to see you."

Mercedes asked, "I do? Lord have mercy. Wait. Okay." She clicked an icon and saw a small box with her video pop up. "There. You see me?" she asked.

"Uh, yep. I do. There you are. You look good."

She fluffed up her bangs. "Rashaad. I know I look a mess. I just came back from the gym. I had no idea I'd be talking on a video. But you look great. Where are you?"

"I'm home."

"Oh my. This is such a nice surprise." She kept staring at the screen, smiling big.

Rashaad said, "Mom, what I was gonna tell you was, you can stay with me in Atlanta. I'll be at the Twelve in Atlantic Station. Don't worry about booking a hotel."

"Oh, okay. I was just about to search for a hotel and flight. That'll be fun. Thanks."

"No problem."

She asked, "So, Star said you told her to invite me?"

"No, I suggested she invite both of you. I made sure I could make this when she told me a few weeks back."

"Okay. When's your next tournament?"

"It's in China on Thanksgiving Day. You can always go on my website, Mom. My tournament dates are there."

"I know. Okay. I'm not sure if your Uncle Claude's birthday falls on Thanksgiving this year. But we'll be watching."

"Speaking of Uncle Claude, is Cameron really tripping like that? Dad told me he's dating some older woman and isn't even trying to get back in school."

"That's what I hear. He'll get it together. He's been through a lot. Maybe you should reach out to him," she told him.

"I did. I called him and he sent me a text saying he'd call, but he didn't."

"Try again maybe."

"I will. I haven't seen him since Grandma's funeral."

Mercedes asked, "Yeah, I'm sure that added to what's going on with him. I know it's hard still. So, how's everything with you? The girls treating you okay?" She kept running her fingers through her bangs.

"I'm sticking with Sasha. I'll bring her by soon. Her middle name is, believe it or not, Mercedes."

"No way. Oh my. The family wouldn't need two women with that name, first or middle."

"She's cool, but it's not like I'm gonna marry her or anything."

"I see. Are you bringing her with you to Atlanta for Star's concert?"

"Oh, no. That's just for the family." Rashaad sounded certain.

"I get it. You talk to your dad lately?"

"Not since he left La Jolla after the Torrey Pines tournament. I saw him on Facebook. That's about it."

Mercedes's voice lit up even more. "Facebook. Your dad has a Facebook account?"

"Yep. You didn't know that?"

"No. How long has he had it?"

"Oh, no, you're gonna have to ask him. I'm surprised you don't have one."

She assured him by saying, "I don't want one. I've got enough to do. That to me is a waste of precious time. You know me."

"I do. But I know a lot of people who said they'd never do it, and then they got hooked. It's a new day. Dad needs to add it to his website so people can go there and find his link to his Facebook page."

She couldn't help but wonder. "So, your dad has a Facebook page, huh?"

He scooted back and shook his head. "Oh Lord, listen. I've said enough. I've gotta go. You're making me nervous."

"And what's there to be nervous about?"

"Okay, so, I'll see you in a couple of days."

"Deal. You and Sasha Mercedes be good."

"And on that note, bye."

"How do I hang up?"

"Just click *hang up*."

"Haha. Bye, Son."

"Bye."

That Thursday evening in midtown Atlanta at the Atlanta Symphony Orchestra, Mercedes sat in section three, the second row, right in-between Mason and Rashaad. Everyone in the concert hall was dressed in their best after-five attire.

Mercedes was in heaven. She kept her eyes on her daughter. Star was one of four pianists who made up the chamber orchestra of fifty musicians. They were led by a female conductor who used masterful arms movements, keeping everyone together in cadence.

They played a series of songs, including one by Beethoven and one by Tchaikovsky, both which were led by a male violinist who was about Star's age.

Mason had been pretty much silent, focusing on the sights and sounds from the stage. He leaned in a bit closer to Mercedes and whispered, "That's the Terrence that Star mentioned before. Terrence Willis. Star's boyfriend."

Mercedes asked softly, "Really?" She tried not to look as surprised as she really was. She kept an eye on Terrence, sizing him up. He was white, tall, and slender. She then focused again upon her daughter who was taking care of business on a Steinway piano, working the keys as she played. Mercedes leaned in toward Mason. "They're both good. I'm so proud."

He nodded without looking over and continued to watch the orchestra.

Mercedes glanced over at Rashaad who kept his eyes only on his sister, smiling bigger than usual.

When the final song wound down, Mason stood first and then the rest of the crowd as the musical conductor took a bow and the musicians stood and bowed, too. The standing ovation was energetic and boisterous.

After a while, Star had gone backstage and then came back out with her guy at her side.

She said, "Terrence, this is my dad. You talked to him already."

"Hello, Sir. I'm honored to meet you."

Mason told him, "It's my pleasure. Great job. You know how to work that violin."

"Thanks. I try."

"Oh my God, your hands are shaking," Star told Terrence.

"They're not." He tried to play it off.

"Dad, you're his idol."

"Oh, no. I'm just Dad."

Terrence grinned.

Star said, "And this is my brother, Rashaad."

Rashaad said, "Hey dude. Good job."

Terrence smiled. "Hey, you've been working it out there on the golf course. Congratulations."

Rashaad looked humble. "Thanks."

Star looked at Mercedes. "And this is my mom."

"Hello, Mrs. Wilson. Pleased to meet you."

"Thank you. Pleased as well. You two are both very talented. I'm so impressed. It was very enjoyable."

He said, "We're glad you liked it."

Mercedes said directly to Star, "Great job. You looked right at home."

Star said to everyone, "So, I know it's late, but dinner is at the Woodruff Arts Center, not far away."

"Okay," Mason said.

Rashaad look at his father. "You are coming, Dad, right?"

"Yes."

Rashaad asked, "Can Mom and I ride with you?"

"Sure. Star, we'll follow the two of you."

"Cool," Star said, walking toward the exit door while Terrence stayed close to Mason asking questions about golf.

Mercedes tied the belt to her sheer wrap coat, holding up the rear.

Dinner at the banquet room in the arts center was buffet style with every combination of seafood, chicken, beef, and pork imaginable.

"Are you okay, Mom?" asked Rashaad, noticing she was a little reserved.

She sat right next to Mason. "Just a little jet lag. I'm fine."

"Good. Glad you are," Mason said. He was the only one who had gone back for seconds and had a few bites left.

Looking surprised, even by his few words to her, she asked, "How was your flight?"

"Good," was all she got from him while he picked up his phone and scrolled through.

Terrence told Rashaad, "I saw you win that celebrity tournament in La Jolla. That was crazy."

"Yeah, it was fun." Rashaad nodded to a nearby table full of people who waved to him.

Mercedes looked over and saw them. To her, it was par for the course when she was with her guys. She asked Terrence, "So, how'd the two of you meet?"

Terrence sat close to Star. "We met in music school in D.C. Been knowing each other for about four years."

"Really?" asked Mercedes.

As Star reached for the sugar, her colorful bracelets jingled. "Yeah, it took him about three-and-a-half years to ask me out." She added the packets to her tea and stirred.

"Hey. A guy's gotta build up the nerve to ask out the most beautiful girl in school."

Rashaad pointed to Terrence and gave him a watchful eye. "Smooth." He looked at Star. "Watch out, Sis."

Star grinned.

"If I may ask, how'd you two meet?" Terrence asked Mercedes.

She looked proud. "We met at Southern Cal. So we're college sweethearts, too."

"Yep. A long time ago." Mason cut into what was left of his steak and took a bite.

Rashaad said to Star, "So, you gonna beat me to the altar, huh?"

"Not even. You're about ten minutes away from what I saw."

Mercedes asked, "Saw what?"

Star spoke while looking at Mason. "When he had that tournament out here at Johns Creek, he and Sasha were attached at the hip. Wait till you see her with him. They look alike, act alike, laugh alike. It's crazy."

But it was Mercedes who said, "We've got to meet her."

Rashaad grabbed a hold of his dinner roll. "You will. Next subject." He bit into it once, and then twice, and it was gone.

Star asked, "How long are you guys gonna be here?"

Both Mercedes and Mason said at the same time, "Till tomorrow."

"Well, glad you could come out," Star said.

Terrence said to them, "Me, too."

Mercedes raised her glass. "So, cheers to your professional music careers, and to your friendship, and to tonight. Here's to family," she proposed, then paused to look at Terrence, "and friends."

Everyone raised their glasses as well, and said, "Cheers."

Later, Mercedes was in Rashaad's two bedroom suite getting ready for bed when he came in. He asked, "Dad's not here?"

"No. Why would he be?"

"He's staying at the Twelve, too. He said he'd stop by."

"Does he know I'm staying with you?"

"Yep."

"Then why would he stop by?"

Rashaad spoke fast. "Because, I asked him to and he said he would."

"It's okay, Rashaad. I know what you're trying to do. Besides, I've gotta leave early in the morning."

"Mom, I'll be right back. I've gotta talk to him. In private."

"Rashaad." Mercedes looked at him like he need not bother.

"Be right back."

She raised her hands in surrender as he left.

By twelve midnight, Rashaad walked back in the room, turned on the light and walked into the bedroom where Mercedes was.

"Mom."

"Yes." She was lying down, but very much awake.

"I talked to Dad."

She looked over at her son. "Good."

"He was in a rare mood. He actually wouldn't stop talking. Told me to settle down and get one woman to come home to and stop playing the field. Told me I've gotta have a safe place to lay my head when everything gets crazy."

Mercedes look pleased. She adjusted herself so she could sit up. "Good for him. I agree. Having a home and stability is critical. Your fame is tough enough. Being single and famous is harder than people think."

"He also said what you thought he would. That I should walk in my own shoes, not his. That I should get out of his shadow and make mine big enough for the next generation."

"Oh, he was on a roll, huh? I'm glad."

"And Mom?"

"Yeah."

"Dad was drinking. Cognac." He looked let down.

Her brows lifted. "He was not."

"He was. He needs to come home. If he doesn't, all of that mess will start up all over again."

"Oh my God." Her voice was sad.

"He'll be back in rehab. I think it's Grandma. And it's you. And his retirement. He's missing his career."

"I'm just shocked. I mean, he hasn't had a drink in twenty years, or so I thought."

She was quiet.

Rashaad just looked at her.

She said, "He vowed to never die the way his dad died from damage to his liver. It's like the sins of his father won't go away. You know your dad talked about your granddad's drinking, and his own drinking when he was interviewed on BET. And he mentioned it in his book. Mason promised me he'd be different in honor of his dad. And he promised himself." The color had drained from her face.

"Star's in the room with him. She's gonna stay the night. She heard everything he said to me. We both told him to come home."

"Really? Star, too?"

"Yeah."

"We'll see." Mercedes gave an exhale.

"Well, I'll let you go to sleep. I just had to tell you."

"I'm glad you did, Son. I'm glad you did."

Sleep didn't come for Mercedes. Insomnia did. Again. Through the night she thought and worried and wondered, tossed and turned and remembered. Remembered the morning she thought she smelled brandy on Mason's breath after he drank from a coffee mug. The same day he was about to go to the meeting about the city council vacancy.

Rashaad was asleep in the other bedroom when Mercedes got up. She went to her laptop in the still of the dark room, logged into her email, and created a new message to Mason.

Mercedes swallowed hard, and fought away her emotions, reminiscing on the good times and wishing things were still the way they were before the Las Vegas trip. She typed, *"The sweetest days I've found, I've found with you,"* reminiscent of the song Mason had Kenny Rodgers sing to her in person on their anniversary seven years ago.

She clicked send, logged off and headed back to the bed, missing the way there were, not so very long ago.

27

Venus

"... seduce him into your life with money ..."

That Monday, Venus had not left. She stood her ground and claimed her home and family.

When Claude came back that night with Skyy, she was at home being a mother and playing housewife. She slept in their bed, just as Claude did, though each half of the bed was like two separate sleepers. No one said a word and no one made spousal advances.

This particular night, it was almost eleven in the evening and Claude was not home yet, which was becoming more and more common for him, though it had never been before.

Without bringing things up again, his usual passive-aggressive behavior showed up as a stand in for what words did not say: he was angry, he was hurt, and he was about at his wits end.

But she wasn't.

Venus was up. She had already taken a relaxing aromatherapy bath. And she had gone through a few boxes in the kitchen that she had asked the movers to leave for her to unpack. One was full of fragile stemware and china that she inherited from her mother who passed many years ago.

Tonight, what had been on her mind was to tell Claude what she did not have the nerve to tell him over the phone.

She sat on the cranberry loveseat in the den.

Claude came in through the front door after parking in the driveway as opposed to the garage next to her car. It seemed to be his way of saying even their cars could not be too close together. As if that was too intimate.

She said loudly after hearing him close the door, "Hello."

"Hi." He walked from the living room into the den where she was.

"Did you eat?" She had made his favorite shrimp and chicken fettuccini.

"Yes." He wore light gray dress pants and a white dress shirt. His plum tie hung from his pants pocket.

"Cameron's gone again?" he asked.

She just laid it out. "Honey, Cam moved out this morning. I wanted to wait until you got home to tell you."

He actually just shook his head. "I'm not surprised. I guess he's got himself a sugar momma now."

"Maybe. He moved in with Penny."

"You have her number?"

"I do."

"Call her. Please."

Venus took her phone from the sofa cushion, dialed up Penny and extended her hand for him to take it.

He did not take it. "Put it on speaker."

Venus held it up toward him as he stood next to where she sat.

"Hello?" Penny's greeting was bright and cheery, even considering the lateness of the hour.

"Penny?"

"Yes. Hi, Mr. Wilson."

"Listen, I know my son is there. I know you let him move in with you."

"Yes, he's here."

"So, you're gonna take care of him I guess?"

"No. He can take care of himself."

"With what?"

"He'll have to tell you that."

"No, I'm asking you. You're the one who just said he can take care of himself. You must know how." His tone was semi-smartass as his anger escalated.

Her tone was sweetness and light. "Yes, I do. Mr. Wilson. I understand your anger."

"No, you don't. Do you have any children his age?"

"Older."

"A son?"

"Yes. Two."

"Well, I'm a man. I don't know about your son's father, but I need to raise my boy to be a man, making sure he has a chance at life, with an education and a future. He needs to experience being the head of the household so he can take on the responsibility of his family. Cameron is being taken care of by you in your household. He's a young man, actually a boy. You cannot rob him of his manhood and seduce him into your life with money, and no doubt sex, and expect me to be okay with it."

"Mr. Wilson. Your son is a man. He's making his own decisions. I haven't offered him anything."

"You offered him a roof."

"He asked to stay here."

"You're old enough to be his mother."

She explained, "I am. But I'm not his mother. I'm his girlfriend and I have no problem with that, neither does he, neither does my family. But you do, and I understand that. Cameron can't live his life for you based on your life-wishes and wants for him. He has his own. And I think he's more of a man in standing up for his wants than trying to fit into the mold that you've carved out for him. With all due respect."

Venus still held up the phone.

Claude still stood over her. He gave a slight nod. "Well, I see you can be very convincing. I'm sure that turns him on. Sounds like he's right where he needs to be. I hope he gets himself together. But I'll tell you one thing, and you can tell him I said so; he'll never get another dime from me or spend another night under my roof, ever. Since he wants to be a man he can be one. And you might want to take off the man-hat you're wearing, because you'll soon find that unless you hand it over to him, he'll just be another son. You two have a good evening."

"You too, Mr. Wilson." She was still easy breezy.

"Oh, and by the way, find another realtor. My son may need your money, but I don't." He stepped away and Venus hung up. He said with tightness to his words, "I'll be damn. That rich bitch has got her a boy toy, and now she's talking shit."

Venus scooted back. "Claude."

He turned to her. His eyes were focused. His face was firm. "Venus, let me tell you something while I'm at it. Bottom line with us, I think you might be the reason Fatima was killed. And with that thought in my head, I can't even look at you."

She said, looking defensive, "I told you, I'm not. I didn't tell Owen anything about where we were going the night before, and I didn't tell him we were going to Mason's house. Mercedes told you back then that Owen wanted Fatima to run off to Vegas with him and get married the night before. The night we all ended up together in that hotel room. She's the one who told him she was coming over to Mason's house for Thanksgiving and couldn't see him. Not me."

"See, I just might have to go and see him again, just to cuss his ass out after I ask him some questions."

"Owen is the devil. Straight up. And you're buying into his lies just like he wants you to."

He leaned against the wall and took his tie out of his pocket, tossing it along his neck. "His lies, huh? I was living my life thinking I had a woman I could trust who was into me and only me as I gave her the good life. But it turns out you and Fatima were whores. She was screwing this crazy Negro who turns out to be Cameron's father, and you and her were both freaking him, you were backstabbing her by wanting me all along, and you told him every move the three of us made the night before she died."

He continued, "That makes me wanna go crazy. All this mess was going on and I had no idea. I bond to you after Fatima dies, and we get closer through grieving over her, and next thing I know, while we were in Vegas I popped the question and that was that. But I will tell you this, if Owen is making this shit up he needs to write a book and give Eric Jerome Dickey a run for his money because this mess is too twisted to be lies. He doesn't seem that bright."

Venus's eyes were large. Her words were even larger. "Well, they are lies. They're lies and they're ridiculous. Years ago you apologized for blaming me for all the secrets Fatima hid from you. I left you back then because I felt like a replacement living in the shadow of Fatima. You said you felt alone and broken and begged me to come home. Well, here I am, seven years later, and we're going through the same damn thing again living with the ghost of Fatima. When I had a miscarriage back then you said we'd rebuild our family and you told me you could love me the way I needed to be loved."

"That is what I said," Claude retorted. "But those two letters from a prison inmate changed everything. I don't know you. How do I love someone I don't know?"

"What do you mean, you don't know me? I'm the mother of your child. I took on Cam like he's my son. Even though he hated my guts, I stayed and worked past off of that. I've shown you a whole lot more over all these years than two letters should be able to destroy. That is if you're really done with the whole Fatima thing. You told me I will always be your wife, and that even though she died, we live on and have to be happy. This is not what happy feels like, Claude."

He stepped away from the wall. "Yeah well, not only do we live on but Owen's ass lives on, too, and he keeps reminding me that I might be sleeping with the enemy."

"The only enemy is Owen. He needs to be reported at the prison for sending letters like that. I thought they screened mail. This is way past sick. Yes, you do need to go see him, and I'll go with you. I'll put everything I love on this, Claude, even on Skyy. I did not sleep with or tell Owen anything. The first threesome I ever had in my entire life was with you and Fatima on your birthday. Now you either believe that, or you don't."

"I don't." He said it almost mocking her.

"So you're serious, like you said the other day, you want me to leave?"

He reached in his other pants pocket. "I've arranged for you and Skyy to stay in a house in Newport Beach that I found for Penny. I ended up renting it for you today." He walked to her. "That way Skyy won't have to switch schools again. It's furnished. Here's the address. Here are the keys. I'll take care of everything." He placed a piece of paper and set of keys on the coffee table before her.

212

She didn't even look at them. "Taking care of everything but you and me, I guess."

He walked away and out of the room. "Goodnight, Venus."

She snatched the keys and sprung to her feet. "Where are you going?"

"To bed."

She put her hands up. "So that's it. You just hand me keys and kick me and your child out and you can actually sleep?"

He got to the stairs and began to go up. "Oh, you can best believe I'm sleeping in my bed. You can come up and go to sleep when you're ready, like we've been doing, but only for one night. I don't expect you to leave until tomorrow. My mom always called you Fatima, anyway. Maybe she knew something. Like maybe you can't turn a ho' into a housewife."

Her eyes offered a swift kick. "Fuck you, Claude."

He stopped and turned around, this time pointing with his finger. "I won't be letting that happen either. No matter what, I sleep in my bed in my house. But there'll be no more of that with you."

Her words bolted from her mouth. "This is my house, too. I am your wife. And anyway, where have you been these last few nights?"

He looked toward their daughter's room. "Keep it down. You'll wake up Skyy. We already have one screwed up child. We don't need two." He continued up the stairs to the landing.

She took the stairs fast and threw the house keys at him and ran up close to his back with her fist balled up. She missed her target. The keys hit the wall.

He spun around. "If you touch me, I will hit you back."

She stared with fire in her expanded eyes like she was seeing a stranger, trying to figure out how the man she loved could be eyeing her like he wished she was dead. "Owen won."

Claude said nothing. He turned around and went into their bedroom, silent, but the entire language of his body still said, *try me*.

Venus just stood at the top of the stairs in the heat of her pain and said, "Still in love with a dead woman." She looked toward the door of their room. Her foggy eyes moved down the hall toward Skyy's room. And she made herself go back downstairs and over to the box she had unpacked in the kitchen. She repacked it.

She looked up as if she could see the sky, up toward her best friend-ghost, who was no longer in their bedroom but still in her life and she said, "You win, too."

28

Sequoia

"... clicking VIEW RESULTS."

It had been nearly a week since Kyle Jr. was home with Sequoia, Torino and TJ.

Kyle was able to get Colette released from the hospital, and she was at home with him at his place in Northridge.

Sequoia and Torino took time a few nights earlier to swab Kyle Jr.'s mouth and they sent the kit overnight to a genetic testing lab in New Mexico.

She was concerned that the time she spent convincing herself they would all be a happy little family of four was not quite coming together because of one homesick seven year-old named Kyle Jr.

"Kyle Jr., now let TJ have time on the DS, too. I told you we'll get you one next weekend."

"But he played with it all this time and I just got it."

She said, "I've seen you with it most of the morning. Now give it to him like I said."

"Here," Kyle Jr. said with an edge, half shoving it into TJ's stomach.

"Ouch." TJ looked surprised. He eyed his mother for help. "Mom."

Sequoia was firm. "Say you're sorry and hand it to him the right way. TJ give it back to him."

TJ did, looking sad.

Kyle Jr. took it and then handed it back. "Here." This time his tone was down a notch. Slightly.

"Say you're sorry."

"Sorry." Kyle Jr. got up and ran toward his room, yelling, "I hate it here. I want my mommy. I want my daddy."

Torino came into the family room, interrupted from his phone call, looking impatient. "What the heck was that about?"

Sequoia explained, "He shoved the game at TJ and I made him apologize."

Torino shouted toward the bedrooms, "Kyle Jr., come back in here. Now!"

Kyle Jr. walked back in at a snail's pace, looking at the floor.

Torino asked, "What's going on with you? Everyone's trying to be patient, but I won't have you being mean and disrespectful. Do you understand me?"

He nodded.

"I asked you a question. In this house, we answer with words."

"Yes."

"Now you two play nicely." He gave a stern look to them both.

TJ just looked at his brother.

"Can I see my dad?" Kyle Jr. asked, with his lip poked out.

Torino looked like he wanted to say no so bad, but he said, "Yes. Yes you can, actually. Hold on. Let me check and see when that's gonna happen. You stay right here with TJ." He then said to Sequoia, "Baby, I'm going upstairs. Pick up the home phone down here in a few seconds. Keep an eye on them."

"Okay."

He ran up to their bedroom. The sound of the door closing was loud.

Sequoia gave it a minute and then picked up, hearing the phone ringing.

"Hey," Kyle said.

"Hey, Kyle."

"Yeah."

"Sequoia's on the line, too."

She said, "Hi, Kyle."

"Hey."

Torino asked, "What's going on over there? How's Colette doing?"

"A lot better. I was gonna call you. Do you think I can come and get Kyle Jr.? I took some time off work. Colette will be here, too. I won't leave the two of them alone."

Torino said, "Okay. That's fine. But I want you to know I filed for sole custody of him until Colette gets through her problems."

"I understand."

"So, you two are that cool now?"

Kyle explained, "Man, just gotta keep it real. She and I are gonna take another stab at this. I can't leave her to get through this by herself. We've been together a long time. Been through a lot."

"Okay. But what's old girl, Yasmin, got to say about that? And your brother's gotta be upset."

"Yasmin is pissed but, hey. I gotta do what I gotta do."

Sequoia said, "Uh-huh," as though moving on from her stuck-up self was at least one thing she agreed with.

Kyle continued, "And yeah, everyone's mad that I missed the wedding, including my brother. This whole thing could've been worse if I wasn't here for her."

"With all the stuff you told me about her, I just don't know. Her issues are the very reasons you filed the restraining order."

"Torino, you should see her. She's docile and beat down. They've got her in mandatory therapy, which wouldn't have happened before, and we're gonna go as a family. She finally admitted some things to me. She was born in prison. Colette always said she didn't know where her mom was. Turns out her mother was a pimp. She's doing life for killing one of the female hookers she fell in love with. And Colette's father, whoever he is, is some John. Colette's anger has been eating her ass alive. She's way past depressed."

"That's gonna be tough to work through. You ready for all that?"

"Yeah, I've gotta be. Everything happens for a reason. I just need to get her some time with Kyle Jr. right now. We both need it. I miss that little dude so bad, I just can't tell you. Can I talk to him?"

"Yeah." Torino said to Sequoia, "Baby, put Kyle Jr. on the phone, please."

"Okay." She called, "Kyle Jr. Your dad is on the phone." He ran to her. She extended him the phone. "Here."

He took hold of the receiver. "Daddy?" He evolved into full on crying again, like he was being burned at the stake. "Will you come and get me?"

"Yes, Son. I will."

"I don't like it here." He cut his teary eyes away from Sequoia, fidgeting with his Hot Wheels toy. "This house is all sparkly and new and fancy. And they're mad at me."

Sequoia looked at him like, *oh, please*.

Kyle said, "Stop it. Now I know this is hard, but they're nice people and they care about you. They're trying to make you comfortable. You'll get used to it. And you will be polite."

Kyle Jr.'s sentences fired away, one after the other without a break. "I want Mommy. I wanna come home.

218

Are you at home now? Did you come back home? I asked Mom and she said you wouldn't, but you did, right?"

"Yes, I did."

"Can I talk to my Mommy?"

"She's sleeping. I'll be there in about an hour to get you."

"Okay, bye." Sequoia took the cordless back and headed to the office while Kyle Jr. ran off, even skipping like he had morphed back into happy-land just that fast. He even told TJ, "My dad's coming to get me and take me home." It was as if he was bragging.

TJ simply said, "Uh-huh."

Torino said, "Okay, dude. See you in a minute."

Sequoia added, "Yeah, we'll have him ready."

"Bye."

They hung up and Torino came back downstairs.

Sequoia was in the office sitting at her desk on the computer and the boys went into the family room right next door.

She and Torino looked at each other and she said, "Kyle coming to get him isn't such a bad thing. This hasn't been easy."

"We knew it wouldn't be. Kyle Jr. just needs time."

"He needs his mom and dad. Speaking of that, I'm checking on those results. I signed up for online access."

Torino sat on the edge of the desk. "Oh? I thought they had to mail it back."

"Not anymore. They won't tell you over the phone, but you can select online order status."

She typed away and clicked the mouse and maneuvered her way through the website, clicking VIEW RESULTS. "Let's see." She read each word closely.

"What does it say?" He tried to figure out which part she was reading.

She scrolled through a section of the page with her fingertip. "It says Torino Wilson. Negative results." She looked up at him. "Torino, you are not the father." Her face was not shocked.

His head darted back and his eyes doubled in size. "What? You're kidding."

"Nope."

He stood and looked over her shoulder, saying, "Let me see."

She pointed, "It says right here under the summary, *Not a paternity match. To get further, more accurate results, the mother's DNA may be required.*"

"Oh, shit! What have I done?" he stepped back.

She swiveled her desk chair toward him. "You've got a son who you're paying child support for based on Kyle's suggestions to get him away from his mother, when even Kyle couldn't stay away from her."

"And I'm trying to file to get full custody of a child who isn't even mine. I knew it. Dammit. Why didn't I stick to my hunches?" He walked over to the window and stared outside. "I didn't think she could've used any sperm from a condom. I should've fought this and just taken the court ordered test."

She asked, wanting to say *I told you so*, but didn't, "So, what now?"

"We get him ready for Kyle to pick him up."

"You telling him?"

"I am. One-on-one, in person. Not only am I telling him, I'm going to suggest he get a paternity test, too."

TJ yelled from the next room. "Mommy, he hit me."

It was Torino who said to him, "I'll be right there."

Sequoia stood up. "I'll pack his things."

29

<u>Mercedes</u>

"... Forever One."

Mason had been back and forth, coming home regularly, mainly to check the mail and then he would head back out to his place in Leimert Park.

Mercedes tried and tried to get used to him popping in and out, and tried and tried to be patient. It was reluctantly becoming a way of life. She felt helpless yet waited for the love of her life to come back around.

She went to work early on a Sunday morning so she could catch up on her unattended projects.

She sat at her desk when to her surprise, Mason called.

"Hi," she said, half excited, half not.

"Hi. What's up?"

"Nothing." Everything was frozen but her mouth.

"Cedes, I'm at home."

"You are?"

"Where are you?"

"I'm at the office."

He asked, "This early? On a Sunday?"

"I came in at five. I have some things I need to get done."

"I want us to go to church."

"You do?" Her eyebrows showed shock. "This morning?"

"Yes. The eleven o'clock service." He sounded matter-of-fact, as though they had not missed a Sunday of church ever.

Mercedes felt a tinge of warmth thawing out her inability to move. She turned away from her desk, looking at the wall clock. "Okay." She wanted to say, *I wish you'd told me earlier*, but considering everything, she didn't. "It's eight-thirty now. I'll be home soon."

"Okay. Bye." He disappeared with a click.

She simply shut down her computer, got up and headed out, walking out a little bit faster than when she walked in.

She prayed that it was not a dream.

Just before ten-thirty, both wearing royal blue suits without even planning to, Mason and Mercedes Wilson arrived at the church in Mason's Corvette. He parked, turned off the ignition and got out. She sat in the passenger seat and waited. Instead of him coming around to her door right away, he hesitated. She still waited.

She wondered who he could have possibly been with who would have allowed such nonsense. He then came around and opened the door. "Thanks," she said as she got out, although he did not extend his hand to her as he always did before.

They headed inside of the sanctuary, each holding their Bibles, and they sat in their usual seats in the front row. The choir began a rendition of "Victory" by Yolanda Adams led by the Rev's energetic wife. Some people stood and sang along. Within minutes, Mercedes stood and sang, too. Mason didn't. "Truly I've been through the storm and rain, I know everything about heartache and pain, but God carried me through it all, without His protection I'd surely fall," and within minutes the song went from full effect to winding down, with most of the congregation singing, "I got the Victory, yeah, yeah, yeah," over and over. Mercedes noticed Mason still seated, clapping, barely nodding with a stoic face.

Once the song was done the applause for the choir led into applause for the Rev as he approached the podium. Mercedes remained standing out of respect. Mason stood out of respect, as well.

"Well now, you may be seated." Everyone did. "Aren't you glad you didn't let that little voice within win this morning? The voice that said, 'I'll go to church next week, I'll sleep in a little longer, I'm too tired to get up, there's a sale at the mall, I can't miss that, I'm gonna watch football, some kind of football, it's Sunday, I think I'll wash my car or wash the dog, or wash down the driveway.' You need to wash your soul and come on and go to church, because you sure would've missed that song. The choir is on fire today, God bless their beautiful souls. I'm telling you. I'm so glad to see you here this morning." The Rev glanced around at the many rows of churchgoers, and his eyes spied Mason and Mercedes. He pointed and smiled, and kept his glance moving.

"The topic for today is *Turning Your Pain Into Power*. When you're hurting and broken, in labor, going through growing pains, having contractions and you feel like you just can't go on, don't quit. Push. Push on and give birth to your vision, your family, and your dreams.

"God will hold up when you're broken. He loves to take away your shame. The payment for our sin is the precious life He gave. You must ask the Lord to let the light from the lighthouse shine on you. It will. There's light in the morning, just as sure as the sun rises, the darkness doesn't last long. Today's a new day. In your life, in your business, with your children, with your health, and in your marriage. You stand together, accept the differences, and realize the grass ain't always greener. Sometimes you think you're sleeping with a cubic zirconium, and you get out there and sleep with the so-called diamonds, and suddenly that CZ at home starts looking like a brilliant twenty-carat diamond just like that. You'd better realize you've got the rock now. Somebody else might wanna step up and buy that diamond you thought was a dud. As soon as you step away, the infiltrators will be right there. Your trash will gladly be their treasure."

Mercedes took in every word, smiling.

The Rev continued and nearly forty minutes later, the pianist began to play ever so subtly, signaling the wind down.

"Don't risk it all by allowing temptation to tempt you. Sometimes what seems like the end is only a disguised blessing to test the heart. Sometimes you won't be given to until you're broken down. Your bank account, your relationship, your back. God makes the broken masters at mending. See your brokenness as a blessing. Without it you won't grow. You can't endure being married thirty, forty, fifty years without being broken. Ask an older couple who've been together for decades have they ever wanted to leave. Did someone cheat? Did someone lie? Did someone hurt them? Yes. Yes. Yes. But they'll say they forgave and stayed. The reward comes in the morning to those who don't walk away. Leaving is the easy part. The hard part is to just stand. Stand for your union, stand for your children, stand for your vows, stand for your life. Stand," he yelled.

Most of the congregation stood and applauded. Mercedes fed off of Mason's reaction and they sat, clapping in their seats.

As the Rev stepped away from the podium, a woman came down from where the choir sat and stood at a microphone. Her voice was loud and deep. "Can't give up now, ladies and gentlemen. Can't give up now."

The music from the song by Mary Mary began and Mercedes nodded her head to the beat and sang the intros and the first few stanzas. "I just can't give up now. I've come too far from where I started from." By the time the third chorus was sung, most were on their feet and this time it was Mason who stood, clapping his hands to the beat, singing along, "Nobody told me the road would be easy. I don't believe He brought me this far to leave me." This was a song that Mattie sang to her sons while growing up. It was also the song that Mattie reminded Mason of when he first started playing professionally.

Mercedes knew it. She stood, her face flushed, blinking a mile a minute to fan off her emotions, clapping as the chorus was repeated, and they sang together. Mason paused from clapping and he took Mercedes's hand into his. They continued to sing. Hand in hand. Husband and wife.

After church they did not wait around to talk to the Rev or go to their usual breakfast at the local Dinah's or Pann's restaurants near their home like they always did before. They both remained quiet, only making small comments, like, "When did they build that CVS pharmacy?" and "Wow, isn't it a pretty day?" Most of the time Mercedes just stared out of the passenger side window as Mason drove fast in his fancy car.

Before Mercedes realized it, Mason pulled through the iron gates of the Holy Cross Cemetery in Culver City, and up the winding road to Jesse and Mattie's graveside in the Way of the Cross section. She took in the view of the sprawling, park-like setting, courtyards, and lush vegetation. It was quiet and serene and beautiful and holy.

They said nothing to each other as he parked. He came around to help Mercedes out of the car, extending his hand, and they walked across the green grass over to the spot where Jessie and Mattie were buried. The black granite companion headstone had both names, Jessie K. Wilson, Mattie B. Wilson, with their respective birth and death dates and a scripted message of *Forever One*. There was a vase that was filled with white tulips.

Mercedes asked, "Did you bring those?"

"Yes." He only looked down.

They knelt together, Mercedes on one knee using her hand to secure the hem of her skirt to her knees and placing the other hand on Mason's back. They began to pray silently. As Mason's eyes were closed, Mercedes looked over to the next section called Resurrection, and saw her brother-in-law, Claude, standing over Fatima's grave . . . alone.

Mercedes did not make another move or say anything about it. They just prayed.

By two-o'clock in the afternoon they were back home.
Mason went into the office.
Mercedes went into the bedroom.
They basically still said nothing.

A while later, around nine o'clock that evening, while Mercedes sat in the backyard on a patio chair sipping chamomile tea, Mason came out and stood in front of her. "Cedes, I'm not leaving tonight. But I need to know how to get this vision out of my head."

She noticed he had a tall can of beer in his hand. "I don't know. I ask you to forgive me. Honey, we have to move on," she said, holding her white teacup.

226

"No. We don't. I don't want to give up, but I have no choice. I can't accept the fact that he must've meant about as much as our marriage did."

"He didn't."

"I'm trying to figure out why it almost seems like you have an attitude." He looked resentful.

"I don't. I just want you to forgive me and learn to trust me again. That's what I had to do."

He told her, "This isn't about you. This is about me. You were allowed your time years ago to hurt and make your decision. You make it seem like I owe you one. This isn't tit-for-tat, like when one cheats the other can just get even and that's that. Like revenge sex." His voice was gruff.

She placed her teacup on the glass patio table. She spoke in his same strong tone. "This was hardly sex and it was hardly getting even. This was seven years later. If I wanted to get even I would've done it back then. And how can a kiss even be compared to someone having sex, repeatedly, with someone else who is not their spouse? I should be the only one in the room with you when you have sex, Mason."

"And I should be the only man you're alone with in a hotel room. I should be the only man you kiss."

"It's different."

"It's not." He looked certain.

"I dealt with years of you being a professional athlete, attracting women, those golf groupies, and I trusted you. But you turned out to be a philanderer. A philandering professional athlete, the stereotypical famous person who does it because they can. I lived with that. And I think you forgot that maybe, just maybe, you're not the only one of the two of us who can attract people." She cut her eyes and looked out toward the view of the backyard.

227

He asked, speeding up his words, "Is that what you were trying to prove, that you can still attract someone?"

"No."

"I see men look at you all the time, you think I don't know that? I'm not blind."

"I don't want to argue. We had a great day. An amazing day." She picked up her tea again. "And I know how you are when you get quiet. It means you've got something on your mind. So I left you to it. But we need to get through this." She looked up at his frowning face. "I'm begging you please, let's learn from this and not throw away over two decades of us being a family."

Mason then looked out at the view. "You didn't think about this before you returned his call and invited him up."

She took it down a notch, saying, "I know. I was wrong," and then she took a sip.

He looked down at her. "And you're telling me nothing else happened?"

She looked up at him. "Nothing else happened. He would've told you if you hadn't left when he was on the phone."

"What man in his right mind would talk to another man on the phone to have him confirm what happened to him and the man's wife? That's a punk ass move and very disrespectful to me as your husband."

She broke eye contact. "I'm sorry. I didn't know what else to do at that point. When you cheated you said she kissed you goodbye and then the two of you walked to the bed together. With me and Ryan, he kissed me goodbye and I walked him to the door. It's still wrong, I know."

All Mason said was, "Kissed," like his mind was playing the tape of their forbidden actions. "What kind of kiss was it?"

She moved her eyes away from the backyard and up at him. "What kind of kiss did you and Natalie have?"

Mason stood in place.

She waited for his comeback and just sat.

He looked to be simmering. Sweat covered his nose.

She looked again at the can in his hand, from which he hadn't taken a sip. "And, honey, why are you drinking?" she asked, as if she didn't know.

"First things first."

She put her now empty cup down. "Mason. I know you're mad. It's up to you. I think you have to ask yourself is this negotiable, or non-negotiable. That is what I had to ask myself back when Dr. Little counseled us. It's on you." She stood up. "Now, I'm going to bed. Are you coming?"

"I'll sleep in Mom's room."

She nodded, taking the cup with her so she could put it in the kitchen sink. "Okay. See you in the morning. I love you." She stood before him on her tiptoes and kissed him on the lips. She gave him an unrequited peck, but still said what she needed to say. "Just remember, we have a good life, but I'd rather have a life with you and no money, than a life without you and be rich. And by the way, I've never slept with another man in my entire life but you."

He didn't react.

As she walked away he sat down in the seat she had vacated and took a long swig of his brew.

She watched him as he crossed one leg over the other.

She was sad. But she was glad.

Glad at the moment because Mason was home for now.

Sad because he brought a nasty bad habit back with him that she prayed he had kicked long ago.

30

Venus

"... he kicked me out ..."

W e're coming from my dad's house. Skyy and I have been with him for a week while Skyy had Fall Break. She'll miss school today, but I'll take her back tomorrow. We've been sleeping on the sofa bed," Venus said while driving on the 405 southbound.

Mercedes was in her home office. She had just returned from a committee meeting for the Alzheimer's Association. "At his apartment in Inglewood and you didn't stop by?"

Venus talked slow. "Mercedes, a lot's been going on."

"Okay. I guess first question is why you two are sleeping on your dad's sofa instead of in that beautiful new house you have in Laguna?"

"It's not so beautiful on the inside. Claude and I have been going through it."

"Is it still the problem you were having with Cameron before, when I came by and Cameron was having trouble with school? The school said he cheated or something."

Venus merged into the fast lane. Skyy was in the backseat with her earphones on, watching *The Princess and the Frog* movie on the DVD player. "No. That was worked out. I mean he can't go back to that school, but he's moved on. Turns out his ex-girlfriend copied info from the Internet and used it in a paper she wrote for him. Cam has other issues now."

"Like what?"

"Cam is awful at picking women, to be honest with you. He was with this girl who it turns out is the reason our house got broken into."

"Oh, damn. She cased you guys out or something?"

"She did. And I mean, Cam's been doing nothing as far as getting ahead, so the more we tried to get him on track, the more he resisted." Venus looked back to make sure Skyy was still watching her movie. "Mercedes, Cam met this forty eight year-old woman out in Laguna, and he fell hard. Our neighbor. And he sent me an email last night that they got married in Vegas."

Mercedes's voice jumped. "Oh, no he didn't. What the hell is that all about? Why so fast, and why so much older?"

"Your guess is as good as mine as far as why so fast. But I do know he's having problems coming to terms with Fatima, and who his dad is."

"He asked you who he was?"

Venus replied, "He did. But I didn't tell him, and since he's not speaking to Claude, who knows when or how he'll find out."

"He must be rebelling. Marrying someone more than twice his age. What's her problem, anyway?"

"Mercedes, this chick is an heir to the Heinz ketchup fortune."

"Oh, no wonder Cameron went for that. First off, she's obviously rich," Mercedes said.

"She well off enough I guess. I think it's some mother image thing as far as the age. But he'd better watch out because I checked online and from what I know, this woman married a fourth generation Heinz. I think he's the founder's great-great grandson who was a few years younger than her, but they only lasted less than a year, so I doubt she has that much dough. She does have some kids from her first and second marriages. This one to

231

Cam makes it husband number four. And one of her husband's was black. Actually, as far as the money goes, I read that some Heinz family granddaughter gets like ninety-percent of everything anyway."

Mercedes reacted by saying, "Damn. That's who he met in the O.C., huh? You guys moved him out to get away and he ran right into being a husband in no time flat."

"Yep. Now my son and his nearly fifty year-old wife live right down the street."

"What did Claude say about it?"

"About them eloping? He doesn't know."

"Oh hell. There's gonna be an earthquake in Orange County when he finds out."

"Ya think?" Venus was now on the 5 Freeway.

Mercedes gave a laugh. "Drama. Geez. But what about you and Claude? What happened that had you ending up at your dad's house?"

"I didn't tell you, but Owen, Fatima's murderer, has been writing me."

"Out of the blue?"

"Yes. I got the first letter that day you came over when Cam got in trouble at school. Some of the mess he wrote Claude bought into and basically kicked me out of my own house, saying I was getting with Owen all along, and that I told Owen where Fatima would be so I could have Claude all to myself. Which is such bunk."

"That is insane. Why would he believe psycho Owen, anyway?"

"I think Claude just wants to believe him. I think he's not over Fatima, even now. I think he's using it as a reason for him to push me away."

Mercedes gave pause. "That is nonsense. You guys have been fine. Venus, I say you go back home. Like you said, that's your house. Don't let him do that. He'll come around. And for the record, you two need to get Owen straightened out."

"Claude said he will. I don't know." Venus didn't sound hopeful.

"Your husband is so headstrong and old fashioned. It's like he holds on to this notion that the woman has her place and the man has his place, and he just doesn't budge. It's archaic."

Venus sighed loudly. "Tell me about it. Mercedes, you know as well as I do that I never told Owen that madness. I never talked to him at all."

"I believe you."

"People get things stuck in their heads and there's no letting go." Venus looked at the display after hearing a beep, and then it stopped ringing. It was Claude. She continued to talk, but wondered. "So, that's what's up in my weird little world."

"Okay, but everyone's world is weird. We all have our own mess."

Venus wanted to ask about Mercedes and Mason, but didn't. Her mind was on what Claude could have wanted. "True."

Mercedes asked, "Where are you headed anyway?"

"I'm going home. I'm headed there now. Me and Skyy. She's watching a movie." Venus looked back at Skyy who was knocked out. Her headphones were removed from her head. "Actually, Claude gave me the keys to some house he rented for me and Skyy somewhere in Newport Beach. But I don't think so." She heard a sound signaling a message.

"He what? Tell me you're lying."

"I'm not." All Venus could think about was the message.

"I'd throw those suckers away. He has lost his ever-lovin' mind?"

233

Venus ended up saying, "Mercedes, girl, I'm gonna call you back. I'm about to get off the freeway."

"Okay. Sorry all this is going on. Call me later."

"I will."

"Okay. Bye."

"Bye." Venus hung up and pressed the touch screen for voicemail.

Venus, umm, yeah. It's me. I wanted you to know, I didn't go out there to see Owen after all. Just too much drama. But, I did have Attorney Sampson contact the Department of Corrections and he sent them the first letter Owen wrote you, not the second one. Turns out Owen's in a minimum to medium security facility in California. So, they're transferring him to a maximum facility in Nevada called the Ely State Prison where they screen calls and mail. Stuff like that. So, that's it. That's all I wanted to tell you. Let's talk about when I can see Skyy. Not sure if you're settled into the house. Haven't heard from you. I can schedule and pay for movers. If I don't pick up when you call, I'm probably in a late meeting. But, let's try and talk tomorrow.

Her mouth was wide open. Hearing him have the nerve to mention movers and basically announce that he would be busy made her fume. There were no sentences saying *come home* or *miss you or let's talk.*

She pressed delete and disconnected.

Venus got into the next lane over, slowing down her ride home but not her thoughts. She wanted to call back and leave nothing but curse words on his voicemail. She wanted to drive around and find him and bust him in the act of being so tied up he couldn't be available for his wife's call. She wanted to run him down with her Infiniti. She wanted to call every client he had in the real estate business and tell them what a dirty dog Claude Wilson was for trying to kick out his wife and child.

And then something escorted her vengeful thoughts and reminded her of Mattie's funeral. She remembered the words Star said her grandmother would always say. *A lady always knows when to leave.*

Immediately, Venus called back, and without even one ring, voicemail stepped in. She prepared herself with a cleansing breath. "Hi Claude. Got your message. I was going to come by and get Skyy's and my things. But, we'll get them tomorrow." She paused, about to say that Cameron eloped, but she said instead, "Bye."

Wearing her wedding ring on her left hand and the emerald ring on her right, she took the exit off of the 5 Freeway. But instead of steering her car toward Laguna Hills, she got right back on and prepared herself to go north on the 5, to the 405 north, to the 55 south, ready for the twenty-three mile drive to Newport Beach, her new home, once again officially separated from her best friend's man, Claude Joseph Wilson.

Then from the backseat she heard a tiny tired voice, "Mommy. We don't live with Daddy anymore?"

Venus's heart sank.

31

Sequoia

". . . with her trademark golden hair . . ."

Kyle had picked up Kyle Jr. once and brought him back two days later. It was Friday, October 29th and though it was Torino's weekend, he had agreed to give them some extra time by bringing Kyle Jr. to Kyle's house.

Torino still hadn't told Kyle that the son Torino had joint custody of, whose last name was legally changed to Wilson, wasn't his.

Kyle had moved into an ivory stucco home that he had rented in the gated Northridge community of Porter Ranch after he and Colette broke up, leaving her and Kyle Jr. in the two bedroom apartment in Fox Hills.

His new place was a three bedroom, two bath corner home with a ton of room, a floor-to-ceiling brick fireplace and several of fruit trees. The environment was much more conducive to family living than where they had lived before.

When Torino and Sequoia pulled up and parked in the long, four-car driveway, Kyle Jr. looked at the house before him and said, "Man. Wow. Is this where my dad lives?"

"Yes, it is," Torino said.

Kyle Jr. unbuckled himself and pulled on the doorknob, pushing the door open and hopping out. He ran up the walkway to the front door at the same time Kyle opened it. "Hey, little man." Kyle reached down and picked up Kyle Jr., hugging him and flashing a major smile.

Kyle Jr. pushed away and squirmed to be let down. "Daddy, this is cool. Can I see it? Where's Mommy?"

Kyle put him down and said, "She's inside. Go on in."

Torino waved from the driver seat and Kyle motioned for him to come in. "Come see the place. Say hi to Colette."

"Oh Lord," was all Sequoia said, unbuckling her seatbelt.

TJ asked, "Can I see Kyle Jr.'s other house, too?"

"Yes, you can." Sequoia got out and closed the door, adjusting her tight jeans and even tighter top.

TJ unstrapped himself. "Cool." He got out at the same time as Torino. TJ's little legs walked faster than his mom and dad did. Once he got to the door he ran right past Kyle, barely saying, "Hi."

"Hey there, TJ." Kyle laughed as TJ made his own way in.

Sequoia walked behind Torino. "Nice place."

"Hey, it's only on loan. Can't buy anything just yet, but I will soon. Maybe this place, maybe not."

"I understand," she said.

She and Torino proceeded inside behind Kyle and stepped down into the enormity of the sunken living room.

The room was furnished with modern sofas and chairs, tables and rugs, mainly in earth tones, and it had a large walnut grandfather clock in the corner. Beyond the living room was a family room that opened up to the newly remodeled kitchen.

And sitting before the fireplace in a brown reclining chair, was Colette Berry, hugging her son for a brief moment. He and TJ ran outside, pushing past the kitchen door, into the backyard, and playing on the big slide like they'd been there before.

"Hi," Colette said, sounding tired. Her normally high-pitched voice had more base.

"Hi, Colette," Torino said, walking toward her and stopping just before he got to her chair.

Their eyes met and he turned back to look around at anything else.

She asked, "Where's Sequoia?

Sequoia stepped up next to Torino. "Hello, Colette."

Colette gave Sequoia a weak smile, aiming her light eyes at her. "Hi. Have a seat." Colette seemed to be even more heavyset and her trademark golden hair seemed to have broken off some. It was pulled back into a thin ponytail. The smell in the room was of Bergamot hair dress.

Kyle still stood, and so did Torino and Sequoia.

Torino was the one who said, "No thanks. We can't stay long. We're just dropping off Kyle Jr."

"Thank you for that," Colette said.

"No problem," Torino replied. "You did good, Kyle. This house is big."

Kyle said. "You know, it's worth about a half-a-million. I think I can definitely do better, though. Maybe something around three or four. It's okay for now but eventually, we'll get something like this so Kyle Jr. can have a yard. He never had that living in Fox Hills."

Sequoia said, "It is nice." She looked around and then at Torino, hoping he would catch her eyes urging him to announce their departure.

Colette said directly to Sequoia, "Thank you for spending extra time with him. I appreciate that."

Sequoia smiled. "No problem."

Colette said to Torino, "And I got the custody papers. I answered without contesting. I even sent my medical diagnosis along with it. You having full custody is fine with me."

Torino gave her a straight-on look as though amazed that she was still perpetrating. "Really?"

Colette's eyes were bloodshot. "Yes." She had a TV tray next to her with some medicine bottles, and a bottle of Visine.

She continued, words dragging. "We'd just like the time we spend to be as equal as possible."

"Okay." Torino looked away again, this time at Sequoia.

Her eyes dragged his eyes to the front door.

Colette asked, "Was Kyle Jr. behaving?"

Torino said, "He was. It's all new to him."

"It is." Colette sounded like she was about to go to sleep. "I was diagnosed as bipolar. I have post traumatic stress disorder, too. I'm on medication. I don't mind you knowing. I hate for you to see me like this."

Kyle said, "She's been through a lot."

"We're just glad you're okay," Sequoia told her.

Torino spoke up. "Yep. Well. We're gonna get going. Sequoia has a catering event."

Kyle said, "Oh, really? If it's anything like the one you did for my brother, it'll be great."

Torino led the way to the door.

"Thank you. So, we'll talk to you both later." Sequoia followed right behind him.

Colette said to Kyle. "Baby, call the boys from the back."

"Kyle Jr., TJ, come inside," Kyle yelled.

The boys came back in slower than when they went out.

"Oh, man," Kyle Jr. said, seeing Torino and Sequoia at the door. "TJ's leaving?"

Torino said. "Yes. Come on TJ. We've gotta get going."

TJ walked up to his dad. "Okay. Bye," he said to Kyle Jr.

Kyle asked him, "Did you meet Ms. Berry?"

She gave him a smile. "Hi, TJ. I haven't seen you since you were a baby."

"Hello." He barely looked at her, only at Kyle Jr.

Kyle Jr. said, "That's my mom."

"Okay." TJ gave Colette a quick smile and then held his own mom's hand.

"Let's go," Torino said.

Sequoia waved to everyone. "We'll talk to you later."

"Okay." Colette closed her eyes half way and then reopened them wide.

Kyle walked them out the door and to their car. Everyone got inside except for Torino, who opened the driver side door and turned around to say, "Man. I didn't want to say it in front of Colette. I wanted to wait until I saw you again, just you and me. I didn't bring it up the other day, either. But the DNA test I took came back negative."

"It did?" Kyle looked like his breath was caught in his throat.

"So, I think the next move is for you to go ahead and take a test yourself. And if it turns out you're his father, I think you should take that to court and get full custody of Kyle Jr."

"You think so?"

"I do. If he belongs to you, why not? That's a true daddy's boy you've got there. And, if you really think Colette can get well now that she's getting the help she needs, the help she didn't have before, then I don't see why you three can't work it out as a family."

"What about the boys? Looks to me like they've bonded already."

"They'll be in each other's lives."

Kyle nodded and thought to himself. He then said, "I'll jump on that right away. Thanks." He looked inside of the car. "Thanks, Sequoia. You've been one-hundred percent through all of this."

"No worries."

He looked in the backseat. "TJ, we'll see you later."

"Bye." TJ was already playing with his DS.

Then he said to Torino, "I'll call you, man. Thanks for everything." They hugged the brotha hug, patting each other on the back with one hand and shaking hands with the other.

"Got it." Torino got into the car and started it up.

As they backed out of the driveway, Sequoia said, "Sorry to say, but she looks bad."

"Yeah."

"I still can't believe she lied about you being the father after all this time."

Torino shook his head in agreement. "Let's just hope *he's* the father."

Sequoia cosigned. "True. Let's."

32

Mercedes

"... running for city council."

I t was a month later.
Thanksgiving Day.

Claude's birthday was the night before.

All of the family was over for the annual dinner at Mercedes and Mason's house.

Mason had been spending his nights there for over a month, yet still not sharing his wife's bed. He spent most of his time being in solitude, finishing his second book which came out in six months. And also, he had been interviewing with several networks regarding a job in broadcasting.

Sequoia had come over early to help Mercedes cook. They took over the kitchen with pots and pans and groceries and seasonings. Mercedes was in charge of the turkey, ham, liver and onions, cornbread dressing, and giblet gravy.

Sequoia was in charge of the side dishes like yams, cheese grits, green beans, collards, macaroni and cheese, and the biscuits.

And Star was in the kitchen every now and then, too, making desserts, like lemon pound cake, carrot cake, and sweet potato pie.

Today, Mason Wilson was not in his office working. He was in the family room shooting pool with Claude, Torino, and Star's boyfriend Terrence.

TJ and Skyy were in Star's old room playing Uno, again, and again, and again.

Mercedes told her daughter, looking over her shoulder at her baking skills. "Those look good, Star."

"Thanks, Mom. I'm starving."

"Did you and Terrence eat after your flight this morning?"

"We grabbed something from Jack In the Crack."

Mercedes laughed. She was pleased that her daughter had her sense of humor back. "Jack in the Crack? No you didn't."

Sequoia gave a snicker. "Wow."

"What? It's just what we call it instead of Jack In the Box. They don't have one in Atlanta, so when I come home it's the first place I go. But that was a few hours ago."

Sequoia asked, "You call it that because it's like crack?"

"Basically."

"These young folks," said Sequoia.

Star said, looking at her aunt, "Auntie Sequoia, you're young. You both are."

"Yeah, you had too much Jack in the Crack alright," Mercedes joked.

"Early forties. I hope I look as good as you two when I'm forty."

"Well, thanks, Star. That's sweet." Mercedes hugged Star from behind, placing a kiss on the side of her head.

Star leaned her head back upon her mom's chest. "Love you Mom. It's good to be home."

Mercedes said right back, "Love you more." She stopped and took in the moment. "It's good to have you home." And then she walked over to the sink. "This house is way too quiet without you and Rashaad." She wanted to also mention Mattie, but didn't.

Star said, "I'm glad Dad's back home. I'm just happy."

"I'm happy, too," said Mercedes, wondering if Star really knew that Mason wasn't back for good.

Sequoia spoke up while adding grated cheese to the macaroni. "Hell, I'm happy, too. And I'll be even happier when we finish all this food so we can eat."

Star asked Sequoia, "You need help?"

Sequoia held her hand up and dropped the bag of cheese on the floor. She bent over and picked it up.

Mercedes and Star laughed.

Sequoia regrouped. "I was gonna say no. I've got this. You just tend to your little desserts over there." She looked at Mercedes who had a look of hilarity on her face. "And you to yours."

Star placed the glass cover over the pound cake and looked at the clock on the microwave. "In that case, I'm done. I'm headed to the living room to watch Rashaad's tournament. It comes on in about two minutes."

Sequoia poured in some milk. "Which tournament is this?"

"He's in China. It's the Omega World Cup or something. It starts today."

Mercedes asked, "Is that the team tournament that lasts three days?"

"It is." She started to walk out of the kitchen. "He's playing with that hottie, Rory McIlroy."

Sequoia said, "Uh-oh, you'd better be careful. Your guy might hear you."

Star clicked her tongue. "Please. He knows. And I know who he likes."

"Really?"

"Yep. He told me himself that he'd marry Paula Patton hands down in two seconds flat."

Mercedes added, "If she was available. And him, too. Which he's not."

Star said while skipping out of the kitchen. "Well, of course. Duh. He belongs to me." Star said from the living room. "Dang. It's starting now."

"That girl has some energy."

Mercedes looked proud. "She does, with her genius self. You should've seen her in Atlanta playing in that symphony. She's so gifted. It's good to see her smiling."

"It's good to see everyone, period. Wish Rashaad could be home. And of course Cameron. Did you invite him?"

"No. I told Venus to tell him. I didn't think I should call him myself since Claude is here. Don't want him tripping out." Mercedes checked the oven and looked at the turkey.

"It's your house."

"And it's his birthday celebration as well as Thanksgiving. But it's also the anniversary of Fatima dying. If Cameron finds out it'll be because they told him." Mercedes did not speak of the fact that she saw Claude at the cemetery.

Sequoia said quietly, "You don't think Venus is going back to him."

"I don't. But, you never know. She did that one time before. Love is blind. You can't see what other people see or feel. That's on them. I just hope they do."

"Hey there, baby." Torino came into the kitchen looking at his wife. "You two are both fine, but I'm telling you," he said checking out Sequoia, "when I look at my wife I think if beauty was a crime, she'd be a felony." He gave Sequoia a look like he could put her on a plate and sop her up with a biscuit.

She giggled. "Torino, are you trying to get some in Mercedes's kitchen? 'Cause you know you can." Sequoia gave Torino sultry eyes.

Mercedes looked away, about to laugh. "Let me leave the two of you alone."

Torino said, "Just kidding."

Sequoia was serious. "I'm not. Oh, you can get it."

Mercedes cleared her throat. "Oh, Lord. I'll be right back so make it a quickie. Gotta check out my son on TV."

"Okay," Sequoia said, standing in front of Torino hugged up. She kissed him like it was a goodbye kiss, and he wasn't even going anywhere.

He said, "California face with a down-south rump." He grabbed her backside and squeezed.

Mercedes looked at them and moon-walked out, then turned to head straight toward the living room to where Star sat on the couch. "It started?"

"Yep."

"Good. You see him yet?"

"Yep." Star said, sitting with her feet up on the couch. "Oh my God. There he is. He's wearing red and black today. I'll go tell your dad." She hurried back into the family room. "Hey you guys? Rashaad's tournament is on."

Mason yelled over to the birthday boy, "Hey, Claude. Would you turn on that television please? Thanks." He eyeballed the plasma TV over the fireplace.

Claude took the remote from the shelf underneath it and turned to ESPN.

Mercedes looked at Terrence who was holding his pool cue. "Can you play?" she asked.

Mason said, "Oh, he got game."

"Really? Where'd you learn that?"

Terrence looked proud of himself. "Actually, I played my first game with Star. She taught me."

"Oh, so now you're gonna brag. Just flaunting the fact that you're new to the game. Making me look like a

246

punk? See, now I know why. It's called beginner's luck."
Mason was animated. He leaned over and aimed the cue
at the ball and took his shot. "Take that." He sank the
yellow ball like it was a cinch.

Terrence said, "Yeah, yeah, yeah. Trying to show off
now that the wife is here."

"Oh, no he's not." Mason took another shot and sank
it. "How you gonna talk mess to a golfer who's shooting
pool? One thing I can do is get a ball in a hole." Mason
lined himself up for the next shot. It went in. "Stick to
the violin, Son."

Terrence just shook his head, watching, smiling so
big he looked like his young cheeks were going to burst.
He was in Mason heaven.

Mercedes laughed, happy that her home seemed alive
again. She looked at Claude and asked, "How are you?"

"Good."

"You hungry?"

"I am, actually. It smells good in this house."

"Thank you. I hope that turkey turns out okay."

"It always does."

Mercedes stood next to Claude. "Wanted you to
know, I talked to Venus. I did invite her."

Claude looked sure. "She won't come."

"I think you're right. Sorry about everything."

He crossed his arms. "Everything happens for a
reason."

"I know. But anyway, I hope you celebrated your
birthday last night with a big bang," Mercedes said,
watching Terrence take over. Mason seemed quieter
now.

"I did. Yep. That much is true. I did." His words
stumbled.

"Good." Mercedes looked up at the television and noticed it was a commercial. She said to everyone, "I'll let you all know when dinner is served."

"Cool," said Terrence.

She heard Nadia barking from the backyard and went outside to the dug-run. She opened the gate. "Come on, girl. You can come in, too. It's Thanksgiving." Mercedes watched Nadia run circles around her, wagging her tail. Nadia led Mercedes to the door and sat, waiting for permission. She looked up at Mercedes with her pretty blue eyes. "Go." Mercedes waved her hand toward the inside. Nadia dashed in and ran up to Mason first.

"Hey, girl," Mason said, looking down at Nadia and then resuming his game. He was back on a roll with his shots.

Nadia made her way around to greet everyone. She approached Terrence with caution and barked.

Mercedes hushed her.

Instead of coming close, Nadia went directly into the living room.

Mason looked up at the TV when he heard Rashaad's voice, saying, "I need to step on the gas and be more patient, see what the course gives me. Our plan is to stay on top. Stay on top and rip it."

Mason said with energy, "That's my boy."

Nadia greeted Star. She could be heard saying, "There's Nadia. My pretty girl." She sounded like she had found a long lost friend.

Out of the thirteen chairs at the formal dining room table, six on each side and one at the head of the table, four were not taken. One for Venus, one for Rashaad, and one for Cameron, and the one at the head table for Mattie.

Mason led the prayer that included being thankful for His goodness, mercy and love. And everyone said, "Amen."

Less than an hour later, the platters and bowls that lined the table were half empty and the individual dinner plates were all but licked clean.

Nadia lay under the table being a good girl.

Skyy ate her food so fast that she looked like she was a starving student.

"Slow down," Mercedes said, smiling to her niece who worked on her second helping of turkey. Most everyone else was done.

"I can't believe how much Skyy has grown," said Sequoia.

Claude looked proud. "She's a big girl." He said, sitting next to her, "Slow down, pumpkin. That food isn't going anywhere."

Skyy asked her dad after swallowing, "Isn't Mommy coming?"

"No." He then asked his nephew, "TJ, are you still hungry?"

"No." TJ looked impatient.

"He just wants to play," said Sequoia. "He's waiting to make his getaway."

"Well, I'm done. That was good," said Star, taking her lap napkin and placing it on her plate.

"It was. Dessert time," said Terrence.

Star said, rubbing her belly, "Excuse me." She stood up. "I need to make some room first. I'm headed back to finish watching the tournament. Rashaad and Rory are in third place."

Mercedes said, "Oh, we can't have that."

Torino talked like he knew the game. "It's early. And if not today, there's always tomorrow. They've got three days."

Mason took a sip of black coffee and sat back. "Not always. Like Rashaad said, in golf, you've got to get a head start right from the beginning and stay on it. Where you start is where you can end up. That's got to be in your mind. It's too easy to lose your lead and I'm telling you, one hole, one stroke, can change the whole game."

Terrence asked, "You miss the competition?"

"I do. I was talking to my manager about opening my own golf course here. Probably out in Valencia near Magic Mountain. Have some competitions and train some of the young folks."

"Count me in. I'd like to learn."

Mason nodded. "Okay. You end up in L.A. and that'll be a done deal."

"Got it." Terrence wore a happy face.

Sequoia asked, "You still get your golf on with the fellas?"

"Not as much lately."

Star said with volume from the living room. "That's because he's busy running for city council."

Mason did not look excited. "No. I just don't think that's for me."

Terrence added, "I can see it. I think you'd win."

Claude said, "Don't give up that idea, Mason."

Mason said, "I hear ya." He stood. "So, let's see how Rashaad and his teammate are doing out there in China." He looked back at Terrence. "And then I'll meet you back in the family room to get my revenge."

Mercedes asked, looking surprised, "You won, Terrence?"

"I did."

Mason mumbled as he sat in the reclining chair. "Boy coming over here dating my daughter and spanking her dad in his own house. That's cold blooded."

Torino said, "Gotta give him credit for bringing it."

Mason leaned his chair back. "Beginner's luck."

TJ asked Sequoia, "Mom, can me and Skyy play shooting pool, too?"

Sequoia said, "I don't think so." She giggled. "And it's not called playing shooting pool. You say shoot pool. But what we can do is we can all take the gifts from over there into the living room." She looked at Skyy. "I'll bring the lemon cake over there so we can sing Happy Birthday to your father."

Skyy hopped up after finally pushing her plate away. "Okay." She and TJ ran to grab the gift bags that were near the table, taking them into the living room.

Nadia dined on leftovers.

The family sang Happy Birthday and ate dessert, watching the game, shooting pool, and enjoying each other just as the Wilson family had always done through the years. A few less family members, but laughs nonetheless. Making the most of being, together.

By midnight, Claude and Skyy had left. Claude had arranged to have her with him for the next two nights.

Torino, Sequoia, and TJ left.

Star was sleeping in Mattie's room with Nadia keeping watch.

Terrence slept in the guest room downstairs instead of going home to his parents' house. He wanted to go play golf with Mason early in the morning.

Mercedes was tucked into bed watching Rashaad's golf tournament on the DVR in the darkness of her bedroom, paying close attention to her son's every move, even though she knew he and his teammate were in second placing going into the next day's round.

She focused on the TV screen when the bedroom door opened. Mason appeared wearing his usual shorts and a tee. "Good night."

"Good night," she replied, as usual.

Instead of walking away, he walked to the bed and stood at the foot of it.

He asked casually, "What's up?"

She looked at him and replied. "Nothing."

"Star's got Mom's room."

"I know."

"Great day, today." Mason sounded like a robot.

Mercedes looked confused. "Yes. It really was."

She kept her eyes on him.

He kept his eyes on her.

She looked at him as if to say, *and*.

He said, "Cedes, remember the letter you put in my briefcase while I was in Ireland after we had our marriage counseling sessions? It was the letter that read you won't tolerate it and that if I did it again you were gone for good. And that you forgave me."

"Yes."

His face looked like he was swallowing his pride but his eyes looked sincere. "Ditto."

Mercedes felt an immediate lump in her throat. Her thoughts did flip flops. She said what she felt from deep within. "Thank you."

She pulled back the covers from his side of the bed and gave him a look.

Mason came along to his side and got in, adjusting his body to lay as close to his wife as possible, pulling the covers over them both.

She wore a long, red, silk nightgown and a red thong.

He smelled of cedar and orange.

He kissed his wife as she made the move to maneuver herself on top of him, still kissing, placing her hand on his chest, and then down to his stomach, and then down into his shorts to her husband's big ego.

She said while stroking it, "I missed you."

"I missed you, too."

"Make love to me." Her words were soft. Intense.

"My pleasure." He switched positions with her. Ready.

Mason and Mercedes sealed their reunion with a slow, lasting, passionate lovemaking session that ended with her on her stomach and him laying upon her back.

He told her in her ear as he was about to release all that he had been saving, "I'm home."

Turns out their last time together before wasn't their last time together after all.

She began to release all that she had been saving as well, contracting and focusing on nothing but him.

Mercedes moaned a loud moan, and cried.

This time, nothing popped into her head, but real, unadulterated love.

33

The Wilsons

"The volume of the music ceased . . ."

May 20th of 2011, a Friday, was a long-awaited, very special date at Wilson's, Torino's nightclub in El Segundo.

It was early evening. Still happy hour.

It was the night of Mason's second-ever book launch party. His book, *Grip It and Rip It*, hit the shelves that day.

Rashaad was there with his girl, Sasha, who Mercedes and Mason got to meet for the first time just before the evening started.

Star was there, but not with Terrence, who it turns out told his best friend that he was only with Star because he idolized Mason Wilson. So, she dumped him, having vowed when she was young to never put up with any man who was not into her only, knowing some would come around for the fame of the family name. Tonight, she was with her friend, Trinity Todd Germany, Ryan Germany's daughter.

Lucinda, Mattie's former nurse, was at Mason and Mercedes's house babysitting Kyle Jr., TJ, and Skyy. Their dog Nadia now had a new companion, an all-white German shepherd named Sugar. Nadia seemed happier, no longer sleeping in Mattie's room.

Venus was out of town at a conference for Make-A-Wish. The foundation rehired her as a virtual marketing director. She mainly worked from home but traveled often.

Sitting upstairs at a large, private V.I.P. table was Mercedes, Sequoia, Kyle, and yes, Colette Berry.

Colette, wearing all white, sat next to Mercedes, who wore all red. Colette spoke loudly over the soulful sounds of the R&B music. "I wanted to tell you, I'm really going to try to get back in shape so I can return to the runway. I'm on the right track, I think. I hope you'd consider assigning me some gigs. If so, I'd really appreciate it." Her voice was now back to high-pitched.

"I'll do that. It's good to see you're well."

Colette put her hand on Mercedes's. "We were so cool. We had good times, you and me."

"Yes. Yes, we did." Mercedes noticed a large black and blue bruise on the back of Colette's hand.

"I'm working on me. I'll be back."

And Colette's eye looked inflamed. Mercedes coyly pulled her hand away and took hold of her glass of champagne, wondering. She said, "I'm sure you will."

Sequoia watched Colette out of the corner of her eye, particularly each time Colette looked over at Torino, who was running around, making sure everything ran smoothly.

Colette's son, Kyle Jr., was formally still a Wilson, even though Torino took a legal paternity test and the support order was canceled. Kyle voluntarily signed an affidavit of parentage but never took a test. He was awarded full custody and claimed he didn't need to know who the real father was. Colette still claimed it was Torino.

At the end of the table was Claude who was joined by Mr. and Mrs. Cameron Wilson, Cameron and Penny. Both wore gold wedding bands.

Rashaad and Cameron had gone to a strip club the night before, hanging out like old times.

"You look happy," Claude said to Cameron.

"I am. We both are."

"Yes. We are indeed," Penny added, as her pink glossy lips shimmered. She looked her age, yet sexy like she must have been a fox back when she was Cameron's age. Her blouse was unbuttoned just so.

Claude told them, "Glad you could make it out."

"Thanks for inviting us," Penny said.

And then Penny looked over at her new uncle-in-law, Mason, as she played with her bronze dangle earrings. She gave a girlie smile.

Mason saw her as he walked up to Torino. He adjusted his red tie and smiled manly back.

Torino's voice blasted over the speaker. "May I have your attention please?" He held the microphone. The music lowered. The buzz of the crowd subsided as he said, "Tonight is a very special night. My brother, Mason Wilson, who's now an author as you all know, has written his second book. And that title, *Grip It and Rip It* made its debut today. I'm happy to be able to throw this little shindig for him, and I just know you all are going to buy a copy, or two, or three. So, without further adieu, I introduce to you, Mason Wilson. The man."

They hugged and Torino did the microphone handoff through the applause.

Mason spoke. He was suited up like he was going to church. "No, you're the man. Look at this place. Look what you've done. I'm the one who's proud of you." He scanned the crowd. "Hello, everyone."

The crowd replied back, "Hello."

"Tonight is special for a few reasons. And I'll keep it brief. First of all, my son, Rashaad Wilson, who's breaking records and taking names out there in the world of golf, is engaged. His fiancé is right there with him. Congratulations, happy couple."

He pointed to where Rashaad and Sasha were standing. Sasha hugged Rashaad close and Rashaad nodded to everyone who clapped. They looked just alike. Rashaad held up her hand, exposing her platinum marquis diamond rock. She beamed and then tried to hide her face into his embrace. They laughed alike.

"And, my daughter Star, who's over there," Mason said, looking right at her, "is a concert pianist with the Atlanta Symphony. She got her degree in music education at Howard, in D.C. But now, she's moving back to Los Angeles to be part of the L.A. Philharmonic Orchestra."

Everyone cheered her while Mason said, "She's a shining star, all right."

Star laughed, being poked in the stomach by Trinity.

"And I have accepted a full-time announcer job with ESPN starting next month."

Claude looked over at Mercedes and gave her a look like he had no idea. Mercedes mouthed, "Yep." They clapped along with everyone else when suddenly a woman with skin like cola, dressed in orange, walked over and sat at Claude's table next to him. Claude, the same man who had talked Mason into the importance of going home, was now separated. Mary kissed his cheek and he hugged her tightly while she waved a quick hello to Cameron and Penny, flashing her slight dimple.

Cameron said loudly, "Good to see you again, Mary."

"You too," she said, just as the applause died down.

"You're looking hot," said Penny.

"Thanks. We've got to hang out again."

Claude was all smiles.

Mercedes and Sequoia gave Mary the once over. Twice. Both frowning.

Mason continued. "Thanks everyone for sharing this special night with me and my family, the Wilsons. I'll hand it back over to Tito. I mean Torino." Mason laughed and people laughed with him.

Torino did not. He took the microphone back. "Ha-ha. Very funny. See the thanks I get? Anyway, you can all stay and party with us, but only after my hilarious brother autographs your hundreds of books. Thanks for coming."

As he and Mason walked to the signing table, the song "Hot Boyz" by Missy played. "Where you live, is it by yourself? Can I move with you, do you need some help? I cook boy, I'll give you more, I'm a fly girl, and I like those Hot Boyz."

Mercedes and Sequoia bounced in their seats, singing along.

Mason sat down as the long line formed, along with a publicity representative from his publishing company. Star and Trinity were Mason's unofficial assistants. Trinity had two books of her own to be signed, one for her and one for her father.

In an instant, the volume of the music ceased and the room was only filled with the club-goers' voices.

Mason asked, "What's going on? That was my song," when three men walked in dressed in L.A. Police department uniforms. They approached Mason saying, "Mason Wilson. You're under arrest. A warrant was issued for DUI charges last year after a failure to appear."

Mercedes stood so fast that she stumbled and fought to balance herself. "No. It can't be. There must be some mistake." She literally hollered, "No!"

Mason, expressionless, put down the Sharpie and arose from his chair, not saying a word.

Mercedes rushed up to him. "Honey?" Her face begged him to say it was a mistake. He didn't. He took his cell from his pocket and handed it to her. She took it and said in a crying voice, "Mason. They have the wrong person." She looked at one of the cops. "Officer, you have the wrong man. This is Mason Wilson, the golfer. He's done nothing wrong."

Star placed her hand over her mouth, in shock.

Mason came from around the table as the officers put him into handcuffs.

Sequoia stood behind Mercedes, placing her hand on her terrified sister-in-law's shoulder.

Mason was led away down the stairs. Star, Mercedes, and Rashaad were behind the officers.

"Dad, no!" Star shouted.

Rashaad asked the policeman, "Where are you taking him?"

"Downtown."

Rashaad stayed next to the last officer, turning to his mom who was one step behind him. "Let's go." And then he said to his sister, "Star, come on."

All of the patrons simply stared.

Mason called out to his brother, "Claude," without even looking back at him.

"I'm right behind you, bro!" Claude replied as if he were yelling across the street. Mary was right by his side.

The music came back on, still the same song, and Torino said to his manager, "Hold things down. And call me with the name of a bail bondsman right away. I'm out."

As much as it seemed unreal, Mason Wilson was on his way to jail.

It turned out he had been arrested in L.A. on his way back from Rashaad's tournament in San Diego for driving under the influence, but he did not show up to court. He had been coming back home to check the mail so Mercedes would not find out. He decided not to pursue a life in politics for no other reason than because of his own resurfaced addiction. And returning to church praying to God for His goodness and mercy was more for Mason's salvation alone, than theirs together.

Headed downtown, Mercedes sat in the passenger seat of Rashaad's car. Star and Trinity were in the back when Mason's cell vibrated. Mercedes's eyes were tender and she fought to view the screen while talking to Rashaad, fearful of her husband's fate. It was an email: *The council unanimously voted you in today. You're our next L.A. City Council member for the 8th District. Congratulations. Ryan Germany.*

Pop!

The L.A. Husbands and Wives were not done yet.

Because I lived through chapter 16, having watched my
mother take her last breath, I'll say, R.I.P.
Mom – 8/17/99.
Writing that scene was the most difficult chapter I've
penned in all my years!
Mamma you're the queen of my heart!

Love,
Marissa

IN HONOR OF

MATTIE BELAFONTE WILSON

<u>Soliloquies</u>

Mama used to say:

1. Take your time young man
2. Don't you rush to get old
3. Take it in your stride
4. I brought you in this world and I can take you out
5. I ain't raising no sorry ass man
6. If it ain't broke, don't fix it
7. Do it right or don't do it at all
8. This is gonna hurt me more than it hurts you
9. The pot calling the kettle black
10. And don't darken my door again
11. Don't half-ass anything
12. What people say about you is none of your business
13. I'll kill you first before somebody else will
14. Two heads are better than one, even if one is a goat head
15. Once you open your mouth you remove all doubt
16. Black don't crack
17. Why you outside so soon after having that baby with your pores open?
18. I pay the cost to be the boss
19. Don't wait for a man to give you what you can get on your on
20. When you do something for someone be sure to do it because you want to

21. Be the best you can be
22. Won't nobody treat you like your momma will
23. Always wear clean underwear. You never know when you'll be in an accident
24. There are two sides to every story
25. Two wrongs don't make a right
26. It's a bad wind that never changes
27. Do right and blessings will come
28. Tell the truth and shame the devil
29. A woman cannot do what a man does, and still be a lady
30. Always have your own money in case your man puts you out
31. Every goodbye ain't gone, and every shut eye ain't sleep
32. What's done in the dark comes to light
33. Never let your left hand know what your right hand is doing
34. The early bird gets the worm
35. There ain't nothing but legs open after 2:00 a.m.
36. Use your head for something more than a hat rack
37. It's better to fart and be ashamed than not to fart and bust a vein
38. Why fart and waste it when you can burp and taste it?
39. All that you're talking, say it while you're walking
40. You can cry until the cows come home
41. That boy ain't got the good sense God gave him
42. It's not what you do, it's the way you do it
43. We don't borrow, therefore we don't loan
44. Put some money away for a rainy day
45. Cry, cry, the more you cry, the less you piss
46. Stop pissing on my leg and telling me it's raining
47. Stop crying those crocodile tears
48. Don't let anyone walk all over you

49. You can only be a doormat if you lay down
50. One monkey don't stop no show
51. God don't like ugly and he sure don't like pretty
52. Don't let your mouth write a check that your body can't cash
53. A hard head makes a soft ass
54. Not even a dog wants a bone
55. Don't let him ride you all night and break your body down
56. A lady always knows when to leave

(Thank you Facebook friends for your amazing and hilarious contributions)

AUTHOR'S NOTE

(Spoiler below – you have been warned!)

I hope you've enjoyed the second installment of the Wilson family's drama. I wanted to show three couples with great challenges that end up in one of three different ways: one stays together against all odds, one separates and then finds their way back, and the other splits up altogether.

Family is so important. I enjoy writing about love and relationships, as well as generational curses and soul ties. Real life stuff with real life broken people.

I do admit that in this sequel I was planning that Mason would cheat on Mercedes with Mattie's nurse, Lucinda. The final paragraph would have been Mason receiving a text with a nude photo of her while he's on his way to jail, and Mercedes reading the text. However, being that his brother Claude does what he does in this book; one out of the three brothers cheating was enough. Not all men are cheaters. This novel was more about what the women did, and so, even though I tried, Mason wouldn't do that this time around. When he was away living in Leimert Park he was basically depressed, dealing with the loss of his career, the passing of his mother, his reduced income, and his disappointment in his wife's choice to let Ryan come to her hotel room in Vegas, which all contributed to him falling off the wagon. Mason simply wouldn't creep again, and my fingers couldn't force him to. ☺

I look forward to bringing you the Wilsons one more time as we check up on them in 2013 in L.A. HUSBANDS

AND WIVES. It'll be more hot family drama, on that you can bet.

Until then, please check out the following chapter excerpt for the next Marissa Monteilh title, which hits in 2012. Sexy Dr. Makkai Worthy, the good doctor, is back by popular demand in the sequel to DR. FEELGOOD called YOU'VE GOT IT BAD. (By the way, you might want to read DR. FEELGOOD first before you read this preview – I'm just saying!)

Ciao.

PREVIEW CHAPTER

YOU'VE GOT IT BAD: The Dr. Feelgood Sequel

2012

by Marissa Monteilh

Prologue

January 2012

I'M BACK.

Dr. Makkai Worthy.

A cardiac surgeon.

The head of cardiology at Cedar Sinai hospital in Los Angeles.

Let me tell you what a ride it's been since 2007.

Years ago I was a bachelor having the time of my life.

I was so wrapped up into messing with the women who threw themselves at me, that I caught a case with my very own sister.

I had no idea that Monday Askins, the woman I was getting with on a friends-with-benefits basis, was my father's daughter.

And that makes my five year-old daughter, Fonda Corrine Worthy, my niece, and my father's daughter's daughter. The baby girl who was only 2.47 pounds at birth, lived. She's my miracle. Even though her mother and I share fathers.

Her mother, Monday, turned out to be the biggest surprise of my life. Not only did I discover she was my sister after seeing photos of her mother at my dad's house, but she also turned out to be homeless, pretending to live in Palos Verdes when she and her dog lived in the backseat of a beat-up old Jaguar.

The day after she gave birth, she left the hospital and left me a note, giving me full custody of our daughter. But, she showed up again, giving me another note which she left on the windshield of my car. It read: *I will get my daughter if it's the last thing I do. This I promise you. Dr. Feelgood, this I promise you. Love, Delicious*.

Delicious was what I called her. Well, let's just leave it at that.

Now it is true that the one who ended up being my lady, Mary Jane Cherry, a nurse at the hospital, stuck by me and had my back. She'd been my rock after little Fonda was born. That is until last year. She realized even before I did that even though I said I loved her, and she'd earned the key to my house, she hadn't yet earned the key to my heart.

And she was right.

Turns out no one has.

Yet.

See, thing is, I've been a playboy for as long as I can remember.

My dad taught me how to please a woman, live and in person, and I'm so turned on by women, so turned on by variety, that I just can't be a one woman man. I just had to face it. My dad messed me up.

See, that's why they call me Dr. Feelgood.

I just can't have one.

That's another reason why Mary Jane left me and the reason Monday was able to make good on her promise. She got custody of my daughter Fonda because of the drama I've been through since 2007.

I'm here now to tell you how it's been living in my lifesaving shoes. And just like last time, the ladies will tell you their stories from their points of view. They'll try to give you a rundown on Worthy's Anatomy, if you know what I mean. But I'll interject the truth when necessary. You know how they are.

But the point is with all the lives I've saved with these skillful hands, it's high time for me to save my own life once and for all.

I just don't want to be like my poppa, the rolling stone, with dozens of grown kids he's never even met.

I don't want wherever I lay my hat to be my home.

I want to break the generational curse because I've got to get my daughter Fonda back if it's the last thing I do.

But in the meantime, I admit it.

I've got it bad.

And that ain't no kinda good.

READING GROUP GUIDE

1. If your mom or dad cheated would you tell the other parent like Star did?

2. Is kissing someone else a reason to leave?

3. If you messed up and your spouse moved out, would you move on or hold out hope that they would come back? Should Mercedes have gone after Mason and insisted he come back home?

4. Once you saw your reformed alcoholic mate drinking again, what would you do?

5. Like Sequoia, would you agree to raise a child with your husband without knowing if he or she was really his?

6. Have you ever had baby-momma drama? Did it contribute to the breakup of your relationship, or are you still with that person?

7. Would you have stayed with a man who had a baby's momma like Colette?

8. Have you ever had a stepchild who was disrespectful? How did you work out the issues at hand, or did it not work out?

9. Do you think men can dish it out but can't take it? Do women handle their spouse's infidelity better than men?

10. Would you consider dating your best friend's man if the two of you bonded after she passed away? Do you think Venus really loved Claude?

11. Is it unusual to fantasize about someone you're attracted to while making love to your mate?

12. What would you do if your grown child married someone more than twice his/her age? Do you think Cameron was rebelling?

13. Do you think Claude was chauvinistic? Were his views about Cameron on point?

14. Is there an older person in your life who is or was a positive influence on you, like Star had in Mattie?

15. Do you think the trappings of the rich and famous contributed to the Wilson family's dysfunctions?

16. Is it better to endure the pain and walk away rather than deal with the agony of feeling stuck because you stayed?

17. Does money buy happiness? Do you think you'd be any happier if you were a millionaire?

18. The whole world loves a comeback. Who would you like to see come back strong in the 2013 *Hot Boyz* trilogy, *L.A. Husbands and Wives*?

THE FINAL *HOT BOYZ* INSTALLMENT

L.A. HUSBANDS AND WIVES: The Hot Boyz Trilogy

2013

by Marissa Monteilh